# THE GREEN WOLVES

An *Oliver DeVille* Thriller

by

Vetle Sivertsen

Published by Polaris Project Partners AS, Oslo

The Green Wolves is a work of fiction. Names, characters, places, businesses, organization, events, and incidents either are the product of the author's imagination or are used fictitiously. Any resemblance to actual people, living or dead, places, or locales is entirely coincidental.

ISBN 978-82-999757-0-4

For more information about the author, please visit www.VetleSivertsenBooks.com

# PROLOGUE

*Mongolia*
*AD 1206*

"Bring in the goats," Temüjin said.

Their bleats cut through the crowd and the darkness of the night as they approached. Seventeen animals were brought before him. The sparks from the flames reflected in the long-bladed ceremonial knives. And then it began.

The goats struggled against their restraints. The first was brought forward. Its eyes widened in fear as the knife came close. It knew. Slowly the blade was drawn across its throat. The white wool turned crimson. It surrendered to the blade.

One at a time, the other goats faced the same fate. A few managed to bleat deeply. Each animal represented one of the tribes present. A red stream flowed from their open throats and silence was absolute as the last drops of life were collected in a wooden bowl. The mixed blood symbolized the unification of the tribes.

The ceremonial master stirred the red liquid in the same direction as the sun moves across the sky, filled a ladle made of horn, and handed it to Temüjin. He bowed to the tribal

3

chiefs and drank from the ladle. The blood contained the collective knowledge of all the tribes. That wisdom was now his.

A lone, throaty bleat carried through the air as the largest buck stood by itself and watched the carcasses in front of him. From birth it had been reserved for the purpose of honoring Tengri, the sky god.

Temüjin slit the buck's throat and the chiefs of each tribe took their turn stabbing its belly. The seventeen elders ensured as much blood as possible was drained from the animal. All of it symbolized Tengri's influence on earth. It soaked into the ground.

The Mongol army, braver than a pack of hunting wolves, would, under Temüjin's command, conquer the known world. It was Tengri's will. They would ride with their swords drawn until they reached the end of the mountains.

As his representative on earth, Temüjin would have all the power to conquer in Tengri's name, and he would not make the mistakes his ancestors had made. He would create a powerful empire that would last forever. He would create the Second Khaganate.

Behind Temüjin, a buckskin banner hung. The image of the green wolf depicted on it flickered in the light from the fire. It showed those around him that this would be Tengri's empire.

Deep within, he felt gratitude—but was not sure how to respond to it. With a grateful stare towards the sky, he knew he would not disappoint the father of the sky. The power and responsibility handed to him would be used in a wise way.

Tengri would be proud of him.

Temüjin would from now on be known to the world as Genghis Khan.

# CHAPTER 1

*Uden, The Netherlands*
*The Present – March 27th – 13:05*

Those who knew him, considered Captain Simon Timmerman to be one of the best F-16 pilots in the Netherlands, which was why they had ordered him to fly this mission. Take-off was just a few minutes away and he knew it would be in a north-eastern direction, but did not know his destination. The tower would radio him the coordinates once he was in the air.

Not unusual, considering the fact there had been several Americans from the 703rd Munitions Support Squadron in the hangar when he arrived two hours ago. It gave him a good idea of what he was about to take with him up into the skies. He expected his destination to be either the UK or Germany.

Captain Timmerman had been flying F-16 fighters for almost twelve years now and at age forty-two he was ready to retire from active duty and settle for a well-paid desk job at a commercial airliner. Flying a passenger airplane after a life with F-16s, was unthinkable.

It would please his wife and two young kids. For the last seven years, normal work hours had not existed. The risk and uncertainty of four deployments to Afghanistan had taken a toll on his family.

"Foxtrot India Tango, you are cleared for take-off. Report when airborne. Over." The earpiece crackled with the familiar voice of the tower controller.

"Uden tower, Foxtrot India Tango, roger. Over." With ease, Captain Timmerman turned the fifteen-ton aircraft around and taxied onto the runway.

Because of the suspected cargo, he wanted to hit the skies and get this mission over with ASAP. At the runway he used the brakes to keep the fighter still for just a moment while the engine built up enough thrust. He let go and the machine accelerated. Seven hundred meters down the tarmac, he reached take-off speed of one hundred fifty knots. He could have taken off at a lower speed, but his load was heavy.

The gray Fighting Falcon—known as The Viper—reached an altitude of a thousand feet in just under two seconds.

Like most pilots, he loved to fly these powerful beasts. The excitement of piloting a fighter jet was something every kid dreamt about. When he folded up his flight suit for the last time, he would surely miss these machines.

Subconsciously, he noticed the contrail coming towards him. The 'incoming missile' alarm went off, but he did not have time to act.

The rocket-propelled Stinger hit his airplane.

# CHAPTER 2

*Brussels, Belgium*
*March 29$^{th}$ – 12:00*

The bells of the St. Michael and St. Gudula Cathedral chimed to whoever was listening that it was noon. After a long and wet winter, the temperature in the Belgian capital was in the mid teens, Celsius, and the sun showed its face through a thin layer of clouds that resembled a wedding veil. This was the first day of spring according to the meteorologists, and scores of office workers were venturing out onto the streets to have a stroll before lunch.

The bravest of the lot would even try to have their lunch outdoors. The crowds were cheerful, and it seemed that everyone was embracing the unreliable fact that summer might just be around the corner.

"Stop that lady! She stole my camera!" a man's voice cried out.

Oliver DeVille was one of the many in the streets. He heard the commotion and saw the hunchbacked gypsy woman hurrying towards him faster than a lady at that age could possibly move.

DeVille also saw the stereotypical tourist, wearing what looked more suitable for an African safari than a stroll in downtown Brussels, waving his arms as if that would somehow stop the camera thief.

The little sympathy DeVille had for old ladies who stooped so low as to steal in order to survive disappeared the instant she was a few meters away from him. Not just because he wanted to stop a criminal act, but equally because his peaceful stroll had been disturbed, DeVille swung his briefcase upwards and slammed it into the face of the hunchbacked runner.

He got behind the old lady and removed his tie. He wrapped it tightly around her neck. Most of the others on the street gasped and some screamed. The lady reeked of tobacco and sweat, but DeVille's nostrils also picked up the woody scent of aftershave.

"Are you crazy? She's just an old lady," a man shouted as he ran towards DeVille.

"It's not—" was the only thing DeVille managed to say before he was pulled away from the gypsy.

The thief wriggled loose from the tie and sprinted away. DeVille managed to grab hold of the headscarf as the gypsy ran off.

"It's not an old lady, you idiot." DeVille looked at the man and threw the headscarf and a wig at him.

He looked at DeVille, the gray lump of hair, and the young man wearing make-up who was bolting down the street.

"You let him go, so you'll have to answer to the police if they show up. If they need me, give them this." DeVille handed over a business card. "I need a drink."

He would not stick around for the police. Every time he went to a police station he ended up with the same nightmares.

*Carina's death.*

He walked away and down the quaint little Bergstraat,

located just between the cathedral and Brussels' famous Grand Place. DeVille stopped outside a small bistro. If you did not notice the little menu in the glass box hanging on the white concrete wall next to the door, you would never know it was a restaurant. Through the window DeVille saw the waiter talking to a couple among the empty tables, and he decided to go in and have lunch.

*And a drink.*

The interior, dominated by dark brown wooden panels, made him think of an old library. The grayish floor tiles gave the impression of a warehouse. Together it felt, surprisingly, like a rustic Italian *ristorante*. The leather chairs, like the ones in exclusive English clubs, oozed luxury. Black and white pictures of celebrities, who probably had never even been to Belgium, scattered the walls, but they gave the place a feeling of coziness.

DeVille thought the mix of everything in the bistro was just like a miniaturized Belgium. He pulled out a stool by the bar.

The bartender finished cleaning a glass before he turned to DeVille. "Can I get you anything?" he asked in French.

"I'll have steak and eggs, please." DeVille ordered in the same language, one of five he was fluent in.

"And to drink?"

DeVille scanned the various choices of spirits on the shelves behind the bar, "Johnnie Walker Red and soda."

*It was good enough for Churchill.*

DeVille pulled out an iPad from his worn leather Bridge briefcase. He did not care much for gadgets, but he liked the iPad.

*A status symbol, perhaps.*

He connected the tablet to the bistro's Wi-Fi and looked at the wallpaper image of himself straddling a quad bike at an EU team building event two weeks ago. The encounter with the religious cult almost killed him. Instinctively, his fingers reached up and touched his right earlobe—now partly missing.

He scrolled to the side and opened a document of an article he was writing about Christian extremists in Africa. He had been working on it for months and it was still not finished. The extremists reminded him of those who had killed Carina.

He opened his browser and clicked on a bookmark of a betting company's website. Qualification games for the World Cup were the only games playing that day. DeVille looked at the list of games to see if he could find anything. It was just pure gut feeling. He stopped when he saw Turkey playing at home against Austria at one forty-five. He placed a hundred euros on Turkey, giving him a reason to watch the game on TV when he got home.

At that moment the bartender appeared with his food.

"Thanks, the steak looks fine," he said. "Another scotch and soda, please."

*Might as well go home afterwards. No point in returning to the office.*

Just as he paid for lunch his phone vibrated in his inner pocket. The caller ID showed an unknown number.

"Oliver DeVille," he answered. Over the years, he had found it was best to answer with his name. He had no idea what language the unknown caller would speak.

"DeVille, glad I could get hold of you," a hoarse voice said in accented English.

The chief of staff of the EU Commission's president. DeVille had worked for him several times over the last few years. They were opposite personalities, but he liked the politically correct, fifty-something, German lawyer.

"How fast can you be here?" the chief of staff asked.

"I don't know, maybe thirty minutes?"

"What's your location? I'll send a car for you."

"Close to Grand Place. Bergstraat. What's going on? It sounds like an emergency." DeVille was curious.

"I guess you could say that. That fighter jet that crashed

in the Netherlands two days ago, you saw that on the news?"

"Yes?"

"Well, it didn't crash. It was shot down. And it was carrying a nuclear missile."

# CHAPTER 3

*Utrecht, The Netherlands*
*13:26*

*Weapon of mass destruction is certainly a suitable name.*

Mahmoud Khan pictured it. Explosions and screams. Flames filled his eyes. The damage it could unleash on his enemies mesmerized him.

And he had just stolen one.

The Americans had moved into the air base with their goods around the time of the Cuban missile crisis.

*A long time ago, but they surely regret that now.*

Khan smiled. He had shown them what a missile crisis *really* meant.

But he was also worried.

*Who has the weapon now?*

He cleared his mind of his worries and stepped onto his prayer mat, devoting his full concentration to God. After five minutes, he turned his head to the right and said the *Taslim*. He finished the noon prayer, *Dhuhr*, and put his shoes back on. Khan rolled up his prayer mat, the only item he had brought with him from his ancestral land. It showed wear from years of kneeling five times a day.

The doors to the bedroom and the kitchen had been removed to create an illusion of space. After years spent in the mountains and in the deserts of Xinjiang, he loathed the cramped quarters of the city apartment which had accommodated him for nearly two years. He heard rainwater drip from his soaked coat which was hanging by the entrance door, making the apartment feel damp and stuffy.

Khan sat down with a cup of tea and wondered if his brothers-in-arms felt as restless as he did.

*Are they also sitting in their apartments, waiting to find out if they have been successful?*

Khan rubbed his beard and felt the hairs curl around his dark-skinned hands. They matched the face of a man who had been outdoors in the sun for a number of years. The jeans and the hooded sweater he was wearing made him uncomfortable. At least he had his skullcap.

As the leader of the team that had carried out the mission, he was proud. It was less than two days since he had returned to his apartment, but it felt like weeks. He stood up and peeked through the drapes, down at Ismail's twelve-year-old Mercedes, parked out in the street. It was the only thing connecting them to the incident. He thought about dumping it.

Ismail was the artillery man and the most important piece of the mission. Khan let a hand run across his own face, thinking Ismail's sunken-in cheeks were quite different than his. Ismail had no beard either, the white of his face only highlighted by a mustache, riddled with brown nicotine stains. Just like the rust on the bumper of the old Mercedes. They went back almost fifteen years. At the Ghulja Massacre they both lost many relatives and almost died themselves. When they recovered from their injuries, they both pledged to seek revenge.

The only way to fight the Chinese was jihad. They joined

a training camp in Afghanistan. Today, they were both veteran fighters and respected in their organization. Khan knew Ismail was one of the best Stinger operators. He had seen him in battle many times, with the weapon towered on top of his skinny shoulder. Ismail was the first man he had picked for this mission.

*It was only two days ago.*

Khan, Ismail, and one of the students, had picked a spot next to an office building at a plant producing animal feed off Nieuwedijk in Uden. The site seemed ideal for their purpose. A few trees lined the driveway, from where Ismail could fire his Stinger. They would be hidden, but with a good view towards where the target would appear.

The plot was laid out like a medieval castle, canals separating the plant from open fields on three sides. It meant they would be trapped if someone was to come through the only entrance, but it was a risk they had accepted. Only one thing mattered—Ismail had to fire the Stinger at the right moment.

"Are we sure about take-off direction?" Khan had asked the student minutes before the Stinger was fired.

"Yes, it will definitely be north-eastern."

Khan was pleased. It was a requirement for their plan to work. One of many key variables in order to make this mission a success. Khan stared through his binoculars at the Volkel Air Base for signs of the F-16.

Ismail launched the Stinger missile a second after the fighter jet went airborne. The difficult part was pulling the trigger about half a second before the F-16 took off, and aiming at a target ahead of the airplane when the missile left the launcher.

They needed the fighter jet down, but in two pieces.

No one needed to worry. The hit was perfect. Only Ismail could have done it. For a man who, for over a half a warrior's lifetime, had fired missiles at airplanes several thousand meters away, a target just a few hundred meters above the ground was no difficulty. Thanks to its recoil spring, the Stinger was one of the most accurate portable surface-to-air missile launchers. Khan had great respect for this weapon. And for Ismail.

He snapped out of his thoughts, and saw the difference between Ismail and the Mercedes—the overall appearance. While the car, though old, looked classic instead of aged, there was nothing classic about Ismail. He was just worn.

In a neighborhood with a lot of break-ins, it had been risky to store the missile launcher in the trunk of the car. They could not carry it up and down to the apartment either. Not without arousing suspicion. The police was active this close to the city center, but it was not unusual for a drug addict or a vandal to try their luck with the parked cars at night. Now Khan hoped someone would steal the car.

He drew the drapes. The noises out there, which he would never get used to, came from a city where people had left work and gone out for lunch in bars and restaurants.

*Infidels.*

Khan went into the bedroom, fell onto the bed, and closed his eyes.

*We have accomplished so much.*

Utrecht was the perfect place to hide while they planned the mission. A large Muslim immigrant population meant they blended in, and the city's mosques had been ideal for the task of recruiting three more men. The Muslims of Utrecht mostly kept to themselves.

To the Dutch, all Muslims looked the same.

*Has it gone too smoothly? Will the mission blow up in our faces?*

"Inshallah," he whispered.

The worn, wooden beads felt soft as he let all ninety-nine of them pass between his index finger and thumb. He put the prayer bead chain into his pocket, but continued to pass them between his fingers.

He got up and took another look out of the window. It

was a little busier in the street now, with more young people.

*School must be over for the day.*

With their scarves and umbrellas, they braved the outdoors—changed, from resembling a nice summer's day, to a cold and wet spring afternoon. All within minutes. He knew the infidel students were already headed for the bars. A cab prowled the street below, and a young couple with hands entwined walked past the Mercedes towards the city center. The man holding the girl's hand was the same age as Yakuf Haq.

The man they had left behind.

That was the only thing that had gone wrong with the whole complicated mission—they had lost a man. Khan felt a knot in his stomach.

*Will it be a problem?*

Right after the attack, when they sped away in the Mercedes, Khan watched the two trucks through his binoculars. The trucks, driven by Haq and another of the students, were almost as important to the mission as the Stinger. They had done well and blocked the routes they were supposed to.

The first truck had turned left towards Volkelseweg and then right onto the one-lane road. It had been going fast and with a hard turn of the wheels the truck and trailer overturned. It then blocked both lanes and the bike path next to it. With a canal on each side, it was impossible for rescue personnel to pass without first moving the truck.

Instead, they went onto the Noordstraat—where the second truck was in the first responders' way.

Khan knew that had been the more difficult task. The truck driver had to block the road bridge while at the same time doing damage to a wooden walk bridge next to it. Haq managed to do just that.

As soon as Haq's truck turned onto the bridge, he fishtailed it. The trailer went through the rails with its rear end, slid on its side to lie partly on the wooden walk bridge and partly on the road bridge.

But it went too fast through the rails. The truck hit a tree next to the bridge, throwing it sideways towards the canal, before stopping. The bridges were blocked, but Khan did not see Haq come out of the truck.

Anyone inside the mangled cabin had to be seriously injured. There was no way to rescue him. Within seconds, police, military, and firefighters would have been everywhere—red and blue lights flashing across the fields, desperate to reach the crash site of the F-16.

A fellow warrior and believer had been left behind.

It made Khan think of what happened a year ago. It had taken them almost six months to recruit the three students, but it was time well spent. The university boys strongly believed in the cause and had accepted martyrdom.

None of them were from the native land, but their parents brought them here from Pakistan and Afghanistan. They all had Uighur names. Their grandparents must have moved across the border during the Cultural Revolution. He proved to the young men that they still had family back home. It was only a matter of time before Khan persuaded them to join the cause.

A year ago, he told Haq about a former leader of the organization and how he was killed by a Hellfire missile fired from a Predator drone in North Waziristan. He had been Haq's cousin. Khan explained to him what they were fighting for and how Haq could help. The young student started to understand his cousin's motivation and when Khan asked him to help with a task that would have made his cousin proud, Haq agreed immediately.

Neither the gloom of Haq's probable capture, nor the delight of the successful mission, was the reason for Khan's restlessness. Neither did it worry him that he might get caught by the police. It was that he did not know why the mission had been sanctioned in the first place.

*Who was on the other end to pick up the nuclear missile we shot off the fighter jet?*

*Why did the Uighur leaders sponsor this mission if the weapon is not to be used against the Chinese?*

*Is it all part of a greater Al-Qaeda plot?*

*Those who have just been served a nuclear missile on a silver platter, what will they use it for?*

# CHAPTER 4

*Brussels, Belgium*
*13:45*

A car picked him up outside the restaurant and took him directly to the basement. This entrance was normally reserved for VIP guests and higher EU officials. A security officer escorted him through a metal detector and they took the elevator straight to the floor which housed the president and his staff.

He liked that they picked him up in an Audi A8. It could be the one the president rode in.

*Surely, they must have more discreet cars in the EU motor pool.*

DeVille's curiosity grew with every second he waited. The black leather chairs and the modern art carefully broke the hypnotic effect of the room's light wood panels. It made the ten-minute wait as pleasant as DeVille could hope for under the circumstances.

For the last two days, the news had been reporting a tragic fighter jet accident.

It was much worse.

Someone had shot down an F-16 that was carrying a

nuclear missile. DeVille saw a mushroom cloud dance across the wood panels.

Religious extremism was his field of expertise. He was not an expert on terrorism, but in analyzing extreme religious behavior. In his mind those two definitions was as different as a cat and a dog. Obviously, some religious whack had shot down the jet, if not he would not have been called in, and the name that came to mind was Al-Qaeda.

If one of the terrorism experts he normally worked with had been there too, it would have made more sense. But no one else was in the waiting area.

*I'm a damn fool.*

If he had only spent the little time he was online at the restaurant on a news page, he might have known what this was about. Instead he had betted money on a soccer game he did not care about. He imagined how foolish he would look if some terrorist organization had claimed responsibility for the shooting without him knowing about it.

He regretted the three glasses of scotch and soda.

The Slovenian secretary to the chief of staff got up from her desk, and DeVille saw her body bulged in the right spots of her pantsuit. She walked towards DeVille. He smiled at her, but did not get a smile back. Her breasts pointed straight at the wall and the pants were tightened by the two petite domes of her buttocks. No one would notice the untrendy pantsuit.

*Even in the gypsy outfit from earlier today, she'd look good.*

He did not know if she was single, but he would ask her out one day.

She averted his eyes. A sign not to ask her out today.

"The chief of staff will see you now, sir."

"Monica, what's with the formality?" She always smiled and encouraged uncomfortable small talk when he was waiting to see the chief of staff. Furthermore, he could have sworn she had flirted with him on several occasions. He

20

wondered what had changed.

"Nothing. You can see him now." She pointed in the direction with her whole hand and DeVille saw the diamond ring.

*Too late.*

He would mourn the loss of her later with a drink. Now he needed to focus on work.

One of the reasons for settling down in Brussels was that it was the ideal place for his expertise, as it housed the headquarters of both NATO and the EU. These organizations had become his main clients.

Most of the member countries of both NATO and the EU had DeVille's expertise internally within their intelligence services—especially on Islamic extremism. The EU and NATO organizations themselves could not depend on getting that expertise when it was needed.

DeVille knew countries would withhold information for a lot of reasons, but sometimes they were just unaware it could be important for others. DeVille stepped in and provided that information.

He followed her to the door of the chief of staff's office. DeVille entered the office which was in the same décor as the lobby area. A lanky man, with a headful of receding gray hair, stood up from behind the large desk.

"Please have a seat," he said as he pointed to two Ikea-style black leather couches and a table. The chief of staff's face did not intimidate anyone, but his voice was so confident it made DeVille feel like he should bow and stare at the floor, when addressed.

The chief of staff sat down on the leather couch across from DeVille, nodded towards the coffeepot, and said, "Self-service."

DeVille poured himself a cup while the chief of staff began, "It's about the fighter crash in the Netherlands."

"The news only said the pilot was one of the most experienced F-16 pilots in the Netherlands. It never said anything about the airplane being shot down or that it was carrying a nuke." DeVille hoped he was right about the last part.

"Well, there are three details of the crash the media doesn't know about. And it should stay that way," the chief of staff said. "The first is that the F-16 was carrying a B-61 thermonuclear bomb."

Even though he had already been told, DeVille's tongue dried up. As he opened his mouth to ask a question, the chief of staff stopped him. "Listen to me first."

"Fine. Go ahead."

"Secondly, it was no accident. The plane was shot down. And thirdly, an individual, who is believed to be an Uighur rebel, has been taken into custody by the Dutch authorities." The chief of staff paused while he poured himself some coffee.

"Seriously? It doesn't make sense for a Chinese extremist to shoot down a Dutch airplane. What would they gain by doing that here in Europe? The Chinese government won't care."

"There's a fourth detail as well." The chief of staff's eyes conveyed the seriousness of the situation. "The nuclear missile, which the plane was carrying, is missing."

DeVille could not process the information. *Where to start?*

"The Uighur is the reason why I'm here?"

There was a long pause.

The chief of staff broke the silence, "The Americans have been moving some of the nuclear bombs, unofficially stored in the Netherlands and Belgium, out. They've been moved to aircraft carriers in the Med over the last year. Part of a secret agreement with the Russians. In return the Russians will remove bombs from former Soviet states."

US nuclear bombs in Belgium, Germany, Italy, and the Netherlands. *One of the most well-known 'secrets' in the world.* The bombs were placed there during the Cold War, part of a NATO strategy of deterrence.

"This F-16 was moving the bomb to Germany. Later it was to be moved to a US aircraft carrier. Just after take-off, a Stinger missile, we believe, ripped one of its wings off. They found the missile launcher near the airstrip. The wing came down in a forested area a few kilometers away from where the plane crashed."

DeVille was not sure if he wanted to hear the rest of what the chief of staff was about to tell him.

"The first emergency units went directly to the crash site—others were sent to locate the wing and the missile, but they were delayed."

"Why?"

"Two trucks with trailers had toppled over. On the two shortest access routes to the forest where the wing was going to be. They probably lost ten or fifteen minutes on the detour they had to make." The chief of staff paused and looked at DeVille before he continued, "When they got to the wing, the missile was gone."

"What about the Uighur? What's his connection to this?"

"In the cabin of one of the toppled trucks, the military police found a man. The steering wheel had him pinned down. The Dutch say he may be Uighur. That's all I know."

DeVille scratched his head. "Is it possible to shoot a wing off a fighter jet?"

"I didn't think so," the chief of staff replied, "but it can't be a coincidence that someone happened to be nearby and decided to steal a missile that fell out of the sky. As I said, it seems strange, but I suggest you give Danny Pearce a call and see what he makes of it. I believe he's advising NATO on this one."

DeVille had worked with Pearce, a terrorism expert, before. The consultancy market was very competitive, but he knew that Danny Pearce was damn good at his job. And he was a friend.

"All right, this is a lot of nasty information. And there might be a slim possibility that TIM is responsible for this and that is why you've called me in," DeVille said using the abbreviation for the Turkestan Islamic Movement. He stared at the cup of coffee in front of him.

The EU and NATO spent a lot of money on external consultants, both to obtain intelligence as well as to validate information coming from member countries. DeVille profited from this. He had become the one to go to when they needed intelligence on a religious group or to analyze an event organized by one of these groups.

"Correct," the chief-of staff said. He continued and answered what DeVille was about to ask. "Because of the sensitivity of this, the Dutch and the Americans are keeping a complete lid on information. What I know is what I got from the Dutch before they shut off communication with both us and NATO. You're the only external person with the expertise needed on TIM. They have mainly troubled China and the Uighur regions, so we have very little information about them. We need to know if they really have taken the bomb, if they plan to use it here in the EU, and if their link to Al-Qaeda could be a reason for whatever they have planned."

DeVille shut his eyes for a moment and realized the size of the problem he was being asked to assess. Perspiration dampened his shirt collar and with a troubled gesture he managed to loosen the top shirt button which was not covered by a tie knot anymore. The collar slowly released itself from his neck.

"Why am I to take the lead on this case, and not someone like Pearce, like it's normally done?" DeVille asked.

Normally DeVille received a chapter in a report compiled by a terrorism expert such as Pearce, who provided input on weapons, manpower, likely targets, and all the operational aspects of terrorism. DeVille had worked with and knew quite well four of these terror experts.

"First, we can't make a big deal out of this until we're

certain this has any implication for the EU. Right now it is a problem for the Dutch, the Americans, and NATO. And I promised that you'd get the next big case." The old German gave a short crooked smile when he made the second point.

DeVille remembered the promise. Deep in a Belgian forest, after having stared into the gun of a politician who turned out to be a grand master of a secret cult sanctioned by the Vatican. "How soon do you want my report, with recommendations?" DeVille asked.

DeVille's best paying assignments were about Muslim extremists, although he really wished he had more time to spend researching other religions.

"No report," the chief of staff replied. "I want you to go to The Hague right away. I will get you an interview with the Uighur. I assume they're holding him in The Hague. You'll report to me twice a day. We'll decide exactly how to proceed after we know what the terrorist has to say."

"You assume he's there because of the MIVD?" DeVille asked, referring to the Dutch Military Intelligence and Security Service. He had never interviewed a prisoner before, but it sounded more interesting than sitting in his office.

There was a slight nod from the chief of staff.

"Okay. I'll get moving."

Moments later, the same Audi as earlier took him by his apartment where he grabbed an overnight bag, and then caught the Thalys express train to Rotterdam. From there, a local train to The Hague.

*Do I need to stop by my office to get more info on TIM? Probably not.*

It was not like he would be away for a long time. He would be home again tomorrow around noon.

DeVille looked down at the cell phone in his hand—one of the old Nokias that still worked after a drop from three-stories up. Modern phones all looked the same and broke as soon as you gave them the stink eye.

The chief of staff had insisted he only communicate with him on that phone—something DeVille found peculiar. It was for this investigation only. One dial-out number was stored on the phone. The bigwigs tended to make his job more difficult than it needed to be.

Most terror threats were treated with confidentiality. No one wanted the media to create any form of hysteria. But this was the first time he had seen this level of secrecy. On the other hand, it was the first time he was involved in a case where a nuclear missile had been stolen by a terrorist organization.

DeVille started to sweat as the mushroom cloud reappeared in his mind.

# CHAPTER 5

*Lyenina, Belarus*
*14:51*

*So far it has gone very well.*

Muhammad Umeira was out of sight, behind the naked birch trees which were waiting for warmer days so they could give birth to a new set of leaves. He sat and waited. The sun's position told him he would take possession of a nuclear missile in a few minutes.

The job was far from done, but from now on they would be operating on familiar territory. The critical part was to make sure the van had made it to the Belarusian border. After that, there was always the option of paying someone off if trouble occurred. Or using guns if it came down to that.

The van, now with Russian license plates, would arrive in a few minutes. The three brave mujahideen in it had transported the nuclear missile across three European borders. They had managed to get out of the Netherlands before alarms went off at the Dutch borders. Exiting Germany had concerned him—the authorities were on high alert by then, but the real German license plates on the van had paid off. Poland was not difficult to cross and following the less populated southern route had seemed a smart choice.

The van was bought from an immoral infidel who did not think twice when they proposed to him he could take the cash for it and be free to report it stolen after a week. By then the van, and its cargo, would have reached its destination in southern Russia.

Umeira looked to the left of him, at the little Orthodox church in the village. Its three domes, one red and two blue, towered above the trees. The Christians believed the domes were a symbol of salvation, but he knew the actual reason for the shape was to prevent snow from accumulating on the rooftops. To him, Christianity was a religion that seemed to change its rules all the time in order to make it more comfortable for believers. That was why they chose to ignore the Prophet's teachings. They were not willing to make the true sacrifice.

"The infidels shall soon burn," he whispered.

He regretted the choice to meet up here, next to a symbol of the infidels and the oppressors. There were few good spots to meet in this village, located just a couple of kilometers from the border to Russia. Umeira counted less than a hundred buildings, and if anyone found him suspicious, they would undoubtedly report him to the secret police. It was still called the KGB in Belarus.

The overcast sky created a sense of dusk. Umeira saw nothing but a dark silhouette when the van, flashing its high beams, came towards him and parked at the curb next to the church. He waited a few minutes before he sneaked out from behind the trees, his white coat a perfect match with the birch bark. It was not that he expected anyone to be watching him. It was more an in-built carefulness he had developed after years of guerrilla warfare.

The passenger side window rolled down, with an electric buzz penetrating the silent grayness hanging over the van.

"As-salaam alaikum," Umeira greeted the men in the front seats.

"Wa 'alaykum al-salaam," they responded.

"Any trouble?" Umeira asked in Chechen.

"So far everything has gone smooth. Not a single problem."

"Great. The cargo is in the back, I guess?" Umeira saw the men's shoulders drop in relief. Understandable, he thought. Their part of the job was done. He just hoped there was not any tension in his own voice.

The side door of the van opened and Umeira got in and saw a man crouched on the makeshift floorboards. He was one of the most promising fighters among Umeira's soldiers and the natural choice as team leader for this operation. A decision Umeira regretted right now. Even though Umeira was high-ranking in the organization, he had not been told all the details up front.

The man stood up, his head still short of the roof lining of the van. "As-salaam alaikum," he said.

"Wa 'alaykum al-salaam, my brave fighter. We do not have much time. Give me a short briefing of what happened."

"We waited in the park's forest as we were told to do. After about seven hours we heard the explosion and out of the blue the huge wing fell down. Just as we were told it would."

"And no problem getting the missile loose?"

"None at all. We cut it from the wing attachment in ten minutes with the blowtorch." The man pointed proudly towards the fuel-burning tool standing inside the van.

Umeira wondered if using a blowtorch next to a nuclear missile was the dumbest or the wisest thing he had ever heard. He shook the thought from his head and asked, "No police or military?"

"Haa-Ha," the man said using the Chechen phrase for 'no.' "It took us five minutes to winch the missile into the van. We heard some sirens when we drove off, but we were in Germany within an hour."

"That sounds good," Umeira said. "Allah has been kind to this operation." He knew the men would receive the ultimate reward and his deceit would be forgiven.

"It is under here," the mujahideen said and removed a large wooden grate.

The cargo floor of the extended Chevy van had been raised by almost half a meter to be able to create a cradle for the missile. Umeira looked down at the metal sheet that was welded to the top of the raised floor. If someone opened the van they would notice the higher floor, but it was a risk worth taking.

"We placed the missile inside this cradle and then we welded it shut," the mujahideen explained.

"Good job, everyone. We need to get moving. The three of you will wait here." Umeira looked at each of his men as he spoke. "I have bribed the border guard to let me over, but he thinks I am smuggling cigarettes. He will not let me over if he thinks I am smuggling people too."

The border guard had asked Umeira if this would become a regular business, stuffed the two thousand rubles into his pocket and smiled. Another two thousand would enter his pockets when Umeira crossed over with the van. Umeira had an ulterior motive for wanting to be alone in the van when it crossed. The three men nodded in agreement, slowly, then looked at each other.

"A car will pick you up in about thirty minutes," Umeira said and climbed into the driver's seat.

Umeira reached the border in less than ten minutes and the same border guard was standing there. He slipped him an envelope through the window. The guard peeked inside it and swiped his card. The barrier went up. The guard seemed pleased with his day's work. The bribe was equal to somewhere around two months' pay. It was quite common for smugglers to use this border crossing, so the contributions these guards added to their pensions made sure they could retire wealthy, years before the average Russian.

The van had passed unnoticed all the way from the Netherlands to Russia. There would be no more border crossings from now on.

It would soon be dark and Umeira decided to drive for a couple of hours before taking a rest. Cars driving around in the middle of the night could attract attention from bored police patrols. It was better to wait for daylight and blend in with other cars on the roads.

When he gave them one last look of approval before he drove off, he saw the resignation in their eyes.

*Do they know what is coming? They know they will become martyrs for the great cause.*

A car would come towards them a little after Umeira had left, but it would not pick them up. The passenger side window would roll down and a machine gun would fire several rounds at them from such a close range that they would know who the shooter was.

The driver and the executioner, both mujahideen, had been told that the three men worked as spies for the Spetsnaz. The Russian Special Forces had shot and killed so many of the mujahideen over the years that suspicion of collaboration with the Spetsnaz was a certain death sentence.

Umeira wondered if he would meet a similar fate when he delivered the missile to Abdul Aziz, the leader of the Arab mujahideen in Chechnya. If that was the case, he would embrace martyrdom as a blessing. He knew it was important that as few people as possible knew about the operation.

*Nothing can stop us from using the missile.*

He did not know how yet, but he knew the missile in the back of the van would help them establish Allah's will—the caliphate of Caucasus.

# CHAPTER 6

*The Hague, The Netherlands*
*17:15*

The area, covered in a dark cloud above the brick and concrete buildings, looked dangerous. Together with the hunched stride of commuters, a sense of danger prevailed and everyone clutched their bags and purses tightly.

DeVille felt it, as his train pulled in to the Hollands Spoor station in The Hague, but he liked it. Normally he would take the tram, a great place to people-watch, but this time he was in a hurry and jumped straight into a cab.

"Frederikkazerne, alstublieft," he said. It was where the MIVD was housed.

The cabdriver grunted and headed north.

During the train ride he had gotten the confirmation from the chief of staff that the suspected terrorist was indeed being held by the MIVD and DeVille had been given permission to interview him.

Will I get anything useful to report back to Brussels?

The chief of staff also gave him a name. The suspect was a twenty-four-year-old man named Yakuf Haq—a Dutch citizen and student at Utrecht University. The name was common, but DeVille's brain interpreted it as a premonition. A man with the same last name had been a leader in the Turkestan Islamic Movement. Haq was a common name in the Uighur region of China, but to DeVille it seemed too much of a coincidence.

While on the train, he had also taken the chief of staff's suggestion and made a call to terrorism expert Danny Pearce. They had skipped pleasantries and gotten straight down to business. Both of them knew the other was on the clock.

"You have to tell me," DeVille said. "Is it really possible to shoot a wing off a fighter jet?" He was sure Pearce had connected the dots and knew the questions were about the downed Dutch F-16.

"Theoretically, yes. But it's extremely difficult. If you use a special missile in the Stinger that contains very little explosives, it's possible to make just enough damage so a large crack appears in the wing. Gravity and the speed of the fighter jet will do the rest to tear the wing off."

"Is it so difficult that only a handful of men in the world could do it?" DeVille asked.

"Don't know how many, but it would require a Stinger expert with knowledge of both explosives and how a fighter jet is engineered. There are probably a dozen or so Taliban fighters with enough experience. You know, the Stinger, together with the AK-47, is the favorite weapon of rebels and terrorists all around the world."

"I thought the whole airplane would explode."

Pearce sighed as he repeated himself. "A seasoned Stinger expert can make the warhead explode *after* it hits the aircraft, especially if the missile hits where the wing is welded to the fuselage. It won't become a large fireball of burning debris."

DeVille took the hint and moved on. "What does a terrorist want to use the missile for? Can it be detonated just like that?"

"Potential targets and use are classified, Oliver. I can't tell you. But the chance of detonating it is small. They'd need to have a computer system which breaks down the security walls of the missile's internal system. They won't have that."

DeVille wondered if it really was classified information or if Pearce was just not willing to give away his market advantage for free.

Before they hung up, Pearce did tell him the most likely way to use the missile was to detonate conventional explosives around it, and hope it would break open and leak radiation. *A dirty bomb.* Pearce was adamant it could still cause massive damage and a large number of fatalities.

The cab dropped DeVille off in front of the gate to the compound which housed the MIVD. After a security check at the gate, he was made to wait until someone showed up to escort him into a gray concrete building he thought befitted the KGB more than the Dutch secret service.

He was led into an interview room which was nothing like what he had expected of a room where they interrogated threats to national security. Or, in this case, a possible threat to international security.

The room was light with one large window. No bars in front of the window, but he knew it was made of some sort of reinforced glass. There was no need to even think about an escape if you were in here against your will. The room felt like a cross between IKEA and a corporate meeting room, with its pine-colored chairs with blue upholstered seats around a large oval table.

There was a knock on the door and two armed military policemen brought in Yakuf Haq in a wheelchair. His hands and feet were shackled, but he was still wearing civilian clothes. Both his legs were in casts. One of the military policemen left the room and DeVille heard him lock the door from the outside. The other took up a position in a corner behind the prisoner. No one had said a word.

A phone on the table rang and when the military policeman made no move to pick it up, DeVille did.

"You may start your interview, Mr. DeVille," a woman's voice said in English before she hung up.

After about twenty minutes, DeVille was about to give up. He needed to change his tactics. He had not learned anything. He started asking some introductory questions, but Haq did not even answer when he asked him to confirm his name.

"We know you did it and I understand why you won't tell me where it is, but you got nothing to lose by letting me know how you did it."

Haq just sighed.

"When did you get to Uden?"

"We got there the night before, and then we slept in our trucks at a gas station before we went to the airfield in the morning."

*Finally the guy said something.*

"I toppled the truck and the rest I'm sure you know. Can I go back to my cell now?"

"Where was the guy with the Stinger?" DeVille continued, but he did not get any answer. "Who was he?"

Haq twitched in his chair, wiped his forehead, and did his best to stare into space.

If it was because of pain in his legs or boredom at the questions, DeVille could not tell. He looked at the folder in front of him, given to him by the military policeman. "You've been enrolled in the university for the last three years?"

There was a slight nod from Haq.

"Faculty of Geosciences? What were your ambitions?"

No response.

"Okay, what about your parents?" DeVille saw that neither Haq nor the parents had a criminal record. "They escaped the Soviet Union in the sixties, right?"

35

"Idiot. Afghanistan." Haq leaned back and seemed more relaxed.

"Tough place for Muslims, wasn't it? Occupied by the Soviet Union." DeVille just stated the fact as he did not expect any answers. "You've never been to China. You've never been to Asia."

Haq moved around in his wheelchair. As much as the shackles allowed him to.

"You don't seem like a Chinese terrorist, do you?"

Haq did a Mona Lisa smile.

Out of frustration DeVille took a chance. "Is all of this because of your cousin?" He saw the surprise in Haq's eyes. He knew his instinct about the name had been right. "Are you trying to avenge the death of your cousin?"

Haq sat up straight in his wheelchair and stared at DeVille.

"Or is all this a confused attempt to embrace Islam in the wrong way?" DeVille continued.

"No, it's not just for my cousin. It's for my people. And the Western world is guilty and has blood on their hands after allowing the Chinese to massacre our people. Because of Chinese money you've decided to look the other way." The voice was closer to that of a boy than a man.

DeVille guessed Haq would give him a lecture about the 2009 riots which saw more than two hundred Uighur people die. He was almost right. But instead Haq started to speak about the Ghulja massacre in 1997.

"Hundreds of Muslims were slaughtered by the Chinese," Haq said. "They hoped to crush the uprising, but they were wrong then and are wrong now."

"Thirty independence activists were executed, and in the following protests up to five hundred people died. Right?"

"Everyone murdered in Ghulja is Uighur martyrs," Haq continued. "Today it's our fighting call and all Muslims who hear about it want to go and fight the Chinese. They must pay and they must give us our freedom. It's Allah's will."

Haq stopped talking and stared at a point way left of DeVille. There was silence for over a minute. DeVille knew he was not going to get anything more useful out of the student, so he signaled to the military policeman that the interview was over. The MP on the outside came in and wheeled Haq out.

The phone rang again.

*Someone must have been watching the interview.*

"Are you done?" the same female voice asked again.

"Yes, but I would like to have a look at whatever you found in his pockets or on him if that is possible," DeVille said.

"Okay," he heard the woman say before she hung up.

"Not very friendly," DeVille said in a low voice to where he suspected the camera to be.

Ten minutes later, the same military policeman that had been in the room during the interview appeared with a small cardboard box filled with plastic bags and a piece of paper which DeVille was asked to sign. It was a list of all the contents in the box: a wallet and some loose pocket items such as a house key and a cell phone.

The wallet contained nothing suspicious—credit cards, a small amount of money, driver's license, student card, public transportation card, and a few receipts. DeVille assumed they had gone through the cell phone, but he still powered it up and looked through the text messages. *Nothing.* Either this was a burner phone or someone had deleted the messages.

At the bottom of the list it mentioned two folded Post-it notes with the remark 'Quran quotes.' That caught his interest. He found the two plastic bags with the yellow paper inside and opened them. They were indeed quotes from the Quran and they were written in Dutch. DeVille knew these quotes, favored by extremists because taken out of context they encouraged violence. He also saw they were mistranslated. The intended meaning was gone.

DeVille needed to see Haq one more time. To confront him. Not sure how to get attention, he looked up and around him before pointing to the telephone.

Two seconds later it rang.

"Are you finished?" the woman asked.

"I would like to see the suspect again," DeVille said, having decided to return the impolite way of conversing—the apparent norm.

"Why do you need that?"

"Something is wrong with these Quran quotes," he said. "I'm sure you'll be watching, so I'll show you."

She hung up.

After ten minutes, there was a knock on the door and Haq was wheeled back in by the same military policemen. Haq's face was drawn and did not show any emotion. Bags under his eyes, he looked twenty years older than he was.

"Your Post-it notes. The ones you had on you when you were apprehended." DeVille decided to get this over with fast.

Haq for the first time looked him straight in the eyes.

"They are wrong in so many ways," DeVille continued.

"What are you talking about?"

"First, no dedicated jihadist would allow God's word to be translated into an infidel's language. Second, you obviously don't speak Arabic since you have translated them wrong, and third, you have no knowledge of the Quran as these verses are famous and even someone who had only studied the Holy Book for a short time would know them by heart."

DeVille saw Haq was both puzzled and angry over being accused of not knowing his religion.

*He doesn't want to be accused of having misunderstood the religion that he almost killed himself for.*

DeVille decided to see how far he could push him. "Can you even recite anything from the Quran?"

"You're a bastard infidel!"

A red light above the door lit up. The military policeman immediately took Haq and wheeled him out of the room.

*What the hell is going on? Have I been too harsh on him?*

Questioning a man's faith was cruel, but a far cry from waterboarding. He assumed professional interrogators did not let a few curses stop an interview. The man was after all a terrorist.

He expected the phone to ring and kept his hand on the receiver. Instead, the door opened, and a woman in a black pantsuit and a beige blouse entered. The blond hair looked like it would fall down from the knot at the back, and cover her face which bore no trace of make-up. DeVille regretted the impolite tone he had used on the phone. She introduced herself as Stella Hanson, special agent international affairs, with the CIA. The voice had lost the raspy echo it had on the phone.

"You were invited here as a guest, Mr. DeVille, so we gave you a little room to maneuver. But no good will come of you harassing the suspect into silence. If he believes we have insulted him, we won't get any information out of him."

DeVille did not reply.

*Just like a reprimand at elementary school.*

"So what is the big deal with some poorly translated prayers?" she asked.

"Just a hunch," he replied. "I've never seen a case before where a man is willing to die for a religion he hardly knows anything about. They tend to have studied it deeply, even if they have gotten the basic meaning wrong."

She looked at him for a couple of seconds before she spoke. "I hope you've gotten what you needed. Thanks for your thoughts on this."

DeVille caught the condescending tone and protested, "I don't think I'm done yet."

"Well, I think you are. I suggest you go back to Brussels and cash your paycheck."

# CHAPTER 7

"Stop here, please," DeVille said.

He could use some fresh air. It had taken him all the strength he had, not to vent his anger at the CIA agent. The cabdriver pulled into the curb at the beginning of Noordeinde. A walk through the high-end shopping and restaurant street in The Hague would bring him to Parkhotel where he had booked a room.

Even with the light colors of the walls and the furniture of the interview room, the condescending tone of the CIA agent made him see red. He stepped out of the cab half an hour after he had left the interview, impressed with himself that he had not burst. If there was one thing which could make him lose his temper, it was being treated like that.

He wondered what to report to the chief of staff.

*He'll be expecting an update.*

In DeVille's mind, the interview had been utterly fruitless. Haq was the cousin of a dead Chinese terrorist leader and most likely a pawn in a bigger picture. Besides this, he had nothing.

DeVille would have dinner near his hotel and write his report. There was a great little Italian place close by which he had visited a couple of years ago. It was the kind of restaurant with only two or three options on the menu each day, but with the freshest possible ingredients. It was like having your own private Italian mother. He hoped it was still there.

He would give the chief of staff a call when he got back to the hotel after dinner. *Perhaps a clearer connection between the Islamists and the stolen missile will show itself before that.*

As DeVille walked by store windows, filled with clothes normal people would not wear, a reflection made him slow his pace. He did not know what, but something did not feel right. His subconscious wired a message to look behind him. Nothing out of the ordinary, which meant one thing—someone was following him.

When going on field trips to old places of worship in different dictatorships around the world, he was always followed by bodyguards. Even though they kept a distance he knew who they were and why. They never tried to hide—they were always slightly visible. They wanted him to know he was being watched.

This was different. Same feeling, except he could not see anyone in particular. He was still a little on edge after the encounter with Special Agent Hanson. *Is that all it is?* He had to do something to get rid of the suspicion.

DeVille reached Grote Kerk, or St. James' Church as it was known to tourists, and made a decision to take a picture of Kerkplein square, a little triangular-shaped plaza to the side of the church, which he had just passed through—a happy square filled with a few restaurants and cheery people. The smell of juniper drinks, beer, cigarette smoke, and crisp afternoon air defined the merry atmosphere.

He walked around the church, and onto the same square again. It still looked the same. The raw air enveloped DeVille's face, yet droplets of sweat still appeared on his forehead. He turned around and took another picture towards the church. Anyone who appeared in both pictures could possibly be following him. They would have been behind him then and behind him now.

Grote Kerk was one of the oldest buildings in The Hague. The church, which was completed in the sixteenth century, was today owned by the municipality and you could rent it to hold concerts or parties. On one side of the church was a little restaurant called Zebedus. To DeVille's amusement, the restaurant served alcohol even though it was inside the church. He entered, ordered a Coke, and looked at the two pictures he had just taken.

His head jolted back as he saw the man who had a chubby, bald head, and was wearing a navy blue duffle coat and jeans. Not only did he appear in both pictures, but also in the window of the pub across the street.

The blood in DeVille's veins boiled for the second time that day. He understood, even though he did not appreciate it, that foreign autocratic governments kept an eye on him when he visited ancient sites in their countries. But this was not Myanmar or North Korea. This was the Netherlands.

*Why do they think I need a bodyguard while on an authorized visit?*

"To hell with them," he said out loud.

He decided to let the man know to mind his own business. DeVille left a five euro note on the table and rushed out of the restaurant towards the pub.

The man in the duffle coat noticed DeVille was watching him and got up from his table. DeVille reached the entrance of the pub and saw the man bolt out of a second entrance and down the street.

DeVille sprinted down a parallel side street, hoping to catch up with the duffle coat at the end. There would be the option of going either left or right, but DeVille hoped the man would turn right. If not, he would lose him.

When he reached the end of the street, the man was nowhere to be seen. DeVille turned his head back and forth several times. The man came around the corner, now with his coat under his arm, and a satisfied smirk.

DeVille used a tram, standing in the road, as cover and waited until the man passed. DeVille quickly walked up to him from behind and cleared his throat. "Why the hell are you following me?"

The man looked around while slowly putting his coat back on.

"Who do you think you are? Thinking you have the right to follow me."

From the man's face, it was obvious he was irritated by the confrontation. DeVille believed he had him cornered, but the man seized him by the arm with a strength DeVille didn't see coming. He dragged DeVille into a side street. There was hardly anyone there—most stores closed up a couple of hours ago.

"If this is Agent Hanson's work I swear she'll pay for it," DeVille lied.

"Shut the fuck up and listen to me," the man said in a low monotone voice while he grabbed DeVille's coat collar.

DeVille then felt a hard and hollow metal pipe pressed into his stomach just below his ribs. The barrel of a gun.

# CHAPTER 8

*Vladivostok, Russia*

"Here's your money. So, now tell us what you saw."

Dmitri looked in the envelope he was handed. The wad of beige ten-ruble bills should add up to the five hundred he had been promised. He looked back at the two men who Dmitri knew were from the mafia. "Sure. Yes, the four men on the photos you showed me was the men who was in the restaurant three days ago. I'm hundred and twenty percent sure."

The mobsters had shown him photographs of four men, but had given no names. He was not allowed to keep the photographs—they told him it was for his own good in case he got searched.

"Give us more details."

"Okay. They all came in and sat at the only table at the restaurant. As they had requested. All of them, except one, had expensive watches." Dmitri could tell they were not replicas. Before becoming a waiter, he was involved in the transport of counterfeit watches over the border. If he was right, three of the men had watches worth several hundred thousand dollars altogether.

"What about security?"

"Two guys. They showed up early and checked the whole restaurant before the men arrived. I suppose there were four drivers as well, because they all arrived in separate Mercs."

"What about our special deal? Did it interest you?" The larger of the two mafia thugs smiled, as if he had just told himself a joke.

"I am sorry, but there was no chance in hell that I could get any information about that guy. He was the one without an expensive watch, but I guess that isn't what you were hoping for." Dmitri knew he would not get the extra cash.

The mafia had said they would pay extra if they received any good information about who the man without the showpiece watch was. Dmitri was not going to take the risk and eavesdrop on them. The fee for just observing the men was decent enough. Not getting too greedy was what kept him alive.

It was not the first time someone had reserved the whole restaurant for a small meeting. They all did it for privacy, but more important to Dmitri, they tended to tip well. So having the whole restaurant reserved for only a few guests did not raise any questions among the hotel and restaurant staff.

Dmitri thought these men all shared the same facial traits and could easily have come from the same area, but he was told that two were Russians and two were Chinese. Over the last couple of years, as they grew wealthier and were looking for new places to invest, there had been more and more Chinese coming on business trips.

Dmitri had cleared the plates of food which they had only picked at, but also two empty bottles of premium champagne and the finest Russian vodka. One of the

Chinese asked for a drink that sounded like a French king, but the bartender had no clue what it was. Dmitri noticed they laughed him off disdainfully when he brought the message from the bartender.

"Anything else you can think of?" The two brutes seemed eager to leave.

"One other thing, but it seems so odd that I might have misunderstood it." Dmitri had not been sure about mentioning it, but he was hoping for similar jobs in the future.

"Spit it out."

"They spoke English so I might have gotten it wrong. Anyway, they raised their vodka glasses in a toast and one of them said something like 'for a successful theft tomorrow.' Another guy said, 'Inshallah' and then they all laughed. Then they downed their vodkas while the guy without the fancy watch said he hoped 'the stupid jihadists won't screw it up.'"

# CHAPTER 9

*Yeysk, Russia*

New car smell was one of life's great treats to many in the world, but most of them never experienced the odor of a new ship. Captain Zhang Min stood on the bridge of his new trawler and took a deep breath, inhaling the smell of burnt metal emerging from the welds of the hull.

*The most beautiful experience in the world.*

The FV Euphausia was the third new vessel Zhang had taken command of during his more than twenty-year-long career as a captain of fishing vessels. This was not a normal trawler and a first for Zhang as well. This was a specially-built vessel for catching euphausia, more commonly known as krill.

She was three hundred feet long and by far trumped any other vessel in the port and, on top of her five-story superstructure, her navigation bridge stood taller than the town's city hall.

Krill was a zooplankton, almost like a micro shrimp, and to catch it the vessel needed to use very fine masked nets. Trawling had to be done at a slow speed. The net was heavy when pulled onboard, because of the krill's tiny size, and they tended to get crushed. A business model leading straight to bankruptcy court.

The FV Euphausia used a different approach. Like a vacuum cleaner, it sucked the krill up from the net while in the water. This way, the krill went straight to a processing area where they were peeled by robotic arms and then blast-frozen. Each catch would be larger and of better quality. At the end of the day, it meant more money.

Zhang looked to his port side and onto the docks at the port of Yeysk—a small town on the shores of the Sea of Azov, connecting to the northern part of the Black Sea.

The vessel was built at a wharf in Ukraine before the Chinese owners took delivery of it in Yeysk. It was fitted with state-of-the-art technology and even had an ice class—a hull strengthened in order to move through sea ice. The FV Euphausia would trawl for krill in the Chinese sector of the North Pacific.

*We are a long way from there.*

There were two surprises for Captain Zhang when he embarked his new ship. The first surprise was that they were to take a route through the Arctic Ocean to get to the North Pacific. To Zhang, this seemed like an unnecessary risk at this time of the year, with all the ice and bad weather, and it would add fifteen or twenty days to their voyage.

The second surprise somewhat explained the first. The FV Euphausia was to take four passengers plus some cargo. These men were to rendezvous with another ship somewhere north of Novaya Zemlya, the Russian island in the Arctic Ocean. They were scientists according to the papers provided, who studied climate change and were part of a larger Russian project.

Zhang did not like strangers onboard his ship and even

worse were people who were neither seamen nor fishermen. The order to change the route and to accommodate these scientists and their equipment had come directly from the shipowner. He respected the man, so he was not going to object, but he had made his irritation known. But that was all he would do. He was too close to retirement to risk any upset with the owner.

He then smiled at the thought of the seasickness that would no doubt hit these guys as soon as they entered the North Sea. He made a mental note to tell the cook to prepare cabbage stew for when they hit the roller coaster of the seas. The smell of cooked cabbage could induce seasickness in even a seasoned sailor.

# CHAPTER 10

*The Hague, The Netherlands*

"Give me the camera," the monotone voice demanded.

DeVille slipped his hand into his coat pocket and pulled the camera out.

The man grabbed it. "I don't like my picture being taken. You'll be coming with me. We need to have a little talk." His voice was still monotone, making the accent unrecognizable.

Gun jammed into his stomach, DeVille did not say a word. His brain was busy computing what he had done to upset the CIA so badly. No good answers came to mind. Spooks do not like to have their pictures taken, but to pull out a gun was overkill.

Monotone Man motioned to him that it was time to move by pushing him with the gun. The gun was covered by the sleeve of his coat, not revealing the barrel that was sticking out and into DeVille's stomach. They walked a few steps before DeVille noticed the alley. The hairs on his arms stood up and pushed against his shirt.

*If we go in there I might not come back out again.*

"Wait. You can have the camera. Just let me go."

DeVille's voice trembled with the last words. "There's no need to do this. I don't even know who you are. Forget about what I said."

The barrel of the gun dug deeper into DeVille's gut.

DeVille still stopped their forward movement. He would rather get shot in an open street than in a dark alley. He was about to scream out to get attention from people around them, when the barrel moved upwards and felt like it was going to puncture his lung.

Monotone Man said, through clenched teeth, "You're making a big fucking mistake."

"Drop the gun." A shout from across the street.

DeVille scanned the crowd on the nearby streets for whoever had shouted. People stopped and looked around. No one was facing him.

"Drop the gun, you're surrounded," someone else shouted from ahead of them.

Monotone Man looked around. DeVille was confused. The last voice belonged to Stella Hanson.

The pressure of the gun's barrel, jammed into DeVille's side, eased.

*A sign for me to act.*

DeVille slammed the arm which held the gun. With the barrel pointed away from him, he twisted his body and rammed his knee into Monotone Man's stomach.

DeVille had hoped to hit him a little lower than the stomach, but he still caught him off guard. Monotone Man crouched and groaned in pain, but stood back up again. DeVille was about to start running when the gun was aimed at him.

DeVille froze.

Two shots were fired and DeVille instinctively closed his eyes. When he opened them, he saw two dark, wet circles growing bigger around Monotone Man's chest. More and more blood trickled out and moistened the duffle coat.

DeVille looked at his own chest.

Nothing.

The gun dropped from Monotone Man's hand and DeVille kicked it away. The man fell over and lay still.

Deville's brain started to register the screams around him and he saw people rushing away. Stella Hanson ran towards him with a gun in her hand.

The CIA agent bent down over the man who had been shot, checked for any pulse, before walking over and picking up the gun DeVille had kicked away. Together with her own gun, she stuffed it into her coat pocket. Her expression gave nothing away as she returned to Monotone Man and grabbed his coat collar with her gloved hands.

"Who are you? Who sent you?" she asked in a low, calm voice.

Monotone Man looked at her and coughed up some blood. His body twitched and his eyes turned foggy.

"Who the hell is this?" Stella asked turning to DeVille.

"This isn't your guy?"

"Why would I shoot one of my own men?" she demanded with anger in her eyes. "Why didn't you just stand still and let us handle the situation?"

DeVille hoped she did not expect an answer, so he let her continue.

"Come with me. It's not up for debate. I have a car close by."

DeVille knew he had no option. Not because of the condescending tone, but because he would rather go with her than try to explain to the Dutch police, who would arrive within minutes, what had happened

Stella stood up and looked at another man who came over to them—something DeVille had not noticed.

She said, "Nick, please take care of this with the police when they arrive. Tell them that they can come by the embassy to pick up both my gun and the one that this guy had. Tell them the truth."

"Yes, ma'am," the man replied.

# CHAPTER 11

*Shanghai, China*
*21:56*

Three days ago Wang Chi had looked at the sad skyline of Vladivostok. Now he stared through the floor-to-ceiling windows in his office on the thirty-fourth floor.

*Much better.*

His eyes rested on the Oriental Pearl Tower on the other side of the Huangpu River. Its two pearl-shaped spheres were bathed in a red light reminiscent of dens of promiscuous sex for money.

*Like a spaceship ready to lift off.*

From the river, which crisscrossed the city, a scenario looking like the stars in the sky beamed up at him. The stars were all the ships and barges that trafficked the river that was the night sky. He focused on a dredger which was slowly moving up the river. He had always been interested in dredgers.

When he was a child he had wanted to become a treasure hunter. The ocean held so many treasures. He had been obsessed with the Chinese explorer Zheng He's treasure ships when he was a teenager. Wang had spent many nights dreaming of finding gold and precious stones hidden in wrecks of treasure ships down on the ocean floor.

He smiled, thinking his dreams had come true. The ocean was a provider of treasures for him.

Two model ships stood on shelves on the wall in front of him. One of them was a standard dredger, while the other was a state-of-the-art subsea mining vessel. The dredger had made Wang a reasonable fortune, but it was the subsea mining vessel which was going to make him one of the richest men in China, and possibly in the world.

The dark hardwood floor made only subtle squeaks as he walked over and sat down behind his desk at the other end of his large office. It was decorated in a minimalistic way, but the Asian influence was unmistakable. Feng Shui principles had guided the interior designer, and it was all yin and yang. The entrance of his office would give, while his desk at the other end would receive.

Not that Wang believed in those things, but it was important to welcome clients in a space in which they would feel culturally comfortable. He knew Tengri had more important matters to attend to than to care about how an office was laid out.

Wang had founded his company, Eje Marine Services, seven years ago. Long days in the office were normal and he had just finished off the last of the day's paperwork. He let his mind drift.

It was his dream to become a treasure hunter, and the dream would soon come true. The seabed contained huge deposits of gold, copper, zinc, and silver. Volcanic vents in the oceans carried metals from the earth's center and deposited the minerals on the ocean floor. The knowledge was not new—it was discovered in the sixties. But only recently, technology had been developed to make it financially viable to mine for these minerals.

There were a few other companies out there which did the same as Eje Marine Services. The difference was that none of them had as advanced a mining vessel as the one Wang had developed.

In addition, these companies were mainly forced to work off the coast of corrupt Lilliput nations in Africa or in the Pacific Ocean, as most developed countries were still unsure of the environmental impact of subsea mining.

Politicians never liked to approve exploration that might challenge the environmentalists to protest. Not even the normally cold and capitalistic Chinese government would risk it.

Wang would soon get sole access to one of the oceans with the highest density of precious metals, as well as a monopoly supplying these metals to the Chinese markets.

By getting full mining rights and fifty percent of the output to sell to the Chinese market, the factory of the world, there was no question that money would pour in. One of the Russian Khagans would get the other fifty percent, at cost, to sell and distribute to the rest of the world.

Wang would be to China what Rockefeller had been to the US—if the plan worked. All thanks to unrestricted access to the Arctic Ocean.

Five days ago, Khagan Wu had called and told him the plan would commence in two days. Wang knew the information needed to be correct if the plan was to work. He had no reason to doubt Khagan Wu. If anyone was going to have accurate information it would be a lieutenant general in the Chinese Ministry of State Security.

Wu headed up the Second Bureau, which was responsible for foreign affairs—in charge of spies abroad. That made him one of the most powerful officials in Chinese intelligence. And also one of the most powerful men in Chinese politics.

Wang had then made a call to the men they had set up in the Netherlands and passed along the information he had received. The Russians would have done the same to the men they had set up.

The next day Wang took the three-hour-long flight from Shanghai to Vladivostok in a chartered business jet. He could not yet afford to have his own private jet, but that would soon change.

There he met up with his fellow Khagans and the four of them dined at an awful restaurant. The main agenda was to tie up any loose ends. The plan was thorough and well made, so there were only a few. The meeting was more a celebration of their plan and that it was in motion. He flew back home the same night.

He looked through the window, onto the Shanghai skyline, and shivered.

*Home sweet home.*

Wang was no admirer of Russia, but knew that the country and the two Russian Khagans were an important part of their plan. Russia would only improve afterwards, he convinced himself.

Whenever Wang's mind drifted, he thought of Genghis Khan. He wondered how proud of them the sky god would be for coming up with such a plan. Ultimately they would create a superpower that befitted his image.

Wang knew he was not the main character in the scheme. It would be either Khagan Wu or Khagan Alexandrovich who would be in charge and wield the power, but he and Khagan Bakunin would be the men who had made it possible.

*No one can create power without financial wealth backing them.*

He was earmarked for the position as Minister of Foreign Affairs, but sometimes wondered if perhaps an ambassador posting to a civilized European country would be more gratifying. Someplace where he could enjoy all the wealth he would have accumulated—combined with the perks of diplomatic immunity. There was still some time before he had to worry about that.

Wang snapped out of his thoughts and looked at his watch. The round red and golden disk told him that it was almost ten at night. The Hublot looked oversized on his small wrist, but he loved the weight of it.

It was time to take the elevator to the penthouse. He hated commuting, so he had made sure to locate the company's offices in a building which also had luxury residential units. Tomorrow it would start, and for several weeks thereafter, they would have to work hard to realize their dreams and Tengri's commands.

# CHAPTER 12

*22:35*

The US Embassy in The Hague was three blocks from where the shooting had taken place, so DeVille and Stella Hanson arrived in two minutes sharp. The building was in the posh area of town, close to the parliament, but the embassy—surrounded by fences and barricades due to security precautions—stood out like a warty face in a beauty contest.

After a quick check of DeVille's papers by the security guards, they entered the underground parking and took an elevator up to the third floor. Stella's access card led them through several doors before a palm scanner indicated that they were about to enter the classified section of the floor.

They entered an office. Stella's office, DeVille assumed. There was no nameplate on the door, but the nicely stacked piles of paper hovering along a wall on the side of a large desk appeared as organized as the woman beside him seemed. A little claustrophobic, DeVille thought, as the desk seemed to swallow the room. With its yellow wooden color, inside the white-walled office, it looked like a yolk inside an egg.

He took a seat in front of the desk while Stella booted up her computer.

"When I read your file, I didn't expect you to get into this much trouble," she said, looking up from the computer screen. "You're a Canadian citizen. You've lived in Brussels for the past five years and do consulting work for the EU and NATO bureaucrats. And you're being paid handsomely."

"Why do you have a file on me?"

"You didn't think we'd let you talk to our only suspect without checking you out, did you? Plus, we looked up everyone who was involved in that incident in southern Belgium a few weeks ago."

"I guess I checked out."

"Your grandparents escaped from Norway during the German invasion and made it to the US. Your grandfather was a minister before the war, but refused to settle with the rest of the government in London. The prime minister denied him an opportunity to go back and fight with the resistance forces in Norway and in protest he moved to Canada and joined the 'Little Norway' base in Toronto as an air force captain. Eventually he settled in Canada."

"What's this got to do with anything?"

"I also know that your wife was killed by a religious cult and that you speak four different languages. My point is that we know everything about you, so if you are into some kind of monkey business and the person I shot leads us to that, it will have consequences for you."

"Five."

"Five what?"

"I speak five languages."

"Fine." Stella took a deep breath. "All right, walk me through what happened before we got there today," she said, and got ready to type his statement.

He explained that he suspected he was being followed and how he detected the man. "I thought he was CIA."

"It was foolish to confront the man," she interrupted.

DeVille paused and swallowed a politically incorrect comment. He just wanted to get back to his hotel.

"Did he have an accent?" she asked. "My colleague at the scene just sent me an e-mail saying there were no ID papers on the guy."

"He did, but it was impossible to recognize where he was from," DeVille said. "If I were to guess anything, I'd say he was probably from Eastern Europe."

"Hmm," was the only verbal response from Stella, as her hands moved away from the keyboard.

"Why do you say that? Is that of significance?"

She looked at him and seemed to ponder whether to share it with him or not. She took her jacket off and DeVille's eyes strayed for a second towards her breasts covered by a blouse.

Her body shape was similar to what Carina's had been. Slim and fit.

Carina would have been around the same age now too.

If it had not been for him.

"It might be nothing," she said, apparently having made up her mind. "The bank account Haq used to pay for the two rental trucks had an incoming money transfer from a Russian account. The Russians are not cooperating with us on this, so we weren't able to trace the actual sender in Russia."

"Why aren't they cooperating?" DeVille asked. "A nuclear missile is on the loose—shouldn't that demand some cooperation?"

"Unfortunately not. The Russians will do their own investigation. Based on what they find, they'll decide what they want to share." She looked at him like he were a first-grader who had just been explained basic math. "After Syria and Ukraine we aren't really on a first-name basis with the Russians."

"Right. Guess we don't want the missile ending up in either of those locations?"

Stella ignored the question, "Anyway, have you come up with any new thoughts on what it could mean that Haq's a novice Muslim, as you put it?"

DeVille decided to play ball. "It struck me that Haq seemed so clueless about the basics of Islam. No one becomes a terrorist by just reading the Quran or attending prayers, so he was obviously newly converted to radical Islam."

"So?"

"I believe someone indoctrinated him. And that person is most likely in charge. Or he can lead us to who is."

"Okay, I'm listening."

"I think it could be useful to make a visit to the university in Utrecht. Talk to some of Haq's teachers and fellow students." He did not mention he had already decided to go to Utrecht no matter what she thought of the idea.

When he was done, she turned to her computer and typed for a minute. Then she leaned back in her chair and looked at him. "Okay, I think you have a good point there. I'd like you to go with me to Utrecht tomorrow morning."

* * *

DeVille got to the hotel an hour later. His stomach rumbled, not having received any food since lunch in Brussels, but the hotel kitchen was closed and he was too exhausted to go out.

Before he could shut his eyes, he needed to check in with the chief of staff in Brussels. Give him a full update of what was happening. DeVille pulled out the Nokia and the chief of staff answered after two rings.

"I've been waiting for your call," he said.

"Sorry about that, but I think you'll understand after I've told you what happened today," DeVille said. The chief of staff listened, not even interrupting when DeVille told him about the dead and unidentifiable man.

"This smells bad," the chief of staff finally said. "Either the CIA is clueless, which I doubt, or they want to keep a check on us and what we know. Neither seems logical and that makes this scary."

"Right."

"Oh, DeVille, make sure you let me know if you find anything in Utrecht. No matter how insignificant you may think it is."

"I will," DeVille said, but the line was already dead.

DeVille put the phone back in his coat pocket.

*Why didn't the chief of staff ask for more details about the shooting?*

# CHAPTER 13

*Utrecht, The Netherlands*
*March 30$^{th}$ – 09:45*

"There's nowhere to park," DeVille said.

"Don't worry about it."

They had traveled towards Utrecht early. DeVille had slept remarkably well considering what had happened the evening before. His alarm went off at five-thirty and he was down in the restaurant for breakfast by six.

He checked out of the hotel, as his new plan was to take a train from Utrecht back to Brussels after they were done there. Stella Hanson picked him up in a gray Renault Megane just before seven o'clock. For some reason he had imagined she would turn up in a big Yank tank of an SUV.

*More suitable for a CIA agent than a small French car.*

Despite leaving early, they hit heavy traffic on the A12 highway towards Utrecht. Rush hour and gridlocks were synonymous with Holland —in fact, the Dutch word for gridlock, *file*, was one of the first words anyone who moved there learned. The drive took them twice as long as it would have done outside of rush hour, so they got to the university just after nine in the morning.

The university was spread over several buildings and campuses. They decided to go to the administration building and see the secretary general of General Affairs.

*It's only in universities where they make up such titles.*

There was no visible parking outside the building, something that seemed to annoy Stella. Then, with no warning, she drove over the curb with all four wheels and parked in the middle of the sidewalk.

"Guess the CIA doesn't pay parking fines," DeVille said.

After Stella showed the receptionist her diplomatic ID, they were led right away to the office of the secretary general. She introduced herself as being from the US Embassy, and DeVille as being part of the EU Commission in Brussels. Not exactly the truth, but close enough for his conscience.

"We're working on a case with the Dutch authorities regarding a money-laundering scam, possibly financing terrorists," she said.

This was far from the truth, but DeVille understood why they needed to keep the real story classified. The secretary general stood up straighter when he heard this, as if he was about to salute.

Stella handed the official a letter. "This is from the Ministry of Defense and the MIVD. They will verify my story, if you feel you need to."

"Oh, no, not at all. I will do all I can to help. In whatever way." The secretary general's voice changed from skeptical to proud. "I will do anything to help my country."

When asked about Haq, he found the young man's enrollment file on his computer and made a printout. "Perhaps I can take you to see the professor who knows Haq the best?" he asked.

They walked to a different building on campus which housed the Geosciences faculty where Haq studied Urban Planning. While they walked, DeVille looked at the enrollment file, but found nothing of interest. Haq seemed as average as sand in the desert—average grades and average attendance.

DeVille knew that the Dutch were known to be the tallest people in the world, but Haq's professor was a short, thin man. His jeans were baggy and stick-like arms emerged from his polo shirt. He resembled a starved child.

After another round of introductions and an explanation of why they were there, Stella was offered the only guest chair in the professor's little office. The secretary general's face reddened and he gave an apologetic nod to DeVille, the two of them cramped near the door. DeVille had seen many academics' offices and knew that small seemed to be the only size they came in.

"I can't really say much about him. He was always a quiet student, but he did well on tests. I don't know if Urban Planning was really what he wanted to do in his life, but..."

"Who'd want to?" DeVille asked.

"...but I think he felt privileged to get an education. Something his parents never were fortunate enough to get."

"Any friends?" Stella asked.

"To be honest, I don't know. The only thing I can do, is to give you the names of students he cooperated with on team assignments. Not that I think that will help you much." The professor wrote down some names on a Post-it and gave it to Stella.

DeVille looked at the four names and reread them twice. All four were female and Dutch. If Haq had befriended these girls to deflect any suspicion of being a Muslim radical, he had done a good job. Perhaps it was as simple as him being a normal Dutch Muslim.

"I do have some good news," the professor said. "They should all be due in class in twenty minutes."

"Okay, we need to be quick. Let's interview two at a time," Stella told DeVille. The professor would get the students to them before he started his class.

It turned out that none of them were close friends with Haq, but they enjoyed working with him as he was a smart student. DeVille read from what they said that neither Haq, nor these girls, could be called socially popular. That was why they had drifted towards each other. It amused him that such behavior existed at university level but then he remembered the same thing from when he had studied.

They compared what they had gotten from the interviews, and both agreed that Haq mainly kept to himself—but that there had been a change over the last year. A year ago he attended parties, although he didn't drink, but lately he had been missing at these social necessities of student life. The common belief among the students was that he had rediscovered his Muslim faith.

"I did get to know where Haq worshipped, the Sayidina Ibrahim Mosque," DeVille said. Not that it would have been too difficult to find out. Even though Utrecht had a large Muslim population there were less than a handful of mosques.

"Okay, it'll help us time-wise. I also heard that a couple of other Muslim students at the university recently rediscovered their faith and have gone through personality changes."

"Any names?"

"No, none of the girls knew their names or what they studied. Wonder if they went to the same mosque."

The secretary general told them the university had almost thirty thousand students, so they decided it would be futile to try to find the other students who had become more devout.

"I'll get someone at the embassy to try to narrow the list down, but I think our best bet is to try the mosque," Stella said.

DeVille agreed.

They thanked the secretary general and went back to the car. The next destination was the Sayidina Ibrahim Mosque—the one that Haq was associated with.

There was a parking ticket on the window. Stella crumpled it and threw it into a trashcan next to the car. "You're right, the CIA doesn't pay parking fines."

# CHAPTER 14

*10:55*

It did not take them long to get to the other side of the city, and while driving, Stella got the imam's phone number and called him. Again she used the same story she had told the university officials. The imam agreed to talk to them.

"Turn right onto Attleeplantsoen," the car's navigation system told them.

It was a small street that immediately gave DeVille the impression of traveling back in time. To the eighties, if he went by the Ford Fiestas and Opel Rekords parked along the curb. When he saw the square, brick apartment buildings, he thought he had underestimated. They had gone back to the sixties or seventies.

*Not the best period in history when it comes to architectural design.*

A crescent moon came into their field of view, mounted on top of a light green dome, pushed up between the trees.

"That thing looks like it's about to take off," said Stella as she turned the Renault onto the side street and parked in front of the Sayidina Ibrahim Mosque.

"That's not like any other mosque I've seen before," DeVille said.

"What do you mean?"

"First of all, it's one of the smallest. It's also square and kind of weird looking. Like someone just stacked a bunch of shipping containers together and covered them with concrete."

There were no other cars parked in front, which made sense, since it was still two hours or so until noon prayers. Most followers lived close to the mosque, or if far away, they would take public transportation. In Dubai, a place DeVille visited often, the rule was that mosques should be within walking distance. The irony was that everyone still drove.

When they opened the metal gate, the imam came out of the front door.

"Welcome," he said without introducing himself. He seemed pleased that Stella had covered her hair with a pashmina. DeVille had pointed it out in the car and was happy she carried one in her purse—and that she did not object.

The imam was dressed in casual khakis and a kurta, the traditional loose shirt which reaches the knees. DeVille knew there was no particular dress code for imams as opposed to Christian priests, but they did tend to dress more conservatively than the average man.

His beard concealed his age, but DeVille guessed that the imam was in his early forties. He also seemed well educated and westernized. According to Stella, the English he had spoken on the phone was textbook, and DeVille made out the shape of an iPhone in the pocket of the imam's kurta.

"Let's go this way," the imam said and led them around the mosque to the back side where a single-door entrance revealed a small room with two tables and four chairs around each. They were offered coffee and they both accepted.

When the imam came back with three cups of coffee, he told them he would listen to them, but he could not guarantee he would help. "It might not be up to me to decide," he said and smiled.

"Inshallah," DeVille said.

They gave him a more detailed picture of the money laundering terrorist funding story Stella had cooked up.

"We suspect the money is being channeled to terrorists in western China," DeVille added.

"So you're saying that there will be many Muslim lives at stake?" he asked.

Stella continued with what they had learned about Haq from the students at the university.

"I'm certain that Haq was not in this alone," DeVille said. "We will find the others eventually, but you can make it happen faster if you give us their names. Delays means that lives will be lost."

The imam carefully stroked his beard without saying anything for what seemed like a few minutes. He suddenly stood up and said, "I don't really believe in your story, but there was a few men who struck me as suspicious."

"Who?" DeVille asked.

"I don't know their names," the imam said.

DeVille went from feeling ecstatic to frustrated.

"You got to have their names written down somewhere?" Stella asked.

"No. We don't keep a logbook, if that's what you think."

"So, why did they strike you as suspicious?" DeVille sighed.

"You know, most of the Muslim society in this city are either Moroccans or Turks who have lived here for most of their lives. These men came in here with a much more conservative view. They tried to blend in, but it was obvious to anyone who saw them that they struggled to agree with the liberal Islam that we teach here."

"If they weren't Turks or Moroccans, do you know where they came from?" DeVille asked.

"Yes, I believe they were Uighur—from Western China."

DeVille looked at the CIA agent, who asked, "Do you know any other kids Haq's age who he hung out with?"

The imam took some time before he answered, "Yes, there were two friends of him who also started to come to the mosque more frequently. I know their names, but I'm sure they're not part of it. It's the Uighur men who is behind if someone has done something wrong."

"We need their names," Stella said firmly.

"Wait here, I will get you all their names," the imam said and left the room.

"This is already more fruitful then the university and even interviewing Haq," DeVille said with a smile towards Stella.

The imam returned with a piece of paper with two names written on them.

The names looked Uighur to DeVille.

"These two," the imam said, "together with Haq they have come to the mosque on and off for many years. I know them. They are good Dutch kids and good Muslims, even though they didn't come to the mosque that often."

A thought struck DeVille. "Did the Uighur men celebrate Ramadan at the mosque?" he asked.

"Yes?"

"Then I'm sure they broke their fast at Iftar here, too."

"I believe they did."

"In a small mosque like this, I'm sure you need advance registration for the Iftar meals. You can't afford to make too much food, nor do you want not to be able to feed someone either."

"I see where you're going," the imam said. "I'll go through our records from last Ramadan and see. We only did three Iftars, so it shouldn't be too many names." He walked out of the room.

DeVille smiled at Stella.

She glanced at DeVille. "Hold your horses, cowboy. The names won't be real. Why would they use their real names?"

Within five minutes, the imam returned. "This is the three Uighur men who came in here. First time was two years ago." He pointed to one of three names on a piece of paper. "It seemed like this man, Khan, was the one in charge."

DeVille noticed that Stella was texting the names into her Blackberry. He was in no doubt that an e-mail would be sent asking for background checks on these five men.

"How did the students get involved with the Uighur guys?" DeVille asked.

"Not sure, but I think their families all had ancestors from the eastern part of an area that is called Turkestan. As I'm sure you know, that overlaps with Uighur China. I guess that in the start, they just wanted to know what life was like back where their families came from."

"And then they got brainwashed?" asked Stella, seemingly done with her e-mail instructions.

"I wouldn't say brainwashed," the imam said.

DeVille could sense some annoyance in his voice.

"It seemed to me that after a while they felt a connection with where they were from and understood the culture they originated from. I guess they developed an admiration for these Uighur guys." The imam rubbed his beard again and stood up. "That is really all I know and can tell you. If anyone has done something bad, it is the three Uighur guys, not any of the youths."

He walked to the door in a move that suggested the meeting was over. "I hope no innocent lives are lost or hurt because of this."

*Too late.*

DeVille had the Dutch F-16 pilot in his mind.

Stella told him that the e-mail she had sent during the meeting with the imam requested her CIA colleagues to confirm the names on the list and get their addresses. The e-mail also asked that they set up an arrest operation for them all as soon as possible, if they could be located.

"It comes under the Anti-Terrorism Act so we don't need any warrants," she said. "I also want the three Uighur men arrested simultaneously. Don't want any of them getting suspicious and doing anything stupid."

DeVille had a fair idea of what she meant by *stupid*.

Fifteen minutes later, she got the addresses in a reply and decided she and DeVille would go to where Khan allegedly lived to see if he was there. She explained to DeVille that the Dutch police would have to make the physical arrest of the men, because of what had happened yesterday. She did not want any further diplomatic upset—plus she preferred for the CIA to stay in the background during such operations.

"No point risking my own men if someone else is more than happy to risk themselves, right?"

Stella handed DeVille her phone. "I've also gotten the immigration pictures of the men. Have a look."

"These guys don't look like students at all," he said. All three faces wore obvious signs of a hard life outdoors in both extreme heat and cold. It looked like their skulls had shrunk and released their grips on their faces.

# CHAPTER 15

*14:22*

Stella and DeVille arrived outside the apartment building that they had been told was rented by Mahmoud Khan, or Mohammad Khan as the immigration papers stated. The terrorists had not put too much effort into their aliases as the other two Uighur men also used Mohammad.

It had taken the CIA less than twenty minutes to connect that Mohammad Khan was Mahmoud Khan of the Turkestan Islamic Movement. He was believed to be a lieutenant in the organization and was wanted by the Chinese government on terrorism charges.

*Just like the chief of staff suspected.*

The two others were also connected to TIM.

After they left the mosque, they had eaten lunch at a coffee bar close by. While there, Stella's colleagues set up an operation with the Dutch authorities to arrests the three men, as well as the two students.

All of it took less than two hours. DeVille was impressed with their efficiency. Five teams were now on standby or on their way to the different addresses.

* * *

They parked their car on the street outside Khan's building and saw that the civilian van with the Dutch SWAT team was already there. Stella rolled down her window.

DeVille glanced at the mirror and saw a jogger approaching. As he ran by, he tossed a small Bluetooth earpiece into the car. It landed on the floor by Stella's feet. She picked it up, placed it in her ear, and pressed a button.

"Testing. Alpha leader here. Alpha team do you read me?"

DeVille could not hear the response.

"Do we have confirmation that the target is in the apartment?" Stella asked in a tone that gave DeVille the impression she had done this many times before.

She apparently got an answer and asked Alpha team to get ready. She looked at DeVille and said, "They don't know if someone is inside the apartment, but even if they did, they wouldn't be able to confirm if it's Khan. I've decided we'll go for it."

"Don't you have all sort of gadgets to see what's going on inside houses?"

"*We* do. But not the Dutch."

"What if the missile is in there?"

"The Dutch are pretty sure it isn't. Even in this neighborhood, someone would have noticed if they tried to move a twelve-foot missile up to a tiny apartment on the second floor." She reached behind her seat and grabbed a bulletproof vest and managed to get it over her blouse with little effort, considering she was sitting in the driver's seat of a small hatchback.

"You're staying here," she said.

DeVille was about to protest, but stopped himself as soon as Stella pointed to her vest.

"I've only got one."

"Fair enough," he said.

"Make yourself useful while I'm gone," she said and gave him a dossier.

DeVille pictured the Dutch SWAT team breaking down the front door of the apartment with a small battering ram and run in with Stella Hanson just a step behind them.

Thirty seconds after they entered the building, a policeman emerged, shepherding a line of wide-eyed residents out onto the street. In case Khan tried something stupid—like blowing himself up—the innocents would be as far away from any fallout as possible. DeVille saw no fault with that particular plan.

He put down the dossier, one particular fact gnawing at him. According to the Uighur men's visa applications, they were all employees of a Russian company.

*That doesn't make sense.*

A number of people gathered around the building out of curiosity. As this was a somewhat shabby neighborhood, chipped brick buildings with laundry drying from the windows, DeVille assumed its residents were used to the police raiding apartments. It would not be the first time they had seen a drug dealer or another lowlife arrested in a sting operation.

DeVille figured the least he could do was help the policeman keep the onlookers as far away from the building as possible. He got out of the car and crossed the street.

A man came out of the little Albert Heijn grocery store, two buildings to the left of the apartment building. He was dressed in jeans and a thick jacket, but also a *taqiyah,* the Muslim skullcap, which caught DeVille's attention. Under it was a worn face. He recognized it immediately.

It was Khan.

* * *

Khan saw the commotion in front of his apartment building the second he stepped out of the food store. He knew it meant they had found him. The fighter in him woke up, although he felt naked without any weapon but his knife.

If the plan had gone as hoped, they would have gone back to the university in a week's time, finished their exams, and left for home. Nothing suspicious.

But that was not to be.

He had nothing to lose. Either he would get away or he would die a martyr's death. He turned, placed his grocery bag in front of the grocery store's obligatory beggar/junkie, and walked away.

* * *

DeVille was sure it was the commotion outside the apartment building that made Khan turn around, and head in the other direction. He tried to catch the attention of the policeman across the street, but the cop was too busy with the crowd to notice him.

That left only two options—let Khan escape or follow him himself—DeVille knew what he needed to do. He walked about a hundred meters behind the terrorist, sending a text message to Stella, knowing she would not pick up if he called—not in the middle of an arrest operation.

> *Spotted Khan outside. Am*
>
> *following him. Call when you see*
>
> *this.*

There were not many people on the streets, so following Khan at a distance proved to be easier than DeVille had thought. The weather promised to complicate things, though. Drops of rain were already landing on his forehead, assuring a cold downpour to come—the standard form of precipitation in the Netherlands. At least it would help hide him—as it was, he felt conspicuous in his tailor-made suit and thousand-euro cashmere overcoat.

*Hardly the norm in this neighborhood.*

Add a fedora and a cigarette and he would look like Sam Spade, trailing his suspect.

Khan turned a corner onto a side street. DeVille picked up his pace, not wanting to lose sight of him for too long.

\* \* \*

At the same time as the attempted arrest on Khan had started, similar operations were carried out at three other locations.

The two identified students had shown up at the university where two policemen had been sent in case they turned up for class. They were detained without any problems.

One of the other Uighur men was spotted in his studio apartment close to the Sayidina Ibrahim Mosque and the SWAT team arrested him after breaking down his door. Immediately after they handcuffed him, he began to violently convulse and vomit before then dying. The SWAT-team suspected he swallowed a cyanide-pill just before they entered his apartment.

The second Uighur was more troublesome to apprehend. They saw him leave his apartment building and decided to act to avoid a potential hostage situation. When approached, the man pulled out a small handgun and shot one of the SWAT team in the hip before he hid behind a clothes donation box. While the SWAT team scrambled to take cover, he managed to grab a teenage girl who had opened her front door to see what the disturbance was about. He made no demands and the SWAT team did not want to take any chances. When one member signaled he could make a clean shot, the approval was given.

The Uighur's life ended shortly after a 9 mm bullet from an MP5 submachine gun erupted in his skull above his left ear.

\* \* \*

DeVille got to the corner of the building where Khan had gone down the side street. He stopped, looked down to see if he could get a glimpse of the Uighur, then continued. It meant that Khan was at least a hundred fifty meters ahead of him—the length of the side street.

DeVille hurried down it to make sure he could catch up with Khan. The subtle crunch of someone stepping on a chocolate wrapper made DeVille quickly turn around. Khan came at him fast from behind a parked car with a large knife in his hand.

The Uighur rushed towards him, but DeVille lashed out with his foot in a volley, hoping to stop Khan's advance. The foot hit his arm instead of his chest. It did not slow Khan down and DeVille took a step to the side so as not to lose his balance.

Khan turned back towards him. DeVille knew there was no chance he could escape him. Khan's left arm slammed DeVille in the chest. The right arm, holding the knife, swung backwards, preparing to make the lethal stab.

DeVille lifted both his hands, bending down. The knife hit his left arm, the fabric of his coat ripping until the cold blade penetrated his skin.

Khan pulled the knife away and prepared for another stab. DeVille lurched forward to head-butt him in the crotch, but all he managed to do was push Khan backwards. He picked Khan up in an attempt to throw him over his back.

The knife jabbed into DeVille's coat again from the back and a lightning bolt of pain surged through him. He growled. Both of them fell onto the car which Khan had hid behind, as DeVille's legs collapsed.

Khan's head hit the taillight of the Ford Escort, and shattered pieces of red and orange corrugated plastic dropped to the ground. DeVille swung his arm towards the knife and knocked it out of Khan's hand, making it slide away on the wet cobblestones. Khan scuttled to get back up on his feet.

DeVille, unable to stand, grabbed hold of Khan's foot with the hand of his unharmed arm. Khan turned and rammed the side of his foot into DeVille's shoulder, just missing his head.

DeVille lost his grip on Khan's leg and watched the man leap towards the knife. Khan picked it up and twisted back around.

*I'm finished.*

He noticed a shard from the broken taillight. Grabbing hold of it, he tensed his entire body as Khan approached.

As Khan neared him, a cold smile cut across his face. DeVille used the last of his strength to leap up and grab Khan's knife-wielding arm. He swiveled, and with his right arm, he jammed the broken taillight deep into Khan's neck.

The edge of the shard dug in deep and gouged a thick furrow. A strangled scream came from Khan as he fell to his knees. The hand, still holding onto the knife, moved up to his neck.

DeVille slashed the shard at the Uighur half a dozen times before falling over sideways, exhausted and paralyzed by an excruciating pain.

Khan fell forward, blood throbbing out of the gashes in a beating rhythm. It went from dark ruby to almost pink as it mixed with the rainwater that had amassed in puddles.

People ran towards them, screaming and shouting, but everything was just a blur of noises for DeVille. He used his last bit of energy to roll over, hoping someone would see the blood trickling out of his back.

Khan lay facedown, his blood streaming towards Deville.

Then DeVille's eyes stopped seeing.

# CHAPTER 16

*Dalian, China*

Wang stood inside a small office next to the outfitting dock at a shipyard in Dalian, about a thousand kilometers north of Shanghai. Dalian was the largest coastal city this far north in China, and it was just a day's hike from the border with North Korea.

He needed the ship to navigate around the Korean peninsula to get north into the Pacific Ocean—it was the best option Wang had. He was short of time.

His pride, the MV Ulgan, glistened in the powerful shine of the spotlights, its blue and green hull towering in the outfitting dock outside. The green wolf stared down from the funnel. It was a state-of-the-art subsea mining vessel that had yet to mine anything, but Wang knew that it would soon begin a great adventure.

It needed some changes to the original fittings and specifications it came with from the Japanese shipbuilder. These changes had to be done as discreetly as possible, which was why he had chosen this small shipyard in Dalian. When the North Koreans needed repairs to their vessels, they came here. It was hidden from attention and free to breach any sanctions.

The Russian naval architect and his team of three engineers briefed Wang on the implemented changes. The hull was already ice class, but deck fixtures and the mining equipment had not been built to handle extremely cold temperatures. This would be rectified. That was the easy part.

"The biggest headache was to make sure she could withstand radiation," the architect said. "Which is why it got a bit more expensive than originally estimated."

"A bit more expensive? I think this is more than a *bit.*" Wang stared at the numbers in front of him.

"We have applied layers of borated polyethylene sheets on the hull and the superstructure of the ship. It is the same material used to encase the reactors of nuclear- powered vessels, except here we have encased the entire vessel. It is a very expensive material."

"And it was absolutely necessary?"

"Yes, sir. If we are to guarantee the safety of the crew, it is vital."

Wang sighed, but knew the architect was right.

*Dead people are poor at operating mining equipment.*

The changes had cost him almost as much as the ship itself, but it was pocket change compared to how much money it would make him. A ship named after the god of abundance—and the son of Tengri—was guaranteed to succeed.

# CHAPTER 17

*Coming closer and closer, the headlights pour through the windshield and engulf the interior. Inside the approaching car, sit two men, with faces full of determination. DeVille cannot see them, but he knows.*

*Carina's arms are frozen to the steering wheel.*

What the hell is wrong with these lunatics?

And why did I feel the need to humiliate them?

*There was no doubt that the two determined faces were the same two from the Christian sect that had tried to crash the conference.*

*DeVille shouts, "Turn right!"*

*But she does not move. Mouth agape, she stares straight ahead. He hears the approaching car now. The rumble from both car engines is mixed with a cacophony of white noise.*

*She shuts her eyes. He grabs the steering wheel, but it is too late. The impact throws the car sideways and the airbag crushes the arm DeVille reached for the steering wheel with.*

*The car stops its screeching drift when the rear hits a tree which topples the car. The airbag deflates.*

I'm still alive!

*Neither the relief nor the pain from his arm is enough to dampen an overwhelming sensation of fear. DeVille wipes blood out of his eyes. Carina lies with one arm, one leg, and her head inside the car, curled up by the sun visor. The fear grows. She always wore a seatbelt.*

*But not tonight.*

*The rest of her hangs on the outside.*

*He unbuckles his seatbelt and falls onto the headliner, next to her.*

"Mr. DeVille? Are you awake?"

DeVille opened his eyes. He was in a hospital room, just as he would have been, had the dream continued, but there was no police this time questioning him about the men in the other car.

The hospital room looked like a hotel room, except for the hospital bed made of intricately welded stainless steel. At the other end, stood a small desk and two chairs.

"Mr. DeVille, I'm Dr. Marloes de Jong."

DeVille looked at the young doctor. She could not have been more than thirty. He also saw 'Bronovo Hospital' on her nametag—where the rich and influential in Holland would go for treatment when needed.

"If you're okay with it, I need to go through your injuries with you."

"Okay. Sure."

"On the back, left side of your lower torso you have a stab wound. This seems the result of a knife?"

DeVille did not answer. If the police had not informed the doctor of what happened in the alley, then it was probably under orders from the CIA.

The doctor took the hint. "It could have been fatal, but it narrowly passed your intestines. The important part is that you'll be fine, but you need to stay here for a week for rest and it's important that we change your bandages often to avoid infections."

"Okay. What about this?" DeVille pointed to a bandage on his left arm.

"It's also what looks like the result of a knife stab. It's deep, but it's just a gash. Again, it's avoiding infections that are the key to recovery. You also have minor cuts and bruises, but nothing to worry about."

"Thanks, Dr. de Jong."

"You can call me Marloes."

She further told him that the night before, an ambulance had taken him directly from a side street in Utrecht to the emergency room at Bronovo Hospital. After a quick check, they sent him through the CT scanner and then carried out surgery on him. It had all happened very fast.

"With enough rest, you should recover fully," she said before she excused herself and left the room.

DeVille's mind drifted to the fact that he had killed Khan. True, either he or Khan had to die in that fight, but the fact was he had been involved—at least partly—in two deaths in just forty-eight hours. He felt a twinge of guilt, but still the deaths did not weigh on him the way Carina's death did.

*Could I've done it differently that day?*

He made his mind up about the one thing which he could do right. The future. It would be easy to give up now, but he would see this assignment through. If there was anything he could do to help prevent any more wasted deaths, he would do it. Right now, that meant he would do everything to help find the missile.

He made a promise.

To Carina.

DeVille stretched for a plastic box on one of the chairs next to his bed. It contained all the personal items he had been wearing the night before, except for his clothes which he was told were too blood-soaked to keep, so the hospital disposed of them.

He picked up his Blackberry and the Nokia that the chief of staff had given him. His smartphone was out of battery and had a crack on the screen, but the Nokia seemed fine.

There were four missed calls: two from late last night, one from early in the morning, and one from an hour ago.

All of them were from the same number.

He called the chief of staff.

"What's your excuse today?" was the first thing the German said when he picked up.

"Same as two days ago, except this time *I* killed someone and got injured in the process," DeVille replied, impressed with the smart-ass answer he came up with.

"I know the so-called arrest operations yesterday afternoon were rather unsuccessful," the chief of staff said. "Which one did you kill?"

"What do you mean 'unsuccessful'?"

"As far as I've been told, the senior terrorists who might have known where the missile is are all dead. All they have are some students that don't know anything."

DeVille told him his version of what had happened at the university, the mosque, and about the fight with Khan. He left out what he had just been told about his injuries and the doctor's suggested week of recovery.

"Okay," the chief of staff said. "Let me think about what we should do next. Your hunch about going to Utrecht was correct, even though it did not pay off. We still don't know where the missile is. I expect to get the name of the company that sponsored these TIM-guys' visa in an hour or so from Dutch immigration. I'll send you a text message."

Barely a minute after he hung up with the chief of staff, there was a knock on the door. Stella Hanson entered before he had a chance to ask who it was or to say 'come in.'

"You're not looking too bad considering you almost got killed," she said with what DeVille interpreted as a smile.

"Well, the pain is killing me." Dutch doctors were notorious cheapskates when it came to drugs. The painkillers he got did little to subdue the pain.

"Don't be a baby. Khan is dead while you're alive. No reason to complain. For you, that is."

DeVille sensed she was not happy with the outcome. He knew she was right, though. He should have made more of an effort to get hold of the policeman outside Khan's building before he went after him. Khan would have been much more valuable alive than dead.

On the other hand, Stella also told him about the two other Uighurs. Since they were dead too, there was no indication that Khan would have surrendered willingly.

"He wouldn't have said anything in interrogation," DeVille said.

She ignored him and continued, "Khan's death will be filed with the Dutch authorities as an act of self-defense. It's possible as part of a Dutch and US police cooperation agreement. Unless the Chinese start screaming about it, but I doubt that. They're just happy to see Khan eliminated. Your involvement will be kept confidential."

"That's good, I suppose." DeVille had not even thought about that part.

"Furthermore, we're interrogating the two other students at the moment, but they've given us only scraps of useful intel. They both say the three Uighurs were behind it all and that they were tricked into being a part of what happened. But they have admitted they both were involved with the incident in Uden."

*Interesting to call the shooting down of a fighter jet and the theft of a nuclear bomb an 'incident.'*

"They gave up the address to an apartment where they claimed the attack was planned. It matches Khan's address. I have a team going through it right now, but I doubt we'll find anything. Also, they both mentioned overhearing something about a Chinese man calling and giving the orders for when to hit. We've been trying to find a number to trace, but so far, we haven't had any luck."

"So we're thinking that perhaps Khan isn't the mastermind, but that it is all organized from Xinjiang?"

DeVille asked, referring to the Chinese name of East Turkestan.

"It has crossed our mind," she answered, then continued, "which would be bad. Because then it's very likely that none of the men involved here in Holland actually ever knew where the bomb was going. There will be no evidence left behind. They also told us it was crucial that the wing landed where it did, but they don't know who picked it up."

DeVille wondered how much she knew and how much of it she was telling him. He decided to test her. "What do you know of the company that sponsored their visas?" he asked.

"Nothing yet, but I'm sure it won't lead anywhere. Setting up a fake company is easier than it'll be for you to put your pants on right now."

"Thanks," he said.

She gave him another indication of a smile, before putting on a serious face. "Based on the fact that you've been involved in the deaths of two potentially informative sources and that you've almost gotten yourself killed, you'll have to back off a bit. You obviously need to take it easy for a while to heal your injuries anyway. Go back to Brussels and keep updating the EU guys you work for whenever I give you something that is relevant to the EU."

"What? You killed the first guy, not me." When she did not reply, he understood that there would be no point in trying to object.

"I mean it this time." She waited a few seconds for his response, giving him time to let it sink in. Seemingly surprised that he did not respond, she said, "Thanks for your assistance so far, Oliver. Get well soon."

A little hint of a smile came over her face, which drew her lips slightly up on one side, like the movement of a fox's whiskers while hunting. Then she turned and left the room.

He heard her say something to the men guarding his door, but was unable to decipher it.

An hour or so later, there was another knock on the door, and a nurse came in carrying a big bouquet of flowers. He did not know much about flowers, but he knew for sure that these were neither tulips nor roses. Not that he was expecting any flowers, but if had been, he would have guessed tulips—this being the Netherlands.

*Perhaps the season hasn't started yet.*

If the flowers were from Stella and the CIA, it seemed strange that she had not brought them with her.

*Flowers doesn't seem very 'CIA.'*

The only other person who knew he was in the hospital was the chief of staff, so he expected the flowers to be from him.

The nurse placed the bouquet on the desk and handed him a small enveloped card. "They arrived while you were visited by the American lady," she said.

He thanked the nurse and waited for her to leave the room before he opened the envelope. Inside, was a white handwritten card:

*Focus on WANG CHI*
*CEO of EJE MARINE SERVICES Ltd*

DeVille read the card again.

*Who the hell is it from?*

While he studied the card, the Nokia vibrated on the nightstand. He looked at the text message he had received:

`Tian Shan Oil & Gas Trading ZAO`

DeVille looked up at the ceiling in confusion. The person mentioned on the card seemed Chinese, while he could tell from the business entity abbreviation that the company in the text message was Russian.

*Who sent the flowers?*

He spent the next two hours thinking through who had been involved so far. Most likely TIM was involved, the CIA and the Dutch were certainly involved, a Russian trading company, whoever had followed him in The Hague and possibly this Wang guy. And not to forget about whoever had sent him the flowers and the card.

He considered calling Stella and telling her, but decided against it. She had been adamant that she did not want his help anymore. If the chief of staff knew about Tian Shan Oil & Gas Trading, then he was sure the CIA already knew about it. Besides, he was on a paid assignment and after everything he had been through, he wanted to make sure it was worth it—and if he played his cards right, there could be a huge remuneration waiting for him at the end of it.

What he had received about Wang could be a practical joke for all he knew. But to read the two names together on the same day, 'Eje' and 'Tian Sha' seemed too far-fetched to be just a coincidence.

Fortunately, Stella had brought him his overnight bag from her car. In it was his iPad which he used to look up Wang Chi and Eje Marine Services online. Nothing out of the ordinary struck him.

It was a shipping company based in Shanghai that had a fleet of dredgers and supply ships. All the ships were on assignments for companies associated with the Chinese government. According to a press release, the company was about to enter the subsea mining business. Wang himself seemed like a successful entrepreneur who had come from a poor background and was now among Shanghai's elite.

DeVille made up his mind.

He had to get to Shanghai.

He had to keep his promise to Carina.

There was not a single reference online to Tian Shan Oil & Gas Trading. Seemed like Stella was right about it being a fake company.

Hopefully she was wrong about his ability to put on his pants. That was a prerequisite for being able to go to Shanghai.

He grabbed the Nokia and pressed the green button twice. Three rings later the chief of staff picked up.

"Have you killed more people?"

DeVille ignored the joke. "I need to go to Shanghai as soon as possible. Can you arrange a ticket for me? Out of Schiphol, please."

"Sure, but you got to give me something to justify it," the chief of staff responded.

DeVille told him about the flowers and the card with the handwritten message. "What's confusing here is that the name Tian Shan is a mountain range in Central Asia in the border area of Xinjiang. It's also the name of a mountain that's holy for a type of shamanistic religion called Tengriism. Tian Shan literally means 'heavenly mountains.' Then there's the name Wang has chosen for his company, 'Eje,' meaning mother in Mongolian. But it is also the Tengriist name for their goddess of fertility and virginity." He paused to let the chief of staff digest the information. "That's two references to Tengriism. Isn't that worth checking out?"

"Could just be a coincidence, couldn't it?" the chief of staff asked. "What is this Tengri religion anyway?"

"It's a form of shamanism practiced in Central Asia, by people of Turkic descent."

"Shamanism? Isn't that all about balance of nature?"

"Yeah, the trees, water, fire, mountains—those kinds of things. They worship Tengri."

"Who?"

"The sky god."

"That doesn't sound like a religion that would steal a nuclear bomb and use it for terrorism," said the chief of staff.

"You're right, they're pretty non-violent. At least nowadays they are."

"I don't see how this helps us. I thought we were dealing with Muslim Uighurs?"

"Modern versions are different from place to place. But its history dates a long way back and includes groups of people such as the Huns and the Mongolians."

"So Genghis Khan and Attila the Hun were Tengriist? Okay, they weren't exactly non-violent."

DeVille hated to make these kinds of explanations over the phone. He never felt like he had enough time to go through everything that was important. "As with all religions, there exist both liberal and conservative factions."

"I still don't get it."

"Look, I don't necessarily think any Tengriists are involved. But there is an evident link between this Wang guy and the Russian company set up to sponsor the Uighur men. I'd just like to have a talk with this Wang."

There was silence from the other end of the line.

DeVille continued, "He might just be someone with an interest in Genghis Khan for all I know. I think it's still safe to assume that TIM are the ones behind this, but the CIA also told me they think someone called the Uighurs from China set it all in motion."

"All right, say I agree to this," the chief of staff said and then paused for a moment. "You were almost stabbed to death twenty-four hours ago. You think it's wise to fly halfway around the world?"

"Book me business class and I'll get some rest," DeVille said. "I can handle myself. Besides, I'm only a consultant, so it's not like you'll get into trouble with the unions for breaking labor regulations."

"All right, I'll get you to Shanghai."

# CHAPTER 18

Three quarters of an hour after DeVille finished the call with the chief of staff, the Nokia vibrated and he checked the text message:

> KL 0893 dep 2130 tonight

The clock on the phone told him it was almost six in the evening. It would take him a good hour to get to Schiphol airport.

*Time to get moving.*

He put on a pair of khakis and the shirt he had used the first night in The Hague. Those were all the clothes left in his overnight bag. He hoped he had time to buy something at the airport.

Putting on the khakis felt like leaning onto a barbed wire fence with a bare stomach, but he was sure it was easier than setting up a fake Russian company.

He left a note on the bed to the hospital staff saying he was going back to Brussels and would see a doctor there. He thanked them for all they had done and gave his company address to bill for the VIP room.

Then he remembered the guys outside his room that Stella had talked to when she left. Supposedly they were only there to make sure he was safe, but he wondered if they would let him leave just like that. Unfortunately the VIP rooms were on the fourth floor so there was no chance of using the windows as an exit.

There was no way they could stop him as he was not under arrest, but he also did not want them to follow him. If even a percentage of what he had heard about CIA paranoia was true, they would try to make sure he did not follow up on the case.

*Over the last few days, having a tail has meant casualties.*

DeVille did not want to be next.

He reached for his Bridge briefcase and found a pack of Marlboros, with a few leftover cigarettes intact. He normally saved them for smoke-filled meetings in bars, something he enjoyed. But now, they would actually be quite useful.

Not that he had much, but the little he had he stuffed into his briefcase and left the overnight bag on the bed— clearly visible from the door. Luckily they had not disposed of his shoes from yesterday as that was the only pair he had with him. If he wandered into the airport with hospital slippers, it would without doubt raise suspicions.

He grabbed the cane that the hospital had provided. He could not put too much weight on his left foot without sending a lightning bolt of pain from the stab wound in his back.

In a tray on the nightstand were four painkillers. His dose for the night. He grabbed all of them and washed them down.

*That should keep the pain in check until I'm on the airplane.*

He exited the room and saw Dupont and Dupond. DeVille had named the two agents after the policemen from the Tintin comic books. It was not because they looked like each other, but because they both had similar facial hair. It was rare to see two men who worked together sport the same mustache. Like old Greek wrestlers, Dupont was blond and short, with protruding muscles under his shirt. Dupond was of average height and build, around fifty years old—fifteen years or so senior to his colleague. All the hair on his head and face had turned silvery gray, like moss on rocks in the tundra.

Both their mustaches were shaped so that they always looked grumpy.

"Good evening, guys," DeVille said and tried to walk past them.

"Good evening," Dupond said. "Where are you going?"

"I'm just on my way out for a smoke." DeVille flashed the pack of Marlboros he held in his hand.

"Why are you bringing your stuff?" Dupont asked while he pointed to DeVille's briefcase with one hand and stroked his mustache with the other.

"Honestly? It's because I don't trust you guys not to go through my things while I'm out. You're free to rummage through my dirty clothes if you want." DeVille smiled and motioned towards the overnight bag left in his room.

Dupont choked out a false chuckle.

"All right, but I'll join you," Dupond said. "I'll have a cigarette myself."

"You guys need to quit that shit and work out instead," Dupont said and banged his muscular chest in a way only a primate would.

"We'll be right back," Dupond told him and shook his head.

DeVille had hoped that they would have let him go out by himself. He had not thought of the possibility that one of them would come with him.

*Damn it.*

"You want a cup of coffee with your smoke?" DeVille asked Dupond while they were in the elevator.

"Not a bad idea."

When they reached the ground floor, DeVille started to limp over towards the coffee machine at the end of the hallway with a few exaggerated groans.

"Don't worry, I'll get the coffees," Dupond said and headed down the hallway.

"Thanks. Sugar, no milk." DeVille hoped the request would buy him enough time.

"Sure."

"Thanks a lot. I'll be outside."

As soon as he got out of the building he looked around for a cab. There were none in front of the building, something he found a little strange. He then remembered he had seen a note at reception that they would more than gladly assist you in booking a cab. He did not have the time for that.

He lit a cigarette and sucked the smoke down to the bottom of his lungs before he slowly released it into the wet Dutch spring. It made his throat itch, but then he noticed the relaxing effect it had when the first blood cells picked up the nicotine from his lungs and it reached his brain.

The main street was just a hundred meters away and he had already seen two cabs pass. He limped across the grass towards the road as fast as his wounded body could bear. The pain made him feel dizzier than the cigarette, which he was still holding between his fingers. He took another drag of it and threw the butt away.

He had just got through the low hedge and onto the street when he saw Dupond come out of the entrance with the coffees.

Dupond's eyes locked onto DeVille, he dropped the coffees, and started to run towards the road.

An occupied cab drove by. DeVille saw one with the roof light on coming in the opposite direction. There was no way he could cross the busy street, limping the way he was. Another one came and DeVille waved at the car. The cab flashed its high beams to signal that it had seen DeVille.

A hand grabbed his shoulder.

"What the hell do you think you're doing?" Dupond stood on the other side of the hedge with his long arm on DeVille's left shoulder.

With the cane in his right hand DeVille swiveled around and let the metal ferrule tip of it crash directly onto Dupond's Adam's apple.

Dupond released his grip on DeVille's shoulder. With the new freedom of movement, DeVille threw his elbow into the hedge and hit Dupond right in the lower ribs. Dupond tumbled over and moaned as he went down on the grass behind the hedge in a fetal position with one hand at his throat and one at his lower chest.

DeVille looked forward and saw the cab pull up to the curb. He wondered how much the cabdriver had seen.

"Goedenavond," the driver said.

"Good evening. To Schiphol, please."

# CHAPTER 19

*Yeysk, Russia*
*April 2ⁿᵈ – 20:00*

Muhammad Umeira arrived at Yeysk docks with three other jihadists and two drivers in two trucks. Each truck carried a twenty-foot container. At twelve feet, the missile took up most of the space in one of them.

They had been directed towards the FV Euphausia by the security guard at the gate. They had been provided papers, but the guard did not bother to look at them. A soccer game on the radio was his priority.

Umeira had never been on a ship before and was surprised at the size of the fishing boat. Abdul Aziz had shown him a picture of it, but he had not gotten the sense of size. He expected the scale to be closer to that of the traditional fishing boats he was used to seeing in the Caspian Sea.

Although amazed, he was also relieved that the Euphausia was larger than most mosques he had seen.

*Not as big as the one in Mecca, but maybe as tall as the minaret.*

Seasickness was something he had only heard about, but it did not sound pleasant. He did not believe that the sea could throw this colossal metal beast from side to side, though.

The afternoon of the day before, he had arrived at the agreed meeting spot. He had driven over fifteen hundred kilometers from the Belarusian border in less than two days. The van was beat up towards the end and he did not dare to go much faster than eighty the last few hundred kilometers.

Sleep was something he had been deprived of over the last few days, but he stayed awake by telling himself 'heroes never sleep.' He would be on the ship for several days. It should be possible to sleep then. That was if he did not get seasick.

Seven of Aziz's troops were waiting at the meeting point and Umeira expected his life to end in the same way as the three mujahideen killed in Belarus. He had served the cause well and would be considered a martyr in the eyes of the Almighty. Instead of a bullet through the head, though, the troops led him to a four-by-four which took him to a log cabin while the troops watched the van and its precious cargo.

Inside the log cabin he was greeted by Aziz. The Saudi looked even skinnier and more fragile than before Umeira had left for the Netherlands. He was greeted with a handshake and a kiss on each cheek.

"As-salaam alaykum," Umeira greeted the man he feared and worshipped.

"Wa 'alaykum al-salaam." Aziz seemed pleased with what had been accomplished so far and said, "We are *all* very proud of you. You have done well."

Only God knew which actions should be praised, Aziz once told him, so compliments from him were rare. Umeira cherished the kind words.

"You need to prepare for a long voyage at sea," Aziz told him as they sat down and shared some tea and bread. "The mission is going into its second phase."

"I am ready."

"Allah has allied us with our brothers in Turkestan in order to complete this mission."

This was news to Umeira.

"I was contacted by Al-Qaeda. They told me how a cooperation between my Arab mujahideen and the Turkestan Islamic Movement could be beneficial for both our causes. We are both fighting against an infidel occupation. If we join resources and intelligence to strike against a target, sacred by both enemies, it will be a great success in the eyes of the Almighty."

"And we are doing it with an American nuclear bomb," Umeira said, smiling.

"If you wondered who shot down the plane carrying the bomb you retrieved, it was our Uighur brothers."

It had indeed bothered Umeira, not because he did not know who, but because he never trusted any job to be done unless he did it himself.

"That is all you need to know at this point," Aziz said sternly. "Here is a bag. Inside is warm clothes which you will need for the voyage. There is also a satellite phone. Always keep it fully charged. I will contact you with further instructions."

Three men walked in as if on cue. They all greeted each other. Umeira knew them to be good men.

"These warriors will come with you."

*Will you have us killed as well?*

*Most likely.*

When they returned outside, the van had been replaced with two trucks with containers loaded on the back. They were told the bomb had been moved into one of the containers. The rest of the evening and the next day Umeira and the three men discussed their cover story and which roles to assume when they got aboard the ship. Two more of Aziz's jihadists came dressed in the uniforms of Russian truck drivers—jeans and sleeveless shirts stained from more than one meal. They fired up the trucks and headed towards the industrial quays of Yeysk.

Umeira stepped out of the truck. He walked onto the metal gangway and grasped the thin rope. It was the only thing that separated him from the dark, murky water below. He felt that his fate had been sealed.

"Allah, give me strength," he whispered.

He took a deep breath and stepped onto the deck of the FV Euphausia.

\* \* \*

Captain Zhang watched from the bridge as the four men walked up the gangway. They did not look like scientists to him; not a single one of them wore glasses. He was glad that they did not look like lab rats in white coats. Maybe he could put them to work.

The first man up, bearded and with a face that bore obvious signs of the outdoors, was stopped by the seaman on guard duty. Normally he would not post a guard while in port, but he did not trust the security in Russian ports. The last thing he wanted was theft of equipment off his brand new ship.

The guard looked up towards the bridge and Zhang waved back and sighed. It was time to meet the guests.

He climbed down the ladder and approached the four men with a forced smile.

"Welcome to the Euphausia," he said. "I am Captain Zhang." His English was not great, but after years at sea, he had learned enough of the language to make himself understood.

"Thank you. I am Mohammad," the bearded man said in poor English. He appeared to be the leader of the group.

With that name, they had to be Muslims. Zhang tried hard to conceal his irritation over the fact that there were now Muslims onboard his ship. He did not know much about Islam as a religion, but he pictured them all as terrorists—chopping off heads of infidels. He knew they were not all like that; however the ones in Western China had a reputation for being lazy and untrustworthy.

The Muslim handed him an envelope and motioned for him to open it. Zhang tore it open. It was written on Eje Marine Services letterhead:

```
To Captain Zhang


These men are my personal guests. I
trust you to extend my hospitality
to them and make sure all their
needs are fulfilled. You will
provide them with what they
request. If they want to deviate
from the discussed route, allow it
to happen. These men are on an
important scientific mission. You
will be rewarded for your troubles.
If you are in any doubt of
accommodating their requests,
please contact me before declining.
I have utmost faith in your
judgment.


        Wang Chi
        CEO
```

Zhang struggled to hide his anger. The message was full of contradictions. Wang said he trusted his judgment, but wanted him to check in if he decided to decline these guests any unreasonable requests.

*Am I supposed to be the servant of these Muslims?*

He had not worked so hard for so long to serve others on *his* ship. He had always respected the shipowner as an entrepreneur and a savvy businessman, but this move was uncharacteristic.

*The reward better be good.*

If not, he would retire as soon as this voyage was over.

He looked at Mohammad, and sensed that his ship would be engaged in bullshit instead of krill fishing for the next few weeks.

"Very well," Zhang finally said. "I'll have someone show you to your quarters. I'll be on the bridge if you need anything." He wondered if this Muslim even understood what he had said.

Just when Zhang was about to turn and head up the ladder, the youngest of the four men asked with a textbook British accent, "Captain, who may we talk to about loading our equipment?"

"I'll get the chief mate to come see you." Zhang paused before asking, "What's in the containers?"

"It is some equipment that we're going to test. If it works well, it'll help us measure light and seasonal variations of the ozone layer," the young Muslim said.

Zhang shrugged, "The ozone layer? I haven't heard about that in years. They still study that?"

"Yes. It is still very important."

"Very well." Perhaps it was deemed not to be important and then all of a sudden someone had figured out that it was important after all.

"Damn scientists," he said out loud as soon as he opened the hatch to the bridge and entered.

* * *

Umeira had never really attempted to learn the infidel language of the English and the Americans. He had picked up a few words here and there, but he could not hold a conversation.

Aziz apparently knew about this weakness, as one of the jihadists he had sent with him spoke the language well. He would have to be both Umeira's ears and mouth during this voyage.

When Aziz had given him the letter, the one handed over to the captain, Umeira asked him if they needed aliases. He was told they would be among friends so it would not be necessary.

If that was so, he wondered why the captain acted so displeased.

*What did the letter say?*

One thing he did know was that there was something he did not like about the captain. The fact that he would not have to talk to him directly, because of the language barrier, pleased him.

Fifteen minutes after they boarded the ship they had a quick look into their cabin. It contained two small bunk beds, and it was more cramped than the tents the jihadists used in the forests of Chechnya.

It was still much better than having to camp out in the forest throughout the whole winter season. It was heated. And with just a glimpse of the mattress, it was clear it would be more comfortable than a night's sleep on the ground—in a sleeping bag that was worn out from years of constant use, something Umeira had done for the last three years. He expected never to do that again.

After the two-second scrutiny of the cabin, Umeira headed to the bridge with his translator to see the captain. He needed to tell the captain where to go. Aziz had just given him the first instructions in a message on the satellite phone he was carrying.

The captain only glanced at Umeira when he entered the bridge. "What can I do for you?" he asked the young Chechen translator.

Without understanding the language, Umeira still sensed annoyance in the captain's voice.

"When are we leaving, Captain?"

"We'll get a pilot around midnight."

"You'll head out of the Black Sea and towards Gibraltar, right?" Umeira had told the Chechen what to ask before they had gone up to the bridge.

"That's what I've been told to do," the captain said with a sigh. "The long way around..."

Umeira wondered if they had to go to port for supplies or fuel during the voyage, so he asked the captain directly in Chechen. The captain looked at the translator, who repeated the question in English.

"Maybe for water or food if you guys eat and drink a lot, but we have enough bunkers to last us over fifty thousand miles."

"Bunkers?"

"Bunkers means fuel." The Chinaman smirked. "This ship was built to spend months alone in the deep seas. You guys probably have no idea what that means, but it's only three thousand miles to Gibraltar. It should take us about eight days to get there."

The young Chechen translated and when Umeira indicated to him that he did not have any more questions, he thanked the captain for his time. Umeira was already on his way down from the bridge.

Back in the cabin, Umeira sat down on one of the bunks and a thought struck him. A pleasant thought.

*We will spend the rest of our lives on this ship.*

# CHAPTER 20

*Shanghai, China*
*April 4<sup>th</sup> – 18:10*

The entrance to the high-rise was humble and looked like a crack in the tall and all glass, covered grand facade. It made DeVille's task much easier. He had been outside in the cold drizzling rain for three quarters of an hour waiting for Wang. Droplets trickled down between his neck and collar making his shirt stick to his back like newspaper on a wet floor.

The small entrance helped see who came and went, as it was impossible for large groups of people to enter or exit at the same time. In his pocket he had a picture of Wang and DeVille was convinced he would be able to pick him out if he showed up. He had some recognizable facial features that separated him from many of his Chinese countrymen. With eyes more round than narrow, and ears that poked out, a child could be forgiven for saying he resembled an elf.

DeVille had found the picture on the Internet site of Eje Marine Services. There was a 'Management' tab on the website with a picture of Wang—chairman and CEO.

Right away he noticed that Wang's face was not typical Han Chinese, oblong with high cheekbones. Wang's face was more oval and because of this, his cheekbones were less pronounced. This made the elf-like ears stand out even more.

DeVille remembered a two-week conference a few years ago where all the Chinese scholars that participated looked and dressed the same. It had forced him to recognize certain facial features for certain regions of China. It was the only way to remember who was who. Flat and broad noses for people from the south and narrow and pointy ones for people from the north. These regional features were slowly mishmashed by the internal migrations in China. Peasants were moving to the cities for work and the government encouraged Han Chinese to move to the outer regions in order to lessen the influence of other ethnic groups. Non-Han Chinese groups had always been regarded as a problem in the history of the People's Republic of China.

*Such as the Uighur in Xinjiang.*

DeVille saw that Wang had certain features indicating that he was originally from the northwest of China. A coincidence, perhaps, but it could mean that Wang hailed from Uighur regions.

DeVille had landed on Friday, three days ago, in the late afternoon. His wounds had hurt like hell and he went straight to his hotel and spent the next twenty-four hours in bed. On Sunday he felt better and spent several hours in the hotel's business center where he tried to learn as much as he could about Wang and Eje Marine Services off the Internet.

He did not learn anything suspicious about Wang, but he had not been expecting to find anything incriminating online either. What he had been looking for was information that would help him get to meet Wang face to face.

The name the chief of staff had brought up still floated around in his gray matter, trying to connect to his theories.

*Genghis Khan.*

The Mongolian tyrant had not been a very religious man, but all historical sources pointed to the fact that the little religion he practiced had been a form of Tengriism, and he used religion as a justification for the bloodbaths he unleashed around Asia and the Middle East. Religion made him the leader of his people and he used the mandate to its fullest.

From there to a modern-day Tengriist stealing a nuclear missile was far-fetched, DeVille thought. But it was the only lead he had and he never believed in coincidences.

These questions irked DeVille as another forty-five minutes passed while he stood outside the entrance of the high-rise where the elf-eared Chinese entrepreneur supposedly lived and worked.

Then, behind a group of young executives, all in Zegna and Armani suits they did not seem to care got wet in the rain, he saw Wang. He seemed smaller and skinnier than DeVille's impression from the picture.

*Even businessmen Photoshop themselves these days.*

Wang crossed the street and DeVille followed him for another two blocks until the shipowner walked into an Italian restaurant. DeVille waited five minutes before entering. While he waited to be seated, he flicked through the menu a waitress, with as much make-up on as a graffitied wall, handed him. A quick peek confirmed that Wang was already placed at a table in the back.

The only non-Italian food on the menu was something called a "Shanghai Pizza," described to be with spicy pork, scallions, and ginger.

It was a strange mix, but so was the interior of the restaurant. It did have the red and white checkered tablecloths that were mandatory for all Italian restaurants outside of Italy. But placed delicately on top of the tables, like the leaning tower of Pisa, were typical Chinese paper lanterns. The walls confused your senses even more with images of panda bears and the Great Wall, and the occasional scary face of former communist party leaders, all mixed together with drawings of the Colosseum and Venice. It made DeVille feel like he was watching two National Geographic travel shows at the same time.

*Surely Wang can afford a more upscale restaurant for his meals?*

DeVille sat down three tables away from Wang and ordered a Tsingtao beer, and pasta with scallops in a creamy vodka sauce. The food was good, but nothing more.

*Why would Wang come here?*

Surely a busy man like Wang could not remember everyone he dealt with, so DeVille's plan was to pretend to know him. He remembered from the website that Wang had been a keynote speaker at a maritime conference a few months ago.

DeVille walked towards Wang with an oversized smile and two beers in his hands.

"Mr. Wang, there are millions of people in this city and I end up in the same restaurant as you," DeVille said with the thickest American accent he could muster. "How's business? I'm sure you wouldn't mind a beer."

Wang looked at him without any expression on his face and with no words coming out of his mouth.

*Shit! Maybe Wang doesn't speak English.*

He had just assumed so because of the conference he read about. It could have easily been done in Chinese with a translator. It happened all the time.

"I'm so sorry. Can you please help me a little with my memory?" Wang finally said.

"Oh, sure, I'm Albert Watts. We met at the Marintec conference in January. Remember? No? We had a discussion about business opportunities in the upper Yellow River areas." DeVille paused to see if there was any reaction readable from Wang's face. "No worries, Mr. Wang. I just wanted to say hello and hear about how things are in the dredging business." DeVille gave him his best hurt puppy eyes and motioned that he was going back to his table. He tried to appear like a lonely businessman, desperate for a drinking buddy.

"I would love to talk Mr. Watts, but I'm afraid I have an appointment in a few moments. Why don't you come by my office at nine tomorrow morning and we can have a cup of tea and discuss?"

"Great. I look forward to it. See you tomorrow then." Not only had he managed to get an appointment, but also more time. He for sure needed more information after what he had just seen.

DeVille paid the bill and finished the two beers before leaving the restaurant and heading towards his hotel.

The image on Wang's cuff links was burned into his eyes. The words 'Umai – Mountain Altai' written around a beautiful crowned woman, seated in a position somewhere in between a prayer and meditation, with a black dress flowing out in front of her.

The cuff links were each made from a 'tenge' coin—the currency of Kazakhstan. They were not valuable, maybe worth around three American dollars each. Wang would only have gone to the effort of having those coins made into cuff links because of the image on them.

Umai was a goddess in ancient Tengriism. She was married to Tengri and would carry out assignments for him. She would hand divine powers to people and be a link between Man and Heaven. In modern Tengriism she had lost some of her importance, and was today considered only to be a guardian of pregnant women and children.

DeVille doubted that Wang would display a guardian of toddlers and pregnancy on his wrists. He clearly had good knowledge of ancient Tengriism.

The Altai Mountains, the mountain range located partly in China, Mongolia, Kazakhstan, and Russia, was once the heart of two former empires—the Göktürk and the Mongol. Both had been Tengriist empires.

The names of the founding fathers of these empires came to DeVille's mind.

*Genghis Khan.*

*Bumin Qaghan.*

These men created large territorial realms that stretched from Europe through most of Asia and they ruled their empires with ruthless brutality. Many historians believed that the sixth century Bumin Qaghan was the more famous Genghis Khan's inspiration seven hundred years later. Both of them were Tengriists and both had been responsible for the suffering of millions of people.

The Nokia vibrated.

> Acc to CCTV; 3 Russians entered
> via Slovakia on March 24 - left
> 4 days later in stolen van —
> into Belarus - connected to Arab
> mujahideen in Chechnya

While impressed that so much info could be crammed into less than one hundred sixty characters, this only made everything more confusing.

These men entered three days before the jet was shot down and left twenty-four hours after it happened.

*So who did it?*

*The Uighurs or the Chechens?*

DeVille could not see Uighur and Chechen rebels cooperating. They had different enemies. They had no overlapping targets.

*And what about Genghis Khan?*

DeVille rounded a corner and was approaching his hotel when his instinct told him to pay attention. There were people on the streets, but an eerie silence loomed over him. When someone behind him stepped on a pebble, it sounded thunderous. Suspended in the polluted air that smelled like rotten eggs, he heard the pulsating tone of a police siren.

For an instant he smelled a stinging body odor, cutting through the light breeze, before hands grabbed his arms and shoved him through the glass door of a convenience store. Two men stood over him and the DVD shelf DeVille had crashed into.

One of the men seized him by his throat, and DeVille flung a handful of DVDs at him. It caused no trouble for the assailant.

The surprise, and the pain from his earlier wounds, paralyzed him long enough for the other man to tie DeVille's hands behind his back with wire ties. Muscles and tattoos strutted from their black tank tops and their eyes looked huge in their hairless heads. They were the most badass-looking Chinese DeVille had ever seen.

He was about to shout for help, but he knew no one was around. He swallowed a protest when he saw the metallic shine of what one man pulled out from his waistband.

A large knife.

The knife carved through the air, almost leaving a permanent rift in the store's stale atmosphere. DeVille choked, then realized he was holding his breath.

DeVille tried to kick the knife, but he was still being held by the throat by the other man. The man with the knife kicked DeVille in the shin and the pain stopped his further attempts to disarm him. A bead of sweat dripped into his now open mouth and the saline flavor felt as strong as if he were drinking seawater.

As the man with the knife smiled and lifted the blade, four pops came from the entrance door. The knife clanged as it hit the floor. Both men grimaced and fell over as if in slow motion.

"Get up. You must leave immediately."

A man cut the wire ties with the knife DeVille's attacker had just been holding in his hand. A second man appeared in the doorway and nodded to DeVille.

"Go. Go. Go." The first man said as he pointed to the door with his sound-suppressed gun.

"Who are you? And who are they?" DeVille asked.

"We will contact you later. You must get out of the store and get away now."

DeVille was not about to argue with two armed guys who had just shown their prowess using their weapons. And they looked even more badass than the Chinese.

The siren still wailed outside as he left the store, but DeVille heard the accented and monotone voices of his rescuers in his head. They were similar to the one he had heard in The Hague.

# CHAPTER 21

Wang looked at his Hublot watch. It was an hour since the man had left the restaurant. Anxiety started to build inside him. His crew should have reported back by now, if they had been successful.

His eyes scanned the entrance of the restaurant—his first not-so-legit business venture. But there was no sign of his crew.

The Westerner was stupid. Even though there were a lot of white Westerners in Shanghai, Wang had noticed him the moment he stepped out of his building. He could just have been waiting for someone but, to be sure, Wang told his crew to follow the man. When he showed up again alone in the restaurant, Wang knew whom he had been waiting for.

Him.

*What did he take him for?*

The marine conference was fresh in Wang's mind. He had not spoken to any Albert Watts. He had not spoken to anyone. After he gave his speech, he had left the stage via the back entrance and got straight into his car.

The man was a liar.

A liar who had waited outside for him.

Perhaps the man wanted to meet Wang to do business in one way or another, or maybe sell himself for a job in Wang's company. But he could not take that chance now when their plan was in motion. It was better to be safe than sorry. To avoid any trouble, he decided to have the trouble eliminated.

As soon as the man left the restaurant, he sent a text message to his crew. The orders were changed from following him to getting rid of the fool.

Wang knew what he needed to do—call Khagan Wu and report the incident. If, for some reason, his men had screwed up the elimination, the resources of state security could be put to use.

* * *

As soon as DeVille opened the door to his hotel room, he saw Stella Hanson sitting on his bed. At his desk sat Dupond, greenish-black bruises visible on his throat.

DeVille stood in the doorway and considered his options. If the elevator was still on this floor, he would have time to run there and close the doors before they could get to him.

"Don't worry. He won't retaliate for what you did to him." Stella stood up, walked over, and closed the door behind him. "What part of leaving this case to the professionals did you not understand?"

"I didn't think this really would lead to anything. It was just a hunch that I figured I'd check out as long as I was on the EU's payroll."

*It was a little more than a hunch now.*

"So, what's so interesting in Shanghai?" Dupond said, his voice still suffering from the blow to his throat four days ago.

DeVille told them about Wang and all the different links he had found to Tengriism. He did not tell them about how he got the name. Instead he lied and said he had researched

Tian Shan Oil & Gas Trading, a company name which he truthfully said he got from the chief of staff—and came across Wang and his company.

"You know, the Tian Shan mountain system reaches all the way from Kyrgyzstan to China. There the system changes name to the Altai Mountains," DeVille tried to explain in his most academic voice. "Here's the interesting part; the second highest peak in the Tian Shan range is the Khan Tengri, just over seven thousand meters. One of the holiest mountains in Tengriism."

What just happened on the way back to the hotel was none of their business. The cuts on his face, from going through the glass door at the convenience store, probably told them more than they needed to know. If the men who rescued him were from the CIA, then Stella and Dupond would already know about it.

*What if the Chinese guys were CIA?*

It also meant he had left four dead bodies in his wake already.

He did not owe the CIA anything. If anything, they owed him for trying to stop him from leaving the hospital. If they had not picked up on the Chechen terrorists coming and leaving EU territory, then it was not his problem. If the chief of staff wanted them to know, he would find a way to get the info to them.

"Do you believe Wang is involved with the Turkestan Islamic Movement in the stealing of the nuke?" Stella asked him.

"I have no idea," DeVille said, which was the truth. He had absolutely no idea. "But I do think this guy is pretty suspicious."

All of a sudden it dawned on him. The CIA had tracked him to Shanghai, followed him, and broken into his hotel room.

*Why spend resources on that?*

116

"What are you two doing here?" he asked. "It seems a little overkill to send two top agents halfway around the world to find a consultant who didn't want to be hospitalized anymore."

"We got a little curious as to why you broke out so violently and left for Shanghai," Stella said with a glance towards Dupond. "Airline records. They're easy to obtain for the CIA. The same with hotel records."

"I know that, but it still doesn't answer why."

"Don't fool yourself into thinking that you're onto something just because we're here. We just decided to check on you before we head to Beijing. That office is the lead task force for checking out TIM's involvement. Hell, we might even go to Xinjiang to see if the Uighurs are hiding the bomb there. So you're probably right, we're wasting time talking to you."

Before they left, they told him to make sure he contacted them if he, against all odds, found anything linking Wang to the case in one way or another.

"Before you leave, I've got one question. Did you ever find out who the guy in The Hague was?"

"Yes, we did. It's kind of strange. Perhaps it was a coincidence, you know, since you were taking pictures. Or he mistook you for someone else. Turns out he was Russian mafia."

\* \* \*

Wang stepped into his apartment and dialed the number to Khagan Wu.

"Yes, Khagan, how is things going?" was the reply.

Wang knew the phone line was secure since Khagan Wu used Wang's title of Khagan, the imperial title the four members of the *Kurultai* held. The *Kurultai* was the council that would elect one of them to be *Yekhe Khagan*—the 'Grand Khagan'—or 'Khagan of Khagans,' when their plan was completed.

"Something happened today that I think you need to know about." Wang told him about the incident earlier in the day.

"You should have told me right away so I could have handled it," the lieutenant general said.

"I made a decision to eliminate him. But I haven't heard back from my men, so something might have gone wrong."

"I will look into it and let you know."

The conversation was over.

Fifteen minutes later, the phone rang. Wang let it ring three times before answering.

"Khagan, your men are dead. They were found shot in a closed convenience store. Looked like a professional job."

Wang wondered how this man could have taken out both of his men. "I agreed to meet him tomorrow morning."

"We need to know what and who this man is. And what he knows. Do the meeting and I'll have some agents follow him afterwards."

Wang agreed to that.

They changed subject and Wu asked how the customizing of the ship was going.

"It is on time. It will leave port in a week's time."

"What about your fishing boat?"

"*Krill trawler*. The Euphausia will pass through the straits of Gibraltar in a week's time as well."

"Good," Wu said. "Some good news from Russia. Khagan Alexandrovich has managed to secure his spot as the navy commander-in-chief. He's also certain that he has enough supporters to be selected the next chief of the general staff—when he gets rid of the current one, of course."

It was all going according to plan, Wang thought, after he finished the call with Wu. Luring the terrorists into being pawns in their grand scheme had been easy.

*Too easy?*

The Chechens and the Uighurs had jumped at the opportunity to steal a nuclear missile. Both Wu and Alexandrovich kept sources inside Al-Qaeda that they had used to insinuate the possibility of stealing the bomb, and how a joint operation between the Uighurs and the Chechens would be a perfect match. They could use it to hurt enemies of both.

At one stage Wang had doubted if these terrorists would be able to pull it off, but they had impressed him.

Now the bomb was onboard his ship.

* * *

It was time to give the chief of staff a call, but the German beat him to it. The conversation got straight to the point as usual.

"Do you have anything on Wang yet?"

DeVille told him he had arranged to meet Wang the next day, but he left out the attack in the convenience store. He also omitted the part about the rescue by anonymous men with guns—and the visit from the CIA.

"I have a gut feeling," DeVille said. "Can you somehow check if the Russian mafia have any connection with either TIM or the Chechen mujahideen?"

"Sure."

DeVille added, "Or with Wang, for that matter."

"Guess you're not going to tell me why. I suppose Europol should have some info on that."

DeVille thanked him and said he would give him an update after the meeting with Wang the next day and then hopefully fly back to Brussels in the evening.

"You might want to consider a detour," the chief of staff said. "I received some flowers a few hours ago. They came with a handwritten note that said '*Keep DeVille focused on Wang and send him to Dubai.*' My first thought is that it's from whoever sent you flowers in The Hague."

*What's in Dubai?*

*And who is sending me these notes?*

*A friend or a foe?*

"What could be the link between Dubai and all of this?" DeVille asked.

"Beats me, but you like the place, don't you? Sure you're not sending these notes to yourself so that you can travel around at my expense?"

"Funny. I think I'll be short on beach time and even fewer drinks this time around." DeVille had experienced a gun in the side in The Hague, a knife fight in Utrecht, and an ambush in Shanghai.

*Dubai can't be any worse, can it?*

Whoever had sent him the first flowers had put him onto something. Maybe these were the same people, and there was another clue to the case in Dubai.

"All right, I'll go to Dubai after meeting Wang tomorrow," DeVille said.

# CHAPTER 22

*Atlantic Ocean*
*April 10th – 11:10*

Muhammad Umeira watched from the bridge, as the FV Euphausia passed the Spanish town of Tarifa on its starboard side—its green hills surrounding it. Umeira had always believed that Gibraltar was the southernmost town on the Iberian Peninsula. It was not. Tarifa was.

"Are we going to change direction?" he asked his young interpreter.

"Yeah. The helmsman says we'll head northwest and follow the coastline of Portugal after we pass Tarifa."

"Okay. Let me know if anything happens. I'm bored. Think I'll go down and check on the guys in the container." Umeira felt watching the ship's clock was like watching a snail race. He had spent a lot of time on the bridge, particularly when the captain was not around. "If the captain comes back up, let me know. We really need to figure out all the technical aspects so that we can at least maneuver the ship somewhat if we have to."

"Yes, sir, Captain," the young interpreter said with a smile.

Umeira let him get away with it. He liked the thought of being the captain.

He also spent a lot of time praying. That was not something he normally did during battle—he preferred to pray when there were no distractions. When it was just him and the Almighty. Not that this was a traditional battle, but his mind was working in the same way as it did on the battlefield. It was attuned to making decisions that made sure he survived that day for the next, and which enticed his body to give a hundred percent.

"What are you guys up to?" he asked as soon as he shut the door to the container down on the deck, even though he knew the answer.

"The same as yesterday. Seems like there isn't any issue with the weapons. Don't think we need to do this every day."

The three other men he had brought onboard with him, mainly spent their time awake at work in the containers—especially the one containing handguns and RPGs.

"Do you know what salty sea air will do to a rocket launcher? No? I didn't think so. Let's stay focused." Umeira felt he needed to assert his authority. He hoped they would not need these weapons, but they had to be prepared for anything.

If they needed to kill the crew and take charge of the ship themselves, that was what they would do. If they needed to cut the crew's throats. If they needed to cut one limb off at a time. That was what they would do. And it was the reason Umeira was trying to learn as much as possible about running a ship up on the bridge.

His thoughts were interrupted as someone touched his shoulders. He turned around with raised fists and saw his young interpreter. Umeira sighed.

"The captain again asks what is inside the containers." he said. "I keep saying it is just instruments, but it does not seem like he believes it."

"Keep telling him that. He will not snoop around. Even if he did, one of us are always on watch down here."

*From now on this is a battlefield.*

A new order from Aziz would not come for another week or so, but Umeira still kept checking the satellite phone every few minutes. He was curious about where they were taking the bomb. Taking it to the North Pole did not make sense. If it was up to him, he would have chosen the Kremlin. But it was not. Most of all he wanted to know where he would be when the bomb went off.

"What are we going to blow up? It will make us famous martyrs, right?" one of the older jihadists asked with a mix of curiosity and nervousness as if he had read Umeira's mind.

"I do not know," Umeira answered honestly. "I assume it will be a Russian target. Possibly Murmansk and the navy base."

"It will not be used against any of the other jihadists in our area, will it?"

It had struck Umeira that the bomb was to be used as leverage in a leadership battle for the Caucasus Emirate since Aziz had recently split from other jihadist groups in Chechnya.

"I am quite sure it will not. My brother led the mujahideen before Abdul Aziz, so he would certainly respect me enough to consult me before he did something so drastic. And I would not agree."

"We trust you and Abdul Aziz."

Umeira sensed the hesitation, so he added, "Besides, we are heading towards the North Pole. None of our disillusioned brethren would be up there."

The emirate had always been led with much more focus from a political aspect than what Aziz and his Arab mujahideen wanted. Umeira agreed with Aziz that the Islamic revolution was more important than borders—and the political powers of the different emirs.

"So, get back to work. We will have to be ready when we get the signal to blow the bomb."

# CHAPTER 23

*Shanghai, China*
*April 11th – 14:30*

Wang had met the mysterious Western man five days ago at the restaurant. The next day, he showed up at Wang's office at nine in the morning.

Wang confronted him with the obvious lie.

The man did not seem surprised about the confrontation, admitting his real name was Oliver DeVille, and that he was a consultant and researcher specialized in religious history.

"I think we need to take this serious. He lied to me with a straight face." Wang was on the phone with Wu. "It took all my willpower not to kill him there and then," he lied.

"I am *sure*," Wu said.

Wang hated the innocuous insults from Wu. "He knew I almost got him killed the night before, but he still had the nerve to come see me and pretend like nothing happened."

"We need to know who exactly he is, and what he knows. It was wise meeting him. *And* to let him go."

DeVille had apologized sincerely to Wang for misleading him the night before, but said he just wanted to secure a meeting with such a busy and important man. If he had not known it was a lie, Wang would have been flattered.

"He told me he was researching Tengriism in the modern world and for some reason he believed I practiced Tengriism."

"Have you been indiscreet?"

"Yes, I guess so." Wang hated to admit anything, especially to Wu. "He made the connection with my ship names." He knew he would get a reprimand from Wu later.

"I always thought it was a bit reckless of you."

"All I told him was that the history which have influenced China fascinates me. That it was just a hobby to me."

The meeting with DeVille had lasted for about twenty minutes before Wang excused himself. The Westerner confused Wang with his calmness, considering what had happened the night before—but not like an intelligence agent of any kind Wang had seen before.

DeVille had thanked him for his time, given him a card, and told Wang to contact him if he had anything else that might be useful for his research.

*What a nerve!*

Yet, the man did not seem like someone who could kill two of his toughest men.

"Well, I got news for you. DeVille left on a flight to Dubai early the morning after he met you. I have one of my agents in Dubai keeping an eye on him."

Wang liked that about Wu. He was a man of action.

"I have some good news as well," Wang told Wu. "Bakunin has managed to change the auction date for the Arctic mineral rights to be held on the fifth instead. By that time those rights should be worthless. We should get them for peanuts."

Together they would start moving the treasure from the ocean floor and into their pockets.

Their plan was ambitious, but the major milestone was getting the terrorists to steal the bomb. Before that, they had nothing to lose. Now they entered a phase where there was a lot to lose. And everything to win.

When the terrorists detonated the nuclear bomb somewhere in the Arctic Ocean, the area would be contaminated. Khagan Bakunin would pick up the mineral rights at a bargain price. Together with Wang's high-tech, and now radiation-proof, mining vessel, the ocean floor would be mined for all it was worth.

"Great news. That should line our pockets as well as finance the last phase of our plan."

Wu seemed genuinely pleased, although Wang knew the spymaster never was.

"It will not take long after the bomb explodes for the world to know that the Uighurs and the Chechens are responsible. You and Khagan Alexandrovich can start moving right after."

"Khagan Alexandrovich will get enough support to run a military coup against Putin."

"And you, my friend, you'll have the backing for the presidency of China. The hero of the war against the terrorists!" Wang needed to brownnose Wu, but he hated every second of it.

*Tengri's wishes come first.*

Wang would obey.

With two of the Khagans in the roles as leaders of two of the largest countries in the world, and the other two being among the richest, they could easily fulfill the last phase of the plan. Wang looked at the screensaver on his laptop and saw the green wolf's head on a blue background. As it had been almost fifteen hundred years ago, the flag of the First Khaganate would be the flag of the Third Khaganate.

And this time, the empire would last forever.

# CHAPTER 24

*Dubai, United Arab Emirates*
*April 11<sup>th</sup> – 18:40*

The brown leather couches lining the lobby of the Grosvenor House Hotel felt cold through DeVille's linen pants. He had been sitting there for twenty minutes, and was starting to suspect no one would show up.

The lobby's black marble flooring was so shiny he could see his dark blond hair, thicker than a lion's mane, in the reflection. It looked unkempt, but purposefully so. As with all high-end hotels in Dubai, there was someone constantly polishing the floors. And all other things for that matter.

He looked down again at his reflection. The beige linen suit, just purchased from a tailor in the nearby Dubai Marina Mall, shone up at him. The cut was perfect and, a little embarrassed, he had to admit he looked good in it.

He traveled to Dubai twice a year on average. It was mainly for conferences and it was the third time he had stayed in this hotel. It had become his favorite place to stay in Dubai. Not only were the rooms large and luxurious and the staff courteous, something most of the hotels in the city of bling had, but it housed some of the best restaurants around.

*Oh, the irony of conferences.*

The day was full of speeches about different aspects of Islam. At night, all the Westerners, and some of the locals, met over more than one drink.

He had arrived in Dubai from Shanghai three days ago and had hung around for someone to contact him. Three days of curious waiting.

*Who is behind the messages?*

This morning there was a note for him in reception, telling him to be in the lobby at six thirty. That was all it said.

*Is the trip to Dubai going to be a waste of time?*

*Should I have stayed in Shanghai and watched Wang?*

It did not matter what he thought. It had been the chief of staff's suggestion and he was the one who currently paid DeVille's salary.

While he sat and waited in the lobby he pondered his second encounter with Wang. He could not figure out what possible motive Wang could have for stealing the nuclear missile. After having talked to him in person, he had hoped to be convinced that Wang was not involved. But he was not—the suspicion only strengthened.

In addition to the cuff links and the names of ships and companies, the office was filled with discreet links to Tengriism. There were paintings of the mountain Khan Tengri as well as the Tamir River. This river was another place considered holy in ancient Tengriism.

There were also two small bronze busts that stood out among the model ships. They were of the two most significant kings in Tengriist history, or Khans or Khagans as they called their kings—one of Genghis Khan and one of Bumin Qaghan, the first Grand Khagan.

Bumin Qaghan had been the founder of the Göktürk Empire around AD 550. His empire ran from Ukraine in the west to the Korean peninsula in the east. It lasted less than fifty years, but it laid the foundations for the man who would terrorize the known world seven hundred years later.

Genghis Khan's empire had been double the size but, more importantly, the dynasty lasted longer. Another common feature of these two men was that they both made their people believe Tengri had ordered them to establish their empires.

"Are you DeVille?"

DeVille's focus snapped back to the lobby of the Grosvenor House Hotel where a man who could have made a fortune as a Danny DeVito look-alike stood two meters away staring at him. He looked out of place with his white T-shirt and Adidas tracksuit pants.

DeVille nodded.

The man pointed towards the hotel entrance and started to walk.

DeVille took the hint and followed.

The sunshine blinded him for a second as he stepped outside. He saw the man open the rear door on a Mercedes Benz G 63 AMG, standing with its engine rumbling.

DeVille knew from earlier visits that this boxlike German tank of an off-road machine, fitted with a five-hundred-horsepower engine, was the favored vehicle of the moneyed elite in the United Arab Emirates. The two and a half ton metal lump could accelerate faster than most sports cars, while it drank gas like a tourist drinking alcohol on Ibiza.

DeVille climbed in and the man sat in the front passenger seat. Another burly-looking man, wearing almost identical clothes, turned his head from the driver's seat and looked at him before he made the Mercedes drive off with a roar from the eight-cylindered engine.

They drove out of the Dubai Marina area where the hotel was located and crossed over the Sheikh Zayed Road—the main road going through Dubai. They took the exit towards Emirates Hills, an upscale neighborhood

DeVille suspected was named after Beverly Hills. The only hills around were on the golf course.

The *Geländewagen* slowed down as it approached a guarded gate, where, to DeVille's surprise, they stopped and showed an access card. DeVille had visited several gated communities in Dubai before and normally it was enough to show a western-looking face and the sleepy guard would let you in. Especially if you arrived in a hundred thousand dollar car such as this Mercedes.

They drove past several villas the sizes of small apartment buildings before they pulled up in front of a large two-story house. It looked like a classical French architect had begun designing it and an Arabic one had completed it. They parked between a Bentley Continental Flying Spur and a Lamborghini Aventador.

It had to be the mafia.

The chief of staff had told DeVille that Europol believed there were connections between Chechen rebels and the mafia. The rebels would assist in smuggling drugs from Afghanistan to Russia and use the money paid for the drugs by the mafia to finance their separatist war. After the Taliban was routed in Afghanistan, the poppy cultivation boomed. This was illegal under the Taliban and this new supply was something the mafia leaped at right away. The Taliban also financed the Chechen wars. After the collapse of the regime in Afghanistan, the rebels were forced to look at new ways to raise funds.

It was the perfect match for both parties.

DeVille was led from the car around the house to a large garden in the back. The massive infinity pool, waterfall included, took up half the garden—but the chlorine blue mixed well with the green view of the golf course. In the far end corner was a gazebo where a man was sitting in front of a table.

The man looked up from a laptop, stood up, and walked towards him. He was tall and thin, but you could see he was fit through his tight pink polo shirt. With chic white linen pants and leather slip-on shoes, he was the complete opposite of his henchmen.

*Or whatever the tracksuit boys are.*

Instead of raising his arm to shake DeVille's hand, the man put it around his shoulder as if they had been best friends for years.

"Welcome to Dubai, Mr. DeVille," he said in perfectly accented English, in comparison to the monotone way of speaking DeVille had expected. "I'm Sergei."

"I got your invitation."

"I'm sorry for all this secrecy and that we haven't had the chance to speak before. Please join me over in my little outdoor office. It's such a beautiful time of the year, so I prefer to be outside before the heat and humidity make this city unbearable."

DeVille knew the temperatures in Dubai in the summer could reach up to fifty degrees with almost a hundred percent humidity. Right now it was in the low thirties and pleasant.

"Can I offer you a drink? Perhaps a gin and tonic, or a glass of wine?"

DeVille entertained the thought that he had walked into a trap. If that was so, he might as well have a drink. He thanked the man and accepted the offer of a gin and tonic.

"Yes, please. Thank you."

Sergei shouted something into an open door by the patio.

"All right, Sergei. I'm sorry to ask you right away, but I'm curious. What is going on?"

"That is understandable. Let me first explain who I am. My boss is the head of several large conglomerates that operate in Russia." The man took a second to pause. "They operate in the shadow of the law," he said, letting his TV commercial-white teeth shine in the sun as he smiled.

"Your boss is Semion Mogilevich?" DeVille asked, referring to the man believed to be the 'boss of bosses' in the Russian mafia. When the chief of staff briefed him on the mafia's connection with the Chechens, that name came up several times. The man was also on the FBI's 'Top Ten Most Wanted' list.

"Names are not important," Sergei said. "I don't know how much you know of our organization, so I will give you a short intro."

DeVille nodded.

*Where is this heading?*

"We have been an organized syndicate for centuries and were quite successful up until the creation of the Soviet Union. With few exceptions, the communists were difficult to deal with for our people and we were only able to carry out small ventures."

The man sounded like a company CEO doing a sales pitch to potential investors.

Sergei continued, "After the fall of the Soviet Union we were able to take advantage of the turmoil and created a vast empire of businesses. Did you know that by the mid-nineties, we controlled almost all the banks in Russia?"

DeVille shook his head. He knew the mafia controlled a lot in Russia, but the size of it surprised him.

"The reign of Boris Yeltsin was good to us. He only cared about liberalizing all the stupid rules the communists had made and he let us operate freely. Putin has also been good to us. After the chaos of the nineties, he told us to behave and, if we did, he would protect our business ventures. And we have behaved. And he has protected us."

"I don't really understand what this has to do with me." DeVille decided to throw out a bait, "Or a gentleman named Wang in China for that matter."

"You're welcome, by the way," Sergei said in a hardened voice. "For the little rescue operation we did for you in Shanghai."

DeVille took the hint to shut up and let Sergei finish his story.

Sergei pointed to the impressive skyline of Dubai which was lighting up the early evening. "Over there you have the Dubai Marina and over there the Burj Khalifa and downtown Dubai. There are over ten thousand Russians living in Dubai." A long pause. "The last thing we want is a return to a regime ruled by some idiot with a religious or political agenda. That's what Wang and his comrades want. We need to stop them."

"His comrades?" DeVille asked before Sergei's eyes reminded him that he was to shut up. A Filipina servant replaced his gin and tonic with a new one.

"They're leaders of a weird religion that believes in mountains and stuff like that. Normally we could not care less about them, but their plan is to unite Russia and China and rule with an iron fist. Sort of like a religious Stalin."

The contempt in Sergei's voice made the hairs on DeVille's arms stand up.

"A guy called Ivan Alexandrovich, an admiral in charge of the Russian navy is planning a coup to take over the leadership of Russia. He has the support of many in the armed forces already. A Chinese guy, whose name we don't know, is going to do something similar in China. Wang and a Russian businessman named Peter Bakunin are involved in some scheme to bankroll these coups. That's how we know about Wang."

Sergei paused to let it sink in for DeVille.

"*How* do you know all this?" DeVille finally asked.

"You know the FSB, the Russian intelligence agency? Well, probably ten percent of them are also on our payroll."

"So, why don't they do something about this Alexandrovich?"

"Unfortunately the top brass is not affiliated with us. They know though. But they either don't believe it or they secretly support a military coup."

DeVille rubbed his head. "Why don't you take him out? I mean, er, since you operate in the shadow of the law." Sweat beads formed on DeVille's forehead.

"We'd never be able to keep that a secret. The guy hasn't done anything wrong yet, at least to our knowledge. If Putin thinks we are killing innocent admirals, he'll decide that we aren't behaving, and do everything in his power to shut us down."

"Isn't there someone else you can tell?" DeVille was frustrated.

"Like who? The Americans? They refuse to even listen to us. The Chinese? Nope. We believe that the Chinese guy is working in state intelligence, so he'd be the first one to shoot the story down. Interpol? They'd just arrest us." Sergei waved his arms to indicate that it was hopeless dealing with these agencies.

"Why me?"

"Easy. We've been keeping our eyes open for a while. We heard, from a source at a restaurant these guys visited, that something was about to happen. Then we heard from our friends in the FSB that an American bomb had been stolen, and a guy believed to be Uighur was in custody. Finally, our friends in Chechnya told us they would soon receive a nuclear bomb."

DeVille drank his gin and tonic in one go.

"We just connected the dots. We sent a guy to keep an eye on what happened. When you showed up, we knew we had the perfect guy."

"Perfect guy?"

"You are a religious expert, working separately from the intelligence agencies, although with the ability to contact them and feed them info. No one would suspect you working for us."

"I'm not working for you."

Sergei ignored DeVille and continued, "Unfortunately, that guy was shot dead by the CIA before he could give you the information we had." DeVille sensed in the man's eyes that he knew exactly what had happened. A crooked smile was DeVille's response.

"A small price to pay," Sergei said. "We wanted to feed you what we knew and lead you towards Wang, without you knowing where the information originated from. If it came out that we knew about the missing nuke, all the intelligence agencies in the world would think we stole it. Bad for business."

DeVille decided to change topic. "So, where is the bomb?"

Sergei told him how they believed that Alexandrovich and his friends had tricked Uighur and Chechen rebels into stealing it and that they would detonate it in a terror attack. The rebels would be blamed and that would be justification for a war against them which would boost Alexandrovich's public support.

"Also, the Chechens are part of our logistical organization, so we don't want them to do something stupid that would lead to their demise. We've everything to lose on this bomb going off. Of course they won't listen to us. Holy war and all that shit. But we have no idea where the bomb is. My thought is that by helping you to find who's behind all of this, you'll somehow find the bomb and foil their plan. And we can all go back to normal and mind our own business."

"And you think Wang can give us clues about the whereabouts of the bomb?" Nothing DeVille had seen in Wang's office in Shanghai had shown anything that could be connected to a nuclear bomb. Even though it made sense, he could not be sure the mobster was telling him the truth.

*Will Stella Hanson believe me?*

She would not use resources on Wang until he could give her some real evidence. The next thing to do was to inform the chief of staff, if he could get out of this mafia get-together.

"We think Wang is the weakest link of the four of them," Sergei answered. "He is also the only one of them who is easily accessible. Bakunin stays most of the time in his compound outside of Moscow. The admiral is heavily guarded in the navy, and his movements are shrouded in secrecy to avoid any terrorist attacks. And we don't even know who the Chinese spymaster is. That's why we...*you* need to focus on Wang."

DeVille repressed the urge to utter a sarcastic 'Yes, sir.'

They both looked at each other. The only noise around came from the driving range not far away from Sergei's house—the metal clang of ball, made of hard urethane, meeting titanium alloyed club head at high speed.

Sergei stood up. "Thanks for listening to me. I'm sorry, but I have business to attend to. I hope you're successful."

DeVille thanked the mobster for the drinks and started to walk towards where he had entered the garden. He turned and looked at Sergei. "It was Wang, wasn't it? That tried to kill me in Shanghai."

Sergei nodded.

"Thanks for the rescue." Something told DeVille that this would not be the last time he would meet Sergei.

# CHAPTER 25

*23:20*

DeVille sat in the hotel bar, creatively named *The Bar*, trying with a bottle of red wine to make all the confusing information he had received three hours earlier disappear.

He took a deep breath, hesitated, then pressed the green button on the Nokia twice. The chief-of staff picked up immediately.

"What do you have for me?"

DeVille gave him the full brief of his meeting with Sergei. "What do you think?"

"It certainly makes sense, although I can't take a criminal's word for it without any real evidence, but I suggest you stay on Wang's tail."

It was clear to DeVille that it was not so much a suggestion as an order.

The chief of staff continued, "I'll give you three reasons. There's no way to verify this information unless we know more about Wang. Second reason, who the hell will believe that a Chinese-Russian religious cult has stolen the nuke?"

"Yeah, I see that," DeVille said reluctantly.

"Thirdly, and it is a bit cynical, but we have to be. If what we've been told is true, then most likely the bomb will be detonated outside EU borders. I assume that the CIA and NATO know at least as much as we do, so *my* concern is just to make sure that the damn thing is not within EU borders."

"I see, but I don't like it."

"I don't care what you like or not. Speaking of which, don't tell the CIA about your meeting with Sergei."

"Why?"

"They don't really approve of other governmental agencies being in contact with people on their most wanted list. They'll give us shit for not letting them in on it before you went to Dubai."

"Okay. But this is getting above my pay grade. Any chance of getting a second pair of hands?" DeVille held his breath.

"Nope. But I'll double your fees and you'll have carte blanche on expenses."

Money was always convincing. DeVille exhaled, smiled, and looked at the half empty carafe of 2007 Barbaresco—a three hundred dollar bottle of red.

"Deal," DeVille said. "But just to have it straight; we have no idea where the bomb is or any clues to it? We don't know if we can trust what the mafia says? And even if the motive they gave us is correct, it doesn't give us anything tangible to use?"

"Sounds about right, except Wang."

"And Tengriism. I'll go somewhere Wang has pointed me to—Altay City."

"Where?"

"The heartland of ancient Tengriism. It's next to Khan Tengri, their most sacred mountain. Close to what was the center of power for both Bumin Qaghan's and Genghis Khan's empires. It's the only place I can think of where I might pick up new clues."

"Fine. Just keep me updated." The chief of staff hung up.

If what Sergei had told him was true, and Wang's connections to Tengriism were genuine, the mountain city was the perfect place to search for more clues.

Deville checked some flights on his iPad and found one flying out of Dubai at six in the evening the next day, arriving in Altay City twenty hours later. He got first-class tickets round-trip for less than four thousand American dollars.

*Damn reasonable.*

The price was normally three times higher, forcing him to fly economy. Not that it mattered now he had his carte blanche on expenses.

DeVille thought about defying the chief of staff's order and calling Stella Hanson. He needed all the help and all the friends he could get. Plus, something told him he did not want to be on her bad side. He took a big sip of the wine and drowned away the thought of it being another reason why he wanted to call her.

He looked over at the wine carafe and poured the last of the ruby-orange colored liquid into his glass. The scent of flowers and forest berries tickled his nose, while spiced, ripe fruit engulfed his tongue. It was worth every dollar.

It would be wiser to postpone making the decision to call Stella or not until he landed in Altay City.

# CHAPTER 26

*April 12<sup>th</sup> – 15:05*

Dubai to Guangzhou, seven hours.

Then a three-hour layover.

Guangzhou to Urumqi, six hours.

Then another layover. This time five hours.

Urumqi to Altay City, one hour.

DeVille looked at the itinerary from Southern Airlines he had printed out in the hotel's business lounge earlier and began to doubt his decision to travel to Altay City. Twenty-two hours of travel and a time difference of four hours, meant leaving Dubai at six in the evening would only get him to Altay City by eight in the evening—the next day.

If the trip turned out to be a waste, it was a waste of a lot of time.

He stuffed the e-ticket into his pocket, grabbed his bag, and walked out of the hotel. He asked the doorman to get him a cab. It was still three hours until the flight departed, but DeVille did not feel like waiting around. He might as well take full advantage of his first- class ticket and use the lounge at the airport.

The doorman waved and a white Lexus pulled up—an advantage of staying in a five-star hotel. Instead of the beat-up Toyotas and Hyundais of the normal cab fleet, you would get a nice, discreet and comfortable Lexus. And the fare was only a couple of dollars more expensive.

"Airport, terminal one, please," DeVille said as he got in the backseat.

"Yes, sir." The driver was a well-dressed Pakistani. Another difference from many of the normal cabs. "Have you been following the cricket between Pakistan and India, sir?"

"No, I haven't. To be honest, I don't know anything about cricket."

The driver was determined to talk about the match anyway.

DeVille was not sure if the driver saw it as his duty to teach DeVille about cricket or if he just wanted to let him know as many times as possible that Pakistan was leading. DeVille knew of the long-standing rivalry between the two countries, but he tuned out as they got onto Sheikh Zayed Road and he looked towards the gated community to his right.

Emirates Hills. Where Sergei lived.

They drove through downtown Dubai where the Burj Khalifa, the world's tallest building, loomed majestically over the other buildings. Skyscrapers, which would look huge in almost any other city in the world, looked small when placed next to the Burj Khalifa.

Just before they came to the Garhoud Bridge, which would take them across the Dubai Creek and to the airport, a white Toyota Fortuner tried to squeeze narrowly in front of the cab. DeVille could tell what was about to happen. As the driver misjudged the length of his SUV, a piercing sound of metal scraping, and plastic shattering, silenced the cricket-talking cabdriver, as the SUV clipped the cab's front bumper.

It was a light touch, but when going that fast DeVille was sure the front of the cab was far from showroom condition. The Toyota put its hazard lights on and the driver lifted his hand in an apology, although none of the men in the car looked apologetic.

The Toyota slowed down and took the first exit. The cab followed. Both had their hazard lights blinking.

"I'm so sorry, sir. It really wasn't my fault, but I have to stop."

"No worries, I'll just get another cab. Airport is only a few minutes away, right?" At least he had lots of time. And a good reason to have an extra drink in the lounge.

The style of driving in Dubai was more aggressive than the French driving around the Arc de Triomphe. The cabdriver muttered, annoyed, and started to flash his headlights since the Toyota did not pull over. The headlights bounced off the white paint before being swallowed up by the harsh afternoon sunshine. They continued for another three hundred meters before the Toyota pulled into a parking spot along the road. The traffic noise from the highway was now subdued and DeVille heard the humming of both cars' engines.

"This idiot probably does not have insurance so he wants to stop somewhere the traffic police will not see us," the cabdriver explained. "He will try to offer me cash for repairs if I do not call the police. I cannot do that. It is the taxi company's car."

DeVille was certain that the driver would accept the cash as soon as DeVille was gone and claim to his supervisor that he had scraped a building or something, pocketing the money himself and letting the insurance company deal with the repairs. The offer from the Toyota driver just needed to be larger than whatever the minimum deductible was and any potential fines the cab company imposed on the driver.

DeVille started looking around for a cab and realized he probably had to walk back to the highway exit to get one.

As he reached for the door handle, the windshield shattered. The hair on his arms raised as he felt the air pressure inside the car deflate and the air-conditioned coldness slowly escaped. Then another sound of breaking glass and DeVille saw the head of the driver slam into the headrest before falling forward onto the steering wheel.

A large hole, with blood and hair around it, was visible on the back of the driver's head. The blood, as it soaked the Pakistani's hair, was so thick that his head looked like a wet brush covered in paint.

On instinct, Deville dived out of the car and into the hedge next to it. A bullet whooshed by, close to him, and hit one of the irrigation sprinklers for the hedge.

He looked up and saw three men step out of the Toyota. They were all dressed in the local kondura; the white dishdasha.

Some trees were clustered together about ten meters away and DeVille leaped for them, jumping behind one just as he heard guns popping.

*Guns with sound suppressors.*

He used the row of trees for cover and sprinted towards the highway, his plan being that they would not shoot him in public. The ramp loomed in front of him and he stopped. He had to find another way. The ramp was too high up for him to reach. Going back towards the lower end of the ramp was impossible—no cover from the shooters.

DeVille headed in the only other direction: under the bridge that crossed the creek.

The pillars holding the bridge up were each the size of a small house. DeVille darted towards the first one. He heard the men run towards him as he turned the corner of the first pillar.

DeVille picked up a rock the size of his fist. It would be no match against three guns, but the coarse, hard surface made it feel like he had some sort of a weapon. It helped reduce the dopamine in his brain, calming him.

It got quiet. The only noise was the constant clacking of the cars above as they drove over the joints of the bridge.

Someone was close.

He bent down and spotted an iron pipe, left over from the bridge construction. Hoping his pursuers would believe him to be farther away, he threw the rock towards the water. It splashed into the Dubai Creek. He picked up the iron pipe just as he heard someone on the other side of the pillar's corner.

Maybe a meter or two away.

One of the men thrust his gun, and head, around the pillar, but DeVille was ready. He smashed the iron pipe as hard as he could into the man's stomach. The man stumbled two steps forward with a loud groan. DeVille pulled him around the corner, trying not to expose himself to the other assailants, and wrapped his body around the arm with the gun. He tried to keep the arm still and the gun pointed away from him. Then he saw what was about to happen next.

The man flung his forehead into the back of DeVille's head, the sound of skull against skull echoing against the underside of the bridge. Both of them were still standing. DeVille's sight became blurry, but he knew he only had a tenth of a second to make his move. His foot lashed out and, with his wooden shoe heel, hit the man's kneecap. His leg snapped like a dried out stick.

But the man was still standing. DeVille used the iron pipe and, with all the energy he could gather, swung it and hit the man in the center of his face. The pipe contacted with the nose like a bat hitting a baseball.

The man was unconscious as he fell down flat, blood flowing out of his nose and mouth.

DeVille took the man's gun and turned in time to see a second man come around the pillar. DeVille fired twice. The bullets dug into the concrete. The man jumped back behind the pillar, stretched his arm out, and fired three rapid shots at an angle towards DeVille.

The bullets missed, and DeVille started to run in the direction of the next pillar—forty meters away.

Another sound caught his attention; the Toyota was coming towards him fast on the pebbled surface. It would get to him before he reached the water, twenty meters away. But it stopped by the first pillar.

Sirens started to sound from several directions. The hope of being saved fell dead fast as he looked back at the man that lay in a puddle of blood by the first pillar. If he had been hesitant to talk to the Dutch police earlier, the Dubai police seemed an even worse alternative.

DeVille fired another four shots in the general direction of the Toyota and jumped into the water. With only a half meter depth, and a rocky bottom, it knocked the air out of him, and the salty water stung his wounds. He staggered to his feet, then started to swim towards the middle of the creek, staying underwater for four long strokes.

As he came up for air, he turned around and saw the pulped face of the man he had hit being dragged into the back of the Toyota—then it sped away. Flashing blue lights penetrated the sunshine and reflected on the water's surface. He saw several police cars up in the direction of where the cab was.

Where the Pakistani driver with the gaping hole in his head was.

Where his luggage was.

Where his passport was.

# CHAPTER 27

*Dalian, China*
*April 12<sup>th</sup> – 16:20*

She was not pretty, but Wang knew the MV Ulgan would become his most cherished ship. It suited her to be named after the god that had created the world and everything beyond.

The Ulgan would recreate the world as it should be and hand them their powers as Khagans—Tengri's representatives on earth.

Wang was at the shipyard taking delivery of the ship after its custom fitting. The team of engineers promised him that the Ulgan could now withstand radiation as well as performing her mining duties in an arctic climate. He knew it had been a difficult job. The mining operation included several exposed parts of machinery, and they did not know the impact of radiation on the computers that operated all the hydraulic machinery.

She would depart immediately, heading for the North Pacific Ocean. When the call came for them to start operating, she needed to be as close as possible to the Bering Strait.

Wang had feared delays in the fitting of the radiation shields, but it was completed on time. Now the ship had enough time to get to the standby location. It would take between fifteen and twenty days to get there depending on the weather. He was hoping they could start mining the ocean floor in less than four weeks.

One of the most difficult tasks was the choice of crew. He needed people as loyal and skillful as Rottweilers. Both the captain and the chief engineer were from South America and there were two Chinese engineers in charge of the mining operations. They were paid good money, they knew the task, the risk, and they were promised more rewards afterwards.

Wang did not trust their loyalty a hundred percent, so he also placed four of his best henchmen onboard to keep him updated and to keep order. These men had worked for him for years and he knew they would do anything for him. He had rewarded them and their families handsomely over the years and would do so this time as well. Loyalty could not be bought, it had to be earned over several years. But to grease the process with some money helped.

He also recruited eight Filipinos: four skilled sailors, and four unskilled laborers for cooking, cleaning, and whatever else needed doing. It was modern-day slavery, but it was legal.

He confiscated their passports and gave them only a small amount of cash up front. The rest was to be paid after six months. The financial crisis in the world had led to a dumping of prices and conditions for the Philippines' biggest export—human labor.

Probably four or six Filipinos would have been sufficient as the mining process was highly automated, but he had given his henchmen authority to kill one or two of the unskilled laborers if they needed to enforce discipline. Wang strongly believed it had a positive effect on work morale to shoot a man in front of the rest of the crew.

Wang was satisfied with what he had seen, so he put his coat on and walked towards the door. The car was already heated up and ready to take him to the airport. In three hours he would be back in his apartment in Shanghai. He looked up at the news broadcast on the TV hanging on the wall in the makeshift office.

He smiled.

Apparently he was not the only one who had been busy over the last few days.

The volume was turned down, but Wang read the lips of the attractive news anchor.

"The highest-ranking military official in Russia has been found dead in his home outside of Moscow in what appears to be a suicide. The chief of the general staff was sixty-one years old. Sources inside the Kremlin say they expect President Putin to appoint the current commander-in-chief of the navy, Admiral Alexandrovich, as the new chief of the general staff."

# CHAPTER 28

*Celtic Sea*
*21:16*

The most southern tip of the UK lay due east and was less than a hundred miles away, at least according to the map on the computer screen which was tracking their voyage.

Umeira thought you would have been able to see land when you were this close, but one of the shipmates explained to him that visibility was only ten miles ahead in the horizon from the bridge of the ship. If the weather was clear and it was daytime they could possibly have made out some of the higher points of Cornwall.

The last thirty-six hours had been dreadful. They hit rough seas when they crossed the Bay of Biscay. All of Umeira's men got seasick, him as well. Not even the seasickness pills they got from the sick bay helped.

They even gave up guarding the containers. Umeira reasoned that if anyone tried to pry, a seasick guard would not be able to do much anyway. An unarmed, but unaffected, sailor could easily take out an armed but seasick guard.

Umeira had not eaten since the rough seas started. What he had in him when it started he had fed to the fishes. Even though the sea had calmed down a bit, he did not trust his stomach to hold down any food.

He ordered his men to eat, and they reluctantly did so.

The captain told him that from now on they should expect it to be rough rather than calm. Calm would be abnormal. When the captain said it, there was a huge grin on his face. A few of the shipmates showed some compassion, but the majority seemed to revel in their misery.

Umeira knew it was foolish, but he felt the urge to revenge this humiliation. He would truly enjoy killing the captain. The Chinaman had humiliated one of Allah's warriors, and by doing that he humiliated all Muslims. That alone was reason enough to kill the Chinese infidel, but since he had insulted Umeira personally as well—it would give him true joy to be his executioner.

It would have to wait.

After experiencing the rough seas, he knew he needed the captain, and his crew, for a few more days.

He had received instructions from Abdul Aziz on the satellite phone the night before. There was no doubt anymore that this was a suicide mission. Last night, during the worst seasickness spell, he would have been happy to see his life end in martyrdom.

They were to head towards Franz Josef Land, a Russian archipelago consisting of almost two hundred islands. The most southern point of the archipelago was less than a thousand miles from the North Pole.

As the waters around the archipelago were covered in deep ice at this time of the year, the instructions said to get as close as possible. Umeira was told by one of the crew that the Euphausia was ice class. Aziz, apparently, did not expect them to get all the way there.

He had not yet told the captain. He decided to only give him brief directions after they passed Iceland—which was why he was looking at the map on the computer screen. He jotted down directions and coordinates to give to the captain when the time was right.

The instructions from Aziz also provided a guide on how to arm the bomb.

It would be a dirty bomb. That suited Umeira fine. It would not be a nuclear explosion, but by using a vast amount of conventional explosives, they would create a fireball—spreading radiation far and wide. The Arctic had the perfect conditions for this. There was little rainfall in the polar regions, so the pollution would remain in the air for a long time. Rain or snow would not catch it and bring it down to the surface. The high winds would make it impossible for experts to predict where it would spread and how much radiation there would be in the air.

Umeira was disappointed that his martyrdom was not going to be connected to a big mushroom cloud. Also, he did not understand why they were using such a fantastic weapon in this isolated part of the world.

A big explosion in the middle of Moscow's Red Square would have been Umeira's choice.

Aziz was a wise man. After all, he had planned and successfully stolen a nuclear bomb—so Umeira would not question the choice of target.

*Perhaps I will understand when we get there.*

*Perhaps it will be close to a Russian naval base.*

There was also the possibility that Aziz would send further instructions. The leader of the Chechen freedom fighters had been very secretive of the overall plan on this mission.

Umeira's thoughts were interrupted as the captain slammed shut the hatch and entered the bridge. He decided to finally go and get something to eat. Later, he would pray and hopefully get a few hours of sleep. If the seas got rough again, he would need energy.

He also could not stand to be around that infidel pig of a captain for longer than necessary.

* * *

"How's he doing?" Zhang asked the shipmate while pointing towards the hatch through which the Muslim had just departed.

"Better, I think. He's very curious about all the things going on up here on the bridge. That shows me he's not that bothered by the seasickness anymore."

Even though he did not like the man nosing around on his bridge, Zhang understood why he did. While they were in transit it was boring to be a passenger. Nothing to see and nothing to do.

Zhang was also bored. The ship was new, so little maintenance was needed. Just trials and checks. He had asked the owner if they could test the fishing equipment and try to catch some Atlantic krill. At least just to see how the equipment worked.

The answer was no. Something about a lack of permit.

*Bullshit!*

Zhang knew they would cross into international waters north-east of Iceland, where no permits were needed. They were international waters. Zhang did not buy the reasoning, besides, the owner had never worried about permits before.

Another thing which annoyed Zhang was the fact he did not know where they were heading. The Muslim had told him to steer north-east of Iceland, but nothing more. He knew there were a lot of scientists on Spitsbergen and the islands would be in that general direction. But he did not understand why he would not tell him.

Zhang understood his dislike of the Muslim was mutual, so he assumed that was the reason for not letting him know.

*The Muslim wants to dilute my authority—and humiliate me.*

# CHAPTER 29

*Dubai, United Arab Emirates*
*April 13th – 03:48*

"Thanks," DeVille said to the consul as he took a sip of the glass of water in front of him and swallowed the painkillers he was given.

"Sure. Have some of this as well." The consul pointed to a bottle of Canadian whiskey.

The pills were just the over-the-counter type so the chance of getting any relief from the pain his stab wound was giving him, was slim. The whiskey would probably do a better job.

He was sitting in a room which reminded him of the interrogation room in The Hague, just a bit smaller. And another major difference—he was the one being questioned.

It was about four hours since he had reached the Canadian consulate in Dubai. And it was a little less than twelve hours since the cabdriver had been shot.

"So, continue please, what happened after the SUV with the shooters drove off?"

"I jumped in the water and swam across to one of the bridge pillars in the middle of the creek." DeVille paused as he remembered the blue lights reflecting in the calm water. "I waited there for about fifteen minutes to get my breath back and to think."

"It's not my problem, but you know the Dubai police will ask you why you didn't swim back to them."

"I panicked," DeVille said without attempting to convince the consul. "I remembered the golf club on the other side has swimming pools by the river. I hoped my boxers would pass for swimming trunks and that I could sneak in there unnoticed. It worked." Even if he had been noticed he was sure he would have been okay. As with most places in Dubai, if you had a western face, the security personnel did not ask too many questions. Either you were a well-off expat or you were a tourist. They never saw a threat in either as both groups spent money and that was all that mattered.

"I pretended to be a guest, and I just walked straight into the changing rooms. I found a pair of slippers, shorts, and a polo shirt. What I'm wearing now. Enough to look like a tourist."

"'Found'? I suppose 'stole' is a better word?"

"People need to lock their lockers," DeVille said as he took a long sip from the whiskey. "I had a wet fifty dirham note, so I hailed a cab and came here." He wanted to see if there was police around before he got close to the Canadian consulate. After all, they had his passport.

He had not seen anything to cause alarm. Surprised to see they still existed, he found a phone booth and called the chief of staff. Even the trusty Nokia had succumbed after having met the water, but DeVille remembered the number by now.

The chief of staff listened to what had happened, told him to stay close and he would do his best to have someone from the Canadian mission take him in.

Two hours later a man approached the bench he was sitting on and asked him if he wanted to visit the consulate.

"All right, I don't want to hear anymore," the consul said. "I was instructed to assist you by the ambassador, but you should know it's more because of your friends in Europe than because of your citizenship. This could've created a serious mess with the UAE government." He stood up and left the room.

Forty minutes later, the police showed up and questioned him. DeVille told them the truth about what had happened.

They seemed more interested in his meeting with Sergei than with the actual shooting.

*Perhaps they have witnesses to back me up.*

On the other hand, the police talked about Sergei as if he were royalty. Although, from their choice of words, they seemed to know what business he was in. DeVille wondered if Sergei knew about what had happened.

Before they left, the police told him that he could stay in the consulate as long as the consul guaranteed he would remain within consulate grounds.

DeVille was okay with that. He was pretty sure they did not serve Canadian whiskey in a Dubai holding cell.

DeVille grabbed the phone that stood on the table and dialed.

"Will you be all right?" the chief of staff answered. It was just past midnight in Brussels, but he sounded as alert as ever.

"Yup, I'll be fine. Listen, a thought struck me as I swam across the creek. I saw all those old wooden dhows that are docked there. Wang owns several ships, so if he's involved, he could have used one of those to move the missile."

"Sure, but so could the admiral."

"If he's trying to get on the military's good side before a coup, wouldn't that be risky?" DeVille asked, unconvinced.

"So, we believe Wang is the smallest fish? Someone who could be sacrificed if the shit hit the fan?"

"That's how it sounded when Sergei told his story."

"Okay, how can we move forward with that theory?"

"Are you close to a computer? Open a browser and go to Eje Marine's website. Find the names of all of Wang's ships, then open 'marinetraffic.com' and punch in the names. It's a site that tells you a ship's location."

The chief of staff did as requested. "Most of Wang's ships are dredgers, currently located around Shanghai. There are also a few supply ships out in the Yellow Sea."

The website gave information about the ships, such as speed, course, and destination, as well as what flag she was carrying and what type of vessel she was classified as. Some ships even had pictures.

DeVille scribbled down what the chief of staff told him, and noticed that one of Wang's twelve ships was only noted as an 'unspecified ship' on the website. It was in the East China Sea heading towards the port of Pevek in Russia.

"Where's that?" DeVille asked.

"Somewhere in Siberia it seems. Arctic Ocean side."

"Maybe a research ship. What's it called?"

"Ulgan."

That caught DeVille's attention. Ulgan meant *magnificent* in Old Turkic. But more importantly, he was the highest-ranking god after Tengri himself. Some Tengriists believed Ulgan and Tengri to be the same god. Ulgan created the earth and all living creatures on it and controlled the movement of the stars.

DeVille noted down the information relayed to him. If he got out of this mess in Dubai he would need to check out that ship.

"Okay, last ship I got for you is called Euphausia."

"Can you google that name?" DeVille asked. "Seems to be the only name that doesn't have Tengriist connections."

"It means 'krill.' But that makes sense, because it says here that it's a fishing boat. Another difference to the other ships is that it is in Europe. It is now in the Celtic Sea."

"Okay..." DeVille sensed that the silence from the chief of staff meant that he was onto something.

"Last port of call is a place called Yeysk in Russia ten days ago."

DeVille knew Yeysk was in the Caucasus. It was not too far away from where Chechen terrorists roamed.

*Is this Chechen connection what we are looking for?*

The consul stepped in and looked dismayed at DeVille for using the phone.

"I've got to go. Call you a bit later." DeVille said and hung up.

"The chief of Dubai Police is here to see you," the consul said and left the room again.

DeVille had just finished his second glass of whiskey. Since the consul was kind enough to leave the bottle in the room, DeVille poured himself another half glass of whiskey and drank it all in one go. Then the police chief entered.

He introduced himself with the title lieutenant general, and his face told DeVille that he was not in the best of moods.

*Fair enough. It's the middle of the night.*

But it did make DeVille feel a little worried as he felt the whiskey burn in his throat.

The police chief told him that he was free to go.

DeVille could not hold the sigh of relief in, and it seemed to amuse the police chief.

"They have been talking on political levels," the Emirati police chief said in perfect English. "And together with eyewitness testimony we have, it seems like you are innocent. We're now working on the theory that the taxi driver was the intended victim."

DeVille wanted to object, but he stopped himself. He did not want to give up his 'get-out-of-jail' card.

"But we will need a written statement from you. Also, your earlier business meeting is of interest to us." The policeman's face showed he did not believe DeVille should walk. "In case we feel the need, we have the right to call you back here for testimony. The EU has guaranteed that you will comply with such a request."

'That's fine with me." DeVille just wanted to get out of this consulate.

"We've brought your belongings that we found in the taxi."

DeVille had completely forgotten about his luggage. And his passport.

He thanked the police chief and stood in an uncomfortably upright position until the lieutenant general had left the room.

"Time for you to get the hell out of my consulate," the consul said.

"I'll do that. And I do appreciate your assistance, but before I go I need to *borrow* your phone again."

He called back the chief of staff and told him that he was a free man.

"You're welcome."

DeVille told him they should put the two ships under surveillance. The chief of staff replied that it was easy for him to arrange for surveillance of the krill ship while it was in EU waters, but when it entered Icelandic or Norwegian waters there was not much he could do but ask for assistance from those countries.

"Will you search or approach the ship?" DeVille asked.

"No. At least not yet. I don't want them to raid the ship at the position it is in now. If it has the nuclear missile onboard we'll let them get out into open seas. I don't want the bomb to accidentally blow up near populated UK or Irish shores. If they all of a sudden deviate and head for the coast we'll intervene."

"Okay. What about the Ulgan?"

"There's nothing we can do about that one. We don't have jurisdiction."

"Can't the Americans do it?"

"I'll ask. But it doesn't make sense that the missile is all the way on the other side of the world, does it? There's no chance they could have moved the missile all the way to north-east China in such a short time."

"If Sergei is right, they have easy access to both money and Chinese intelligence," DeVille reminded him.

"All right, I'll talk to the CIA."

DeVille smiled. "No worries. I'll give them a call."

# CHAPTER 30

*Shanghai, China*
*April 13<sup>th</sup> – 08:00*

*April 13$^{th}$ – 08:00*

It was exactly eight in the morning. Wang never arrived later than that to his office. Of course the commute down in the elevator from his penthouse was easy, but Wang took pride in his own discipline.

The routine was the same each morning. He would go down and look through the e-mails that had come in overnight. His secretary would bring him the day's newspapers while his maid brought down breakfast from his apartment.

*Breakfast, the most important meal of the day.*

A normal breakfast for him consisted of fatty mutton soup and yogurt, something he liked to believe Genghis Khan and Bumin Qaghan used to eat for breakfast.

The maid knocked on the door and he waved her in. She was in her early twenties with a body to be proud of. Sexy, but in an innocent and flirtatious way. Wang had never married, which, in his mind, made it acceptable for him to look at the maid in a sexual manner.

"I made you two cups of tea, sir." Her face looked older than her body, but Wang suspected it was the result of growing up in destitution.

"Thank you. I will have it here at my desk as I have an important phone call to make." Wang sometimes wondered if it was just her face that looked older than she was.

She lived in the maid's room of his apartment. She had worked for him for almost two years now, and while many maids would have refused to live in the same house as a single man, she had not objected when he hired her. Certainly, people believed he took advantage of the daughter of a blacksmith from the countryside, but he did not care. Sometimes he suspected she would not have minded it either.

But he took pride in his discipline. He needed to stay focused. Their task was to revive Tengri's honor in the world. His own body's needs would have to wait.

Today he would not attend to anything business-related. He was responsible for organizing the next *Kurultai*, the meeting of the Khagans. His phone rang.

"Good morning, Khagan Wu," Wang said as he picked up the phone after the third ring.

"Good morning, Khagan Wang. I assume you are busy planning the Kurultai?"

"Yes, indeed. It was a wise decision to have it every two weeks now that the ball is rolling. There are already a number of items on the agenda."

They rotated on organizing the Kurultai. Wang always chose the temple for the event. The last Kurultai, arranged by Khagan Bakunin, had been in a restaurant in Vladivostok that Wang found as seedy as the girls that work their trade along the Nanjing Road. The restaurant was reserved just for them, so it served its purpose, but it was the lack of dignity which bothered Wang. It was an insult to the fellow Khagans, and Tengri, he thought at the time.

"Good. I assume that what I told you last night is on the agenda?" Wu asked.

"It certainly is. I have it as agenda point one. I find it very curious."

DeVille had been attacked in Dubai.

And not just attacked in order to scare him or send a message. He had been attacked with the purpose of eliminating him.

But the attack had failed.

*Like the one in Shanghai.*

Wang wondered what and how much DeVille knew.

"It was good that I arranged for him to be under surveillance," Wu said. "I wonder what the other Khagans will think of this."

"I think that since DeVille met with this Russian mobster before he was attacked, there might be a link there. Regardless, Khagan Alexandrovich needs to investigate what the mafia knows and take appropriate measures."

"I fully agree with you, Khagan Wang."

The agenda point that Wang found to be the most interesting was the fourth. This was to create a strategic outline on how to annex other countries in the region so they could complete the third and most powerful Khaganate.

Even though China and Russia would be the powerhouses of this new Khaganate, they needed Mongolia and Kazakhstan as they belonged to the Turkic motherland. In addition, both Genghis Khan and Bumin Qaghan had ventured into the Korean peninsula as well as other Central Asian countries.

It was something they would only start with after they solidified their power in Russia and China, but long-term planning was important to ensure that they had a plan to counteract any possible disturbance to harmony. Harmony led to success.

The idea to take control of Russia and China had been laid out almost twelve years ago. Things change as time passes, but the plan was still similar to how they envisaged it all those years ago. They were guided and protected by divine forces.

It had taken them many years to excel in their designated fields—business, military, and intelligence. The biggest change was that Wang originally planned to work for the judiciary in China, but when government-led capitalism blossomed, they all agreed Wang should work the business angle. Just like Khagan Bakunin in Russia.

The original plan featured a foreign government as the scapegoat—not terrorists. But when Alexandrovich got hold of an informant within the Chechen rebellion, the current plan was agreed. It would only work if Wu managed to get an informant within the Uighur Islamists as well. Wu had succeeded.

That was three years ago. The Khagans had waited as patiently as a stalking cat for the right moment to set the wheels in motion.

The four of them had known each other for over thirty years. They all came from the same region, but from different sides of the border.

But they shared each other's interest in their common Turkic heritage.

In an attempt to improve relations between the Soviet Union, Mongolia, and China, the governments had launched a number of cultural cross-border initiatives in the late eighties. One of them was a symposium on the Mongolian empire under Genghis Khan, where all four of them met and discovered their common interest in Tengriism.

Afterwards, the four of them studied Tengri further. They did this in secrecy as it was filled with danger in the two communist countries. The governments looked upon religion as some sort of plague. This led to them becoming close to each other. A few years later, Wang bought an abandoned Buddhist temple up in the Altai Mountains. The four of them spent two years in the temple, renovating it and turning it into a place of worship to Tengri.

That was when the idea of a third Khaganate had grown on them as fast as bamboo in warm soil.

The ancient Khagans did not have a specific house of worship for Tengri, but Wang and the others felt they needed a building that showed Tengri their appreciation. The holy mountains were located in an inhospitable climate with bitterly cold winters. Having a temple helped them to get near and to stay there for longer periods of time.

They had also recruited other believers over the years, although very carefully. The temple now had almost sixty devotees that lived there permanently. They were titled *Baghaturs*, or *valiant warriors*. All of them were recruited from the regions around the Altai Mountains and were made to live in solitary for six months before they were allowed to become warriors of Tengri.

The Khagans did not stay there for longer periods anymore as they were needed elsewhere to complete the plan.

"Hold on a second, please." Wang covered the mouth of the phone as the maid walked in to clear Wang's breakfast. He thanked her and looked at the skirt he made her use as a uniform—any shorter and it would have revealed if she wore stockings or pantyhose. He was not sure if it was slutty or sexy.

*Perhaps both.*

"Sorry about that, you have my full attention again."

"Your maid?"

Wang hated how it seemed like Wu knew everything about him, so he let the question remain unanswered.

"I am not so worried about DeVille having a small clue about our plan. Or if he has informed the mafia." Wu said. "We can handle them."

"You mean you are worried about the CIA? So am I."
They knew the CIA would be involved in one way or
another in connection with the missing missile, but they had
not at all expected *this* incident to happen.

The men Wu had instructed to tail DeVille had wisely
decided to split up and one had followed the attackers. The
tail followed them to the US consulate, not far away from
Dubai Creek where the attack occurred.

"Yes," Wu said. "Why would the CIA try to kill
DeVille?"

# CHAPTER 31

*Altay City, China*
*April 16<sup>th</sup> – 10:10*

The English was not understandable, but DeVille assumed the voice was telling them to stow away their tray tables, put their seats in an upright position, and fasten their seat belts.

They were approaching Altay City airport. DeVille could see the town. It did not look big, but he knew it was sizable compared to western cities. Every town in China was big compared to western cities.

There was a gray city center surrounded by white and green—nothing around it besides a little bit of farmland or grazing areas. The rest was mountains and rocks.

*What do they live off? What do they eat?*

He could see some forest, but most of his vision was filled with open and arid mountain landscape. There was still snow on the ground, but not much, he saw brownish-gray patches here and there. According to an Internet site he had checked while at the airport in Urumqi, it was supposed to be clear and around ten degrees Celsius today.

The trip had been long, but he felt rested. It made a world of difference to travel in first class. After twenty hours of luxury travel, he felt as relaxed as he possibly could be. His wounds had healed well. He had been worried that his swim in the Dubai Creek could have infected his wounds, but it all seemed good.

The Dubai Police had escorted him to the airport in a police cruiser, probably not because he was in danger, but more likely because they wanted to make sure DeVille left the emirate.

A petite stewardess came by and asked him if she could get him another drink before they landed. DeVille loved first class.

He declined, thinking to himself that over the last twenty hours he had probably eaten eight meals and had twice as many drinks. The big problem with traveling was there really was not much else to do but eat and drink.

At least you ate and drank well while sitting in comfortable seats when you were traveling first class. In economy—or 'sardine class' as DeVille had overheard someone aptly call it—one would eat bland and unappetizing food, flushed down with bitter wine or lukewarm beer. Twenty hours of heartburn. All while you felt like you were sitting on a wooden bench.

Before he left Dubai, he had called Stella Hanson. She said she would have someone take a closer look at Wang's vessels. It seemed she was more interested in where DeVille had gotten the information from. He did not mention Sergei, but he started to wonder if Sergei had duped him.

*But why would Sergei do that?*

The bomb had been gone for almost three weeks, and it might or might not be onboard the krill ship heading out of European waters. If it was not, the least DeVille could do was to look into if there were any clues up in the Altai Mountains. Hopefully, the *professionals* were on the right path to locating the bomb.

A chime echoed through the cabin and awoke DeVille from his thoughts. A further five chimes came through the speakers.

It could not be positive news. Contrary to popular belief, DeVille knew there was no set rule for how many chimes meant an emergency. All airlines did this differently. Some used one for the flight attendant to contact the flight deck and two for going through ten thousand feet. What they all did similarly was to use as few chimes as possible for the most frequent messages. As many as six could only mean one thing. He saw the crew start to move around faster and the purser picked up the intercom.

Tension flowed through the airplane and unease was noticeable in the pressurized air. Passengers moved around in their seats and fiddled with their tray tables. No one spoke and the humming of the jet engines seemed thunderous. The clang of seat belt clasps went through the rows like the sound of falling dominos.

After what seemed like an eternity, the crew took their designated positions for emergencies, and a voice, this time in understandable English, filled the fuselage. "This is your purser speaking. We have a problem with one of the engines and will have to do an emergency landing. There is no reason to panic. Our pilots have done this several times. I need you to remain in your seats and follow the instructions on the emergency leaflet found in the seat pocket in front of you. As soon as we have come to a standstill, we will do an emergency exit using the chutes. Please locate your nearest emergency exit."

DeVille's ears popped as they descended fast. He imagined the massive strain the wings and the fuselage were under. It still seemed like it took forever to get down on the ground. All the lights in the cabin went off and this darkness, together with the gray outside as they went through a cloud, created an eeriness—only surpassed by the sound of what DeVille assumed to be people praying.

They hit the runway, and the screeching sound of rubber meeting tarmac and the roar as the pilots initiated reverse thrust filled DeVille's ears. He heard nothing wrong with the engines and there were no emergency vehicles visible through his window. He *did* see that this was not Altay Airport. There was no terminal building. It looked like a private airstrip.

The cabin crew opened the emergency exits and inflated the chutes.

Several military vehicles, with their characteristic green color and the red star of the People's Liberation Army Air Force on their doors, approached the airplane. But no fire trucks. The vehicles came to a stop, and around a dozen uniformed, and armed, men took up positions at the bottom of the chutes.

DeVille, close to an emergency exit since he was in first class, was the second to go down the chute—after an American man that had sat in the seat in front, giving himself away when he used his loud Midwestern accent to brag about how successful he was. DeVille had felt bad for the stewardess who courteously listened to the man throughout the flight.

The American went down the chute and DeVille saw a man at the bottom holding a picture which he compared to the man. He pointed him towards an arriving bus.

DeVille knew who was in the picture.

*The emergency landing and the engine problem were a decoy.*

The chance that there was a criminal or a terrorist or someone on the airplane, that they were looking for, was slim.

It was his turn. The chute was like silk and he tried to slow the speed down by using his feet to brake. At the bottom, the little hope he had left shattered when the man looked him up and down before nodding to two armed men.

They each grabbed one of DeVille's arms and led him to a civilian car and put him in the backseat. DeVille tried to protest, but he got no response from anyone. One of the armed men took the front passenger seat, while the other sat down next to DeVille in the back. A third man got behind the wheel and they drove off.

They left the airport and went onto a one-lane road with tall trees on both sides. Through openings between the trees, DeVille saw small patches of farmland which had been invisible from the air. They started to climb up a valley with steep cliffs on both sides. In a matter of minutes they went from lush and green forests and fields to infertile mountain landscape decorated with pine trees and unwelcoming grayish shrub.

The road zigzagged and for a moment DeVille thought he would be sick. He made his mind change focus, from the discomfort between his eyes and the balance in his ear, to a huge concrete building. It was either the local communist party offices or military headquarters. He was surprised when they did not enter the main gate.

There were hardly any other cars on the road.

They drove further and entered the city center he had seen from the air—it was much bigger than he had thought. He had pictured a tiny village, but it looked remarkably big and modern, although far from what he would call charming. The only part that was visually pleasing were the majestic mountaintops in the background.

Tengri's mountains.

All the buildings were the result of hurried construction, just like you could still see in parts of European cities that had been leveled by bombs during the Second World War. At least those cities had started to modernize, with the old buildings being replaced by cutting- edge new architecture.

That was not the case with Altay City.

It took about fifteen minutes to drive through the center. After another ten minutes, through another valley with forest on each side, they came to a stop behind a tanker truck with a flat tire. The trees encased the road, creating the illusion of a tunnel. The road was barely wide enough for two normal cars to pass each other, so when a flatbed tried to pass on the outside of the tanker they had to wait.

Not knowing why, DeVille tested the door handle on his side.

The door opened.

Without thinking, he dashed out of the car and into the forest at the side. It would take them a few seconds to get out of the car and aim at him. Getting a rifle out of a car window was difficult enough, but he had seen something that made it even more difficult—the manual handles to roll down the windows.

He managed to zigzag a hundred meters before the first shot came. He saw it hit the ground far away from him. They obviously did not have visual contact with him.

Three more shots came. None of them close to him either.

There was some shouting and he heard two of them starting to run after him, the driver probably calling for backup.

The forest started to thin out, which made it easier to run, but he got slowed down as he came to a steep hill with low brushes. He saw another pocket of heavy forest about two hundred meters ahead. With a thirty-second head start he figured he could make it there before his hunters came out of the first pocket of forest.

Just as DeVille got into the second pocket, a shot slammed into a tree just a meter to his right. He kept running. The energy started to drain from his legs as he ran uphill. And he only had loafers on his feet.

He stopped behind a large tree and made up his mind. He fought to control his breathing and stood as still as the tree. The wind cooled him and dried the sweat off his face. The frequency of snapped branches that he heard revealed that the soldiers were approaching slowly. He could not outrun them, so his only chance was to stop their advance. They outnumbered him and outgunned him. Sooner or later they would catch up with him—either on foot or with a bullet.

DeVille thought about using the same trick as in Dubai, and picked up two large rocks. If he knocked out one of the guys and got a rifle, at least the playing field would be even.

Heavy breathing signaled that one of them was getting close. A branch broke just a few meters away from DeVille, so he tossed the decoy rock in the opposite direction.

As he had hoped, the man stopped and turned to check out the thud. DeVille bounded from behind the tree and slammed the other rock into the man's neck with both hands.

The impact felt like DeVille had crushed all the bones in the man's neck, but the soldier only stumbled to his knees. He tried to get back up on his feet, lifting his rifle towards his target.

DeVille was still holding the rock and slammed it into the guard's face. Now he was sure he felt bones shatter.

He tried to wriggle the rifle out of the soldier's hands, but he held onto it while he screamed in agony. Not holding back, DeVille smashed the rock into the man's face repeatedly—as intense and strong as a hydraulic pump.

After what felt like an eternity, the rifle dropped to the ground, like a leaf in autumn. The blood on DeVille's knuckles was not his and he stopped and looked at the face he had been punching—to still call it a face could be disputed.

Like a predator, he looked around for the second soldier. He did not see or hear anyone. The forest covered whoever was out there.

He grabbed the gun and had started to run when he stopped and turned around. The loafers on his feet were about to disintegrate. He bent back down and took the soldier's coat and boots. He checked the man's wrist and there was still a pulse beating.

The boots were a bit small, but still better than the loafers he had on. He started to run when he heard a siren from down in the valley. He placed his index finger on the trigger guard of the rifle and used his thumb to flick the safety switch.

He ran for another thirty minutes, but as the terrain got difficult and steep, he moved as slowly as a car stuck in gridlock. He kept looking over his shoulder for the second soldier, but he saw no one.

When he spotted an open, rocky area he paused to weigh up his options. He realized that he was doomed no matter what he chose. He could keep running, but he did not know where he was or where to run to. Or even what to do if he got anywhere.

*Why did they want to arrest me?*

Not that it mattered. After what happened at the airport and here in the forest, he could forget about trying to find any links to Wang and his Tengriist friends. His priority now was to get away. In the mountainside he saw a small crevice that could shelter him on three sides and above. He walked in and sat down.

The Chinese would most likely find him sooner rather than later. He had nowhere to go. They would probably send dogs after him or use a helicopter with heat-seeking sensors. He had no equipment and no food. He could not survive for long here.

And the longer it took for them to hunt him down and catch him, the more severe the punishment would be. If he got captured, at least there was a slight chance they would let him contact the chief of staff—to let Werner wield his magic wand and have him freed.

That slight chance was his only chance.

He threw the gun away, sat down, and prepared himself to surrender to the first soldier he saw.

# CHAPTER 32

*April 17<sup>th</sup> – Sunrise*

The sun was about to rise which meant DeVille had been waiting for almost twenty hours. He had expected to be apprehended rather quickly after he sat down at the rock crevice.

Many thoughts had gone through his mind during the night. He should have prioritized sleep, but he had not. They probably expected him to freeze to death during the night. It was cold, but the soldier's coat helped.

He wondered if they perhaps had him under surveillance from a drone or something like that. Flashing images of dangerous wild animals and reptiles danced in his mind. He hated snakes, but all logic said there were no snakes where it was as cold as this.

Since it did not seem like anyone was coming after him, he decided to try to retrace his steps back to the road and find someone he could turn himself in to—as soon as it was light enough. It had been pitch-dark, so any attempt to do that before the sun came up would have resulted in him lying in a ditch with a broken leg or worse.

He also gave a lot of thought to why the Chinese wanted to arrest him. There seemed to be only three possible answers. One was that it was a misunderstanding. DeVille did not believe that, so it seemed more probable it was something Wang had orchestrated. After all, he had tried to kill him in Shanghai.

It could also be the work of the fourth Tengriist Sergei had told him about—the one they believed worked in Chinese intelligence. Such a man could be behind something like this.

*Is Sergei right?*

Although he did not believe it, DeVille hoped it was just a misunderstanding. If so, he might have a chance of getting out of this mess, even though he had escaped and assaulted a soldier. If it was one of the other two explanations, he knew he was screwed. DeVille started doubting his decision to turn himself in.

*What other options are there?*

Out of nowhere he heard footsteps coming towards him. With no time to change his mind, he lifted his arms up above his head in surrender. He did not even look up.

His senses were on alert and he heard only one person. No dogs or a large lynch mob. Nobody shouted at him to get up or stay down or anything else he had expected them to yell at him.

DeVille looked up and shook his head when he saw a man approaching him. He lowered his arms.

*Am I dreaming?*

The man stopped about ten meters from DeVille and stared straight through him. He looked like a cross between a Viking and a native American. The latter would also suit the man's occupation.

He was dressed in a colorful robe which appeared to be made out of many different pieces of scrap fabric, and with leather boots covered in intricate patterns. Most telling was the upwards sloping toe of the boot. Consisting of both horns and feathers, in the dark the man's headgear would scare all but the bravest. It was like a cross between a bird and a buffalo. He was a Mongolian *shaman*.

Not knowing what to do, DeVille stood up and raised his right arm in greeting. It was something he probably had picked up from a western, but he hoped it would have the desired effect.

The shaman nodded back in acknowledgment.

"Sir, do you speak English?" DeVille asked.

The shaman did not respond. He just kept staring through DeVille as if there were something interesting inside the rocks behind him.

"*Merde*," DeVille uttered a French swearword in a low voice while looking around to see what the shaman was staring at.

"Not nice," the shaman replied in heavily accented French.

"You speak French?" DeVille was baffled.

The shaman nodded. "A little bit. Jesus preachers came to my village few years ago. They spoke French. I learned from them."

DeVille knew of the missionaries to Mongolia. It had been heavily reported in European newspapers as they preached without permission from the Mongolian government. They were eventually arrested and deported.

"You are lost?" the shaman asked and finally looked directly at DeVille, almost as if he had come out of a trance. "Can I help?"

"Yes, please." DeVille was unsure what the shaman could help him with, but if nothing else, the shaman could point him in the right direction to the closest road. He decided to tell him what had happened the day before.

In easy sentences he explained that he had come to seek out Tengriist clues to a criminal case in Europe and that upon arrival he was arrested by the military. He also told him how he escaped and ended up here. The minor fact of the man's crushed face, he chose to leave out.

"To continue to run is hopeless. If you can help me to get down to the town, I would really appreciate that. I need to turn myself in."

"I can help you," the shaman said immediately. "But not to give up your quest. I can help you continue."

DeVille sighed. Being hungry, tired and cold, he was not in the mood to play Indiana Jones games with the old man.

"Thank you, but I really need to get down to the city or at least to a road."

"There is a temple where bad people worship Tengri. About one day of walking in that direction." The shaman pointed farther up the mountains. "What were you hoping to find in Altai?"

DeVille was not sure he had the answer to that question. Ever since he had boarded the airplane in Dubai his brain had been working overtime to find an answer to what exactly he should look for. He did not know. It was his gut feeling which had told him to come here. "I don't know. Obviously some more clues to the mystery I'm trying to solve, but more realistically—inspiration perhaps?"

"Are there evil people who worship Tengri involved?" the shaman asked, but his face revealed he knew the answer.

The question took DeVille by surprise. "I believe so, yes."

"Then the spirits have led you towards this temple." The shaman told DeVille of an old Buddhist temple in the mountains which a group of people had taken over many years ago. What the shaman did not like was that these people worshipped Tengri as a god. He claimed that this disturbed the balance and harmony of the mountains.

DeVille had read somewhere that many shamans did not believe in Tengri as a separate god or spirit. Some believed that Tengri lived in every organic part of nature. The point was that as long as there was balance humans would live in harmony. It was sort of similar to the Chinese concept of yin and yang. The shaman was obviously of this belief.

"Why would you want to help me?" DeVille asked while sensing a possibility of at least delaying his incarceration with the Chinese military.

"We have common enemies. Both the military and the men in the temple are disrupting the harmony of the sacred mountains here. The military is an enemy, forcing my people to go to the cities to work in polluting factories—instead of being out and living off and *for* the nature for which the spirits have provided them. I have already told you why it is my duty as a shaman to do something about the men in the temple."

This made sense to DeVille—the most important role of a shaman was to maintain balance in their communities. If the balance was off, it was the shaman's duty to restore it.

He could not help himself from asking, "Why haven't you done anything about these men in the temple before?"

The shaman's eyes showed signs of sadness. "I have failed. I am an old man that cannot find a way to fight them." He sat down and opened a furry bag, which DeVille had not seen through the rainbow of fabric which clothed the shaman.

"But I have not given up. It is every man's duty to keep fighting the battle bestowed upon them by the spirits. I have failed so far, but I have not lost yet."

DeVille shivered. It sounded like something Carina would have said. She used to be able to quote the most appropriate sayings from any religion at the perfect times in any conversation. He forced himself to concentrate and wondered what was in the bag.

"I have waited for you to come along." The shaman smiled and took out a loaf of bread, something that looked like beef jerky, and a water bottle. "Here, you need to eat and drink some. After that you will think straight."

DeVille took a big swig of the water bottle and had a coughing fit when his body realised it was vodka and not water. He composed himself, and tasted the bread and jerky. His stomach seemed to instantly absorb energy from it.

While DeVille helped himself to the food and vodka, the shaman began preaching, "The key to understanding the spirits is to follow three rules. You have to be aware and protective of Mother Earth. You have to be an honest person. Lastly, balance and harmony should be the outcome of all your actions. Each of them sounds easy, but the difficulty is to follow all three at the same time."

There was a longer than necessary pause.

"When do you cut down a tree to make a fire to warm your loved ones? Why would you harm your evil neighbor who has harmed you?" The shaman took a sip from the bottle. "Only Tengri knows for sure."

DeVille had read a lot of books about this, but he had never before met a Mongolian shaman. The man was interesting, but not as much as another swig from the vodka bottle.

"The men in the temple have misunderstood this and it has upset the balance. Balance means that war is just as much part of the universe as peace, but that does not mean that men should deliberately work to cause it. These men believe that the spirits will name one of them to be Tengri's representative on earth—that would be wrong."

DeVille saw that talking about the temple and the Tengriists disgusted the man. He took another good sip of the vodka and enjoyed how it warmed him up inside.

DeVille's eyelids turned to lead and within a matter of seconds everything turned black.

# CHAPTER 33

*Atlantic Ocean*
*16:20*

When he first read the message he had received early in the morning, it unsettled Umeira. But now, he was content. It meant that they had something to do and that the time onboard the ship might come to an end soon.

Abdul Aziz had sent him a message ordering him and the team to arm the bomb and make sure it could be detonated quickly. The message also told them to sail closer to land.

The last part forced Umeira to make a decision which he was unsure was the right one. When he ordered the captain to go closer to the shore, the reply was "which way?" Apparently their location was in the middle of the North Atlantic and halfway between Iceland and Norway. They had passed the Faeroe Islands the day before and were about to enter the Norwegian Sea.

The captain asked him if he were to turn the ship towards Iceland or Norway. Umeira decided on Norway. The only reason being the country was closer to Russia.

The message explained why they were to deviate from the original plan. Aziz had learned that European authorities were keeping the ship under surveillance. That part unsettled Umeira.

Not the fact that they might get caught bothered him. It was unsettling to know that someone was aware of their plan and most likely looking to *stop* it—the biggest jihadist action since nine-eleven.

It only took a few hours to arm the bomb, as they had made a lot of preparations over the last two weeks. It was not a sophisticated setup. They placed over three hundred kilos of different types of explosives around the nuclear missile, including C-4, TNT, and industrial dynamite. Enough to blow up a small town.

There were two reasons for this. Firstly, because they were not sure which type of explosive was best for the job, and secondly, it was what they could get ahold of before they left.

The detonator was also a very simple device. Just a satellite phone wired to a radio wave fuse. No complicated wiring. The simpler the detonator was, the bigger the chance was of the detonator lighting the fuse. And the simpler the fuse was, the bigger the chance was of the bomb going off.

It did not mean it would be easy to disarm the bomb, though. They booby-trapped the container with enough explosives that if anyone tried to get into it they would surely set it off.

Both he and Aziz had the number to the satellite phone.

All the explosives in the container meant there was a second, and easier, way to detonate the bomb. Blasting a few rounds of machine gun fire into the container should be sufficient to set off some of the explosives.

Lastly, just to be on the safe side, they attached a trap underneath the container so if someone tried to lift it, the bomb would also detonate.

After fifteen days onboard the ship, with nothing to see but water most days, he was ready for the bomb to explode so he could complete his ultimate sacrifice. He smiled when he thought about the captain. He would die soon too, but he would go to hell.

*Hopefully there will be enough time to torture him—before we all die.*

Umeira forced himself to focus on something else. Being blinded by hate was something he could not afford now.

He looked out of the porthole in the cabin. He saw a silhouette. It almost looked like a ship. He took the binoculars out of his bag and focused on the structure.

He knew immediately what he was looking at. They had the same ones in the Caspian Sea. They were colored gray, like the communists who were now rich because of these structures. This one was flame red, but still it was the same. The flare gave it away—a gas production platform.

Umeira laughed for the first time in fourteen days.

He knew exactly what to do next.

# CHAPTER 34

*Altai Mountains, China*
*April 18th – Noon*

DeVille stared across the highland plateau that they had just reached after climbing a steep hill. The horizon was blocked with snow-capped mountains that resembled gray pyramids. The mountains looked majestic and DeVille understood why they were treated with such reverence in the Tengriist religion.

There were still large patches of snow covering the ground, but here and there some grass was starting to enjoy the sunshine. The shaman told him the winter had been unusually mild. Normally the ground would be covered beneath a thick blanket of snow until late May.

DeVille had no idea how far they had walked. It was not that far, possibly fifteen kilometers from where he had met the shaman. He had passed out from too much vodka in an exhausted body. He woke up two hours later with the shaman standing over him smiling.

The shaman had said to DeVille, smiling, "You needed to rest and get some sleep. Come, let us start to walk."

They had walked for about six hours the day before and four that day, but because there were no trails and the elevation was steep, their average speed was slow.

With all the snow melting, the ground was soggy and threatened to swallow their feet at certain places, forcing them to take detours. They also had to do a bit of climbing. The shaman seemed to know exactly where to go all the time.

The night before, they camped just below the tree line in the cover of some low trees which reminded DeVille of Christmas trees. DeVille hoped the shaman had a tent or at least a blanket in his bag, but no such luck. The ground was soft with moss, but it was wet. The shaman gathered some branches and twigs for them to sleep on.

It was the most uncomfortable mattress DeVille had ever slept on. He did not sleep much, instead spending the night watching the stars. He was tired, but even next to the fire the shaman had made, it was so cold that most of the night he shivered to keep warm.

For dinner they ate more of the jerky, supplemented by some wild red berries they had stopped to pick during their walk. The berries looked like redcurrants, but the taste was much sweeter.

There was no more vodka, so they filled the bottle with ice-cold water from a stream they crossed. The shaman had a second bottle, which DeVille suspected to have been full of vodka earlier, and not shared, and they filled this one too with stream water.

In the morning, the shaman dug around, not far from where they had spent the night, and came back with breakfast—some tiny-sized mushrooms with long stems picked from the bottom of trees.

DeVille closed his eyes while he tried the first and feared the worst. But they were quite delicate and tasted almost like normal button mushrooms.

They did not talk after they set up camp for the night. In fact, they hadn't talked much at all since they started walking. When he tried to ask how much farther they needed to walk, the shaman simply answered 'Yes.' At one point DeVille wondered if the shaman even knew where they were heading. It did not matter though—the alternative of not following him was much worse.

At one time in the late afternoon, they took cover behind some large rocks as helicopters flew over their heads. DeVille's first thought was that it was the Chinese military which was out searching for him, but it could have been anything.

*Probably nothing to worry about.*

There was ample opportunity to think while they walked, and DeVille tried to plan what to do and say when they reached the temple. One possibility was to just knock on their door and ask if they could feed and host a trekker for a couple of days. They would have no idea who he was and he could then spend a couple of days deciding if these worshippers were part of a dangerous cult or just a bunch of peaceful believers. He also pondered how to get out of China, being a wanted man and all. He did not come up with any answers to that.

If he could get out of China, he would go straight back to Brussels. From there he would do everything in his power to catch Wang, no matter if the man was guilty of stealing the missile or not. He just knew that that man was up to no good.

It should be the professional agents out in the field, being shot at while escaping soldiers who wanted to arrest you. DeVille found it ridiculous that it was him out there.

Another thing which nagged at his mind was that he had not told Stella Hanson and the CIA about going to Altay. Since she had only seemed partially interested when he had told her about Wang, his friends, and the ships, he believed she would not care at all that he was going there. The chief of staff might contact her since DeVille had not been in touch for a few days.

*He will be fuming by now!*

The shaman stopped and looked ahead. DeVille wondered if he had spotted danger of some kind.

"This is it," the shaman said after a few moments. "You will have to continue on your own from here."

DeVille tried to look for something that resembled a temple, but did not see anything. He was not too enthusiastic about continuing alone. "I don't see anything. Where should I go?"

"Look very careful over there," the shaman said while pointing with his walking stick.

DeVille looked and saw an arc made of either concrete or large square rocks, possibly a gate at the other end of the plateau, perhaps a kilometer away.

"Between those two pillars there will be a path that will lead you around to the south-facing side of the mountain. Which is where the temple is—about another tenth of a day's hike."

It was around noon now, so Deville thought he should have plenty of time to find the temple before sunset.

"*Bonne chance*," the shaman said.

"*Merci*," DeVille said and tried to sound helpless in an attempt to persuade the shaman to come with him further. It did not work.

The shaman handed him a small leather pouch with leftover mushrooms from their breakfast and one of the water bottles.

DeVille's mood quickly improved. The thought of spending the night in a warm bed and eating some freshly cooked food seemed like paradise compared to the last two nights. Just something with a roof would make him happy.

"How far is it to Mongolia?" DeVille decided to ask before the shaman left.

"Not more than a day's hike as the bird fly, but..."

Even with a heavy accent, the shaman had a significant vocabulary in French and he had been easy to understand throughout their journey together, but for the first time DeVille sensed that the shaman was not sure how to phrase himself.

"It's in that direction," the shaman pointed with his stick towards the opposite side of the plateau where the two pillars were. Then he turned around and started to walk down the path they had come up.

DeVille's good mood deteriorated as quickly as it had come. All he could see was a tall wall of gray skyscraping mountain—made of rock with white hats.

They were not snow-capped as it had looked from a distance.

They were snow-*covered*.

# CHAPTER 35

*Khan Tengri Temple, Altai Mountains, China*

The Kurultai had just opened and the first thing Alexandrovich did was to request that they skip the first agenda point and come back to it later. He said he was waiting for some information which would shed light on the whole thing. Wang was not pleased with this, but the other Khagans seemed to accept the reason, so Wang chose not to object.

They moved quickly through the agenda before they spent almost three hours debating item four. Annexation of other states.

They all agreed that the combined military and economical might of Russia and China would be so big that neither the US nor the UN would dare to interfere, neither through military action nor by applying financial sanctions.

This Khaganate would have the world's largest military force and the largest arsenal of nuclear weapons. Over five million soldiers and more than two thousand active nuclear warheads. It would also be the world's greatest economy with most western countries heavily in debt to them. It would probably be the debt and not the weapons that other countries would be most frightened by. Money always trumped weapons.

They were all reasonably certain that if they explained that they were only after the countries which belonged to the former Khaganate, the western powers would sacrifice these countries. They would not want to risk financial mayhem and a potential nuclear war.

And that was the truth, Wang knew. They were not after world domination or to increase the size of the empire. They just wanted what rightfully belonged to Tengri.

They ate lunch while they discussed items under 'miscellaneous.' Alexandrovich informed them that he would take out the Chechen rebel leader Abdul Aziz in three days.

They would use Aziz's satellite phone and communicate directly with the terrorist onboard the ship, pretending to be the terrorist leader. Even though it had worked well so far, they could never trust a mentally unstable jihadist. Together with Wang's communications with the captain, they should have full control.

Wang showed them some pictures of his newly 'nuclear-proofed' ship and told them she was well under way towards the Arctic Ocean. He could tell that this pleased Bakunin by the size of his smile. He sometimes worried if Bakunin were truly dedicated to the cause or if he was just playing along because of the financial reward.

Wang looked around.

*Much more suitable for a Kurultai than that disgusting restaurant in Vladivostok.*

The grand hall, where they were seated, was also used for celebrations. The square room was about ten times ten meters. Dark shadows crept up towards the high ceiling as natural light only came through small windows on one side of the room. Adjacent to the grand hall was the rituals room where the worship to Tengri was performed. Across from the rituals room was the auxiliary part of the temple. It contained a kitchen, laundry, repair shop, and the normal dining room. In front of the grand hall was a library and reading room where the Baghaturs would study for at least three hours a day. A separate building contained the accommodation.

The grand hall was sparsely decorated, as if the room were a sculpture itself. Apart from the long table they were sitting at, there was no other furniture, which made the room feel larger and *grander*. By the entrance door, small paintings of sacred mountains hung on the bare rock wall. A few showcases with historical artifacts dating back to Genghis Khan and Bumin Qaghan lined the walls.

Next to the entrance to the rituals room, stood a small, but still impressive, hand-carved fireplace. The only item, besides the fire, which added any color to the room other than the grays and blacks, was a large flag of the Third Khaganate that hung over the fireplace. The light blue background almost melted into the wall. The green wolf's head in the center of the flag stared at them with its triangular-shaped eye, and flared its jagged teeth. It would make anyone feel awed by Tengri's powers.

All four Khagans had arrived the day before by helicopter. There was no other way of reaching the temple, unless you came by foot. Wang and Wu had chartered a helicopter together, while Bakunin and Alexandrovich had shared another. They could not risk using government transport, even though they had easy access to it.

They all slept in separate rooms in the accommodation building. Basic luxuries were something they believed they all deserved, so even the Baghaturs had their own bedrooms with en suite bathrooms.

Their lunch was almost over when Alexandrovich's phone beeped. He took a quick look at it and smiled. "I'm sorry to have had you wait for this, but I think you will be pleased. In five minutes you will all know the explanation for what happened to DeVille and who he is. Again, I apologize for making you wait."

Wang could tell Wu was getting annoyed. People who worked in the intelligence industry hated to be kept in the dark. They hated it when someone knew something they did not. Especially if it was information they were desperately waiting for.

"I can start then," Wu said suddenly. "DeVille is on his way up towards the temple as we speak. We should be expecting him in less than an hour."

Wang noticed that Wu enjoyed letting what he had just said hang in the air while he looked at the confusion in the others' faces. It was probably his revenge for being kept in the dark by Alexandrovich.

"An alarm went off when he entered China on a flight from Dubai. We've kept track on him. When we found out that he was going to fly into Altay City, I decided to arrest him—to find out what he knows. Unfortunately, he escaped."

"Who the hell is this guy?" Bakunin sounded frustrated, directing his question to his fellow Russian who had promised an explanation.

Before he could answer, Wu continued, "It would've been easy to catch him again in these mountains, but I decided that we follow him and see if he really knows where to go. He passed between the two pillars about an hour ago."

Wang decided to play it cool, "What's the plan? To catch or kill him?"

"Let's first see what Khagan Alexandrovich is going to surprise us with," Wu said as he stared at the admiral.

Wang wondered if this was the beginning of a power battle between the two of them. The ultimate prize was to be elected *Yekhe Khagan*. He expected it to happen sooner rather than later. He preferred it to be later, but he was not worried. Even though they both wanted the top spot, they would not jeopardize the plan. Tengri came first and both of them would accept and respect the one who ultimately got selected.

Alexandrovich connected his computer to a big plasma screen and clicked himself into a video conference program.

Tengri accepted technology. He knew of enough shamans and medicine men that claimed to be Tengriists and believed Tengri wanted you to integrate with nature and that technology was evil. They were wrong. Everything on this planet was from nature, no matter if processed into microchips or remaining in its original form such as bauxite or gold.

A ship made of metal, taken from the earth and put together was no different from a soup consisting of different ingredients. If Tengri did not allow humans to build and use a ship, he also would not allow mankind to cook and eat soup.

"I'd like you to meet a person who will explain all about what happened to DeVille and if he is a risk or not," Alexandrovich said, making Wang turn his attention to the screen.

The rough image of the video function came alive on the big screen and Wang saw a white, western-looking woman staring down on them. Her eyes were wide and her mouth was surrounded by well-sized lips. She was not fat, but there were no cheekbones visible. There was authority in her eyes, something Wang disliked. The woman smiled and started to speak.

"Good afternoon, gentlemen. My name is Stella Hanson."

# CHAPTER 36

"I'm a special agent with the CIA," the lady on the screen said.

Wang felt perspiration moisten his woolen shirt.

*The CIA?*

*Is our whole plan about to fall apart?*

All eyes around the table darted around before settling on Alexandrovich. Wang saw anxiety in the face of Bakunin and anger in Wu's.

*What does my face show?*

"Alexandrovich, explain yourself!" Wu shouted the words, not addressing him with the title *Khagan* as was protocol.

"Calm down everyone. I'll explain. She is on our side. Relax." It seemed like the admiral had trouble holding back a smile.

"The name given to me at birth was Irina Alexandrovicha," the lady on the screen continued. "The dear admiral is my uncle. I came to the US when I was adopted from an orphanage at the age of seven. Both my parents had died and so had my grandparents on both sides."

"My brother, Irina's father, died in combat early in the Soviet Afghan war. His wife died a year later. I was the only family left for Irina, but I was a young officer in the navy and could not take care of a child," the admiral said in an apologetic tone directed towards the CIA agent on the screen.

"I was taken care of by a good family, but never forgot my real roots, so I've kept in touch with my uncle over the years. When I graduated college, I joined the CIA as a trainee. My uncle was already climbing the ranks of the Russian navy. We realized that both of us could profit career-wise by swapping information."

"She's not only been helpful to Russia and myself, but to our cause. She's been more helpful to you, my fellow Khagans, than you can imagine. If it was not for the American intel that she's been kind enough to share, we would never have managed to get a man inside Abdul Aziz's camp. That's just one of many things she's helped me with."

The story seemed strange, but if she was not on Alexandrovich's side, then surely the Americans would have stopped them by now and retaken the nuclear missile. It was not the first time there had been double agents working the intelligence world. Wang had huge trust in Alexandrovich and chose to give him the benefit of the doubt.

Alexandrovich was the one with the most to lose. He could walk away from the cause discreetly, today, and still have a good chance of becoming the next leader of Russia. If he thwarted the plan in any way, and it became public, he would be a dead man politically.

*Probably literally too—treason carries the death penalty.*

"What is in it for you?" Wu directed his question to the screen.

"I'm in a dead-end job with the CIA and my uncle has promised me a very prominent position within your new government. A ministerial post perhaps?" she asked, looking at Wu.

It confirmed something Wang did not like; it was a two-way video stream.

"Why are we getting to know this now?" Bakunin spoke for the first time since the screen had come alive. "I mean, if you two have kept this secret for so long, why tell us now?"

"And what else have you not told us?" Wu added to the questions.

The CIA agent spoke first. "It was my suggestion to keep it secret from you. The less I knew about you and the less you knew about me, the better it would be for everyone. But my cover might get blown when your little bomb goes off. If that is the case, I will need all of you to help cover me."

Wang tried to guess, from the timing of her father's death in Afghanistan and the image on the screen, how old she was.

*Mid-thirties?*

"There is absolutely nothing else hidden," Alexandrovich said in a firm voice.

"I assume the good Khagan can show us proof that we can trust his *niece*?" Wu asked.

"Of course I can. Take a look at this." Alexandrovich took a folder from his bag and placed it on the table. "It contains all the information that she has given me over the years and how it has benefitted us. But first, can we get to the task at hand. She will give us some details on DeVille. Even though you do not trust her, you have nothing to lose by listening to what she has to say." The Russian looked around the room to see if anyone objected before nodding to the screen for the woman to continue.

"It was indeed my men who tried to kill DeVille in Dubai. And we did not know that we were being tailed by Chinese intelligence." She smiled in the direction of Wu, who did not smile back.

"I've been following DeVille ever since he showed up in The Hague trying to interrogate one of the guys you had stealing the bomb. It was standard procedure at first, but then someone from the Russian mafia tried to contact him, so we stayed on his tail. So he knows me. We also, as you do, I suppose, know that he met with the mafia in Dubai. I also met with him in Shanghai after Khagan Wang failed to kill him."

Wang felt the stare from his fellow Khagans.

"I got worried when I heard the mafia was interested in him in The Hague," Alexandrovich broke in. "Then, a possible mafia rescue in Shanghai, followed by a meeting with a high-ranking mafia boss in Dubai."

"He's also employed by the chief of staff of the President of the EU Commission. He's been in regular contact," the woman said. "We didn't know what DeVille knew, but he seemed to be in contact with the right people and go to the right places at the right times. So we decided it would be best if we got him out of the picture."

"What should we do with him when he arrives here?" Wang guessed the answer, but wanted it confirmed.

"He called me a couple of days ago and told me that he suspects the missile to be on Wang's fishing boat. He also knows about the four of you and what you're planning. He didn't tell me he was coming to your temple, but I assume he has no evidence for his theories. He probably thinks he can find something up there."

*He probably can...*

"We need to find out how much he knows and how much this EU guy knows. But the most important thing is to find out how much the mafia knows and if they are planning to take any action. What, when, and where?" Alexandrovich looked around the room.

Wang and the other Khagans nodded.

"I think perhaps Khagan Wu will be the most qualified to find out how much this little rat actually knows," Alexandrovich said while looking at Wu.

For the first since they had arrived at the temple, Wu smiled.

# CHAPTER 37

The path was not really a path. Perhaps decades ago there had been a visual path. There were no signs of the ground being worn from people walking. Still Deville knew that he was heading in the right direction.

Every ten or fifteen meters there was a knee-high pile of rocks. The stone on the top was painted in a neon, yellow-greenish color—to help anyone navigating the path in the dark with a flashlight. The piles of rocks were another indication of the path not being frequently used, as the size of them meant they would surely be covered in snow during the winter. Like a woolen blanket, moss was draped over the stones, the neon still shining through. They must have been placed on top of each other years ago.

*Will anyone be at the temple?*

*What if I am going through all this—and no one opens the doors when I knock?*

The surface was easy to walk on with smooth moss-covered rocks and an occasional bush here and there. In some places, where the sun struggled to reach, snow had yet to melt. The direction given to DeVille by the rock piles made for a steep climb. It was only forty minutes since he had passed the pillars, but he already felt the lactic acid cramping his thighs.

The views down to the plateau were incredible, so DeVille took his fair share of breaks. It was some of the most beautiful scenery he had ever seen. It was a shame not to enjoy it. Even Genghis Khan must have felt somewhat humbled by the view.

He looked across to the mountain range that separated him from Mongolia. The pencil-sharp tops and their vertical, slippery sides made him feel incarcerated. He sighed and continued the walk towards the next cairn. The temple was his only chance.

Within another half an hour, he saw man-made structures in the distance. It looked like three or four buildings. Not the beautiful Buddhist temple he had expected, instead it looked like something in between a military barracks and a detention camp.

When he got a little closer, the size of the buildings made him wonder if he had come to the right place. The largest building was two stories high and rectangular in shape. There were two other buildings and something that looked like a garage or a workshop. It was a compound, and a quite modern one.

*Should I turn around?*

A large tarpaulin hanging from four posts as tall as flagpoles caught his attention as soon as he approached the courtyard. He froze. It was protecting two helicopters—the same as he and the shaman had seen, and hid from, the day before.

It did make sense. There was no other way to get up here besides walking. Without helicopters, it would be impossible to reach the temple with supplies and to get people in and out. Two or three days of hiking from Altay City, with no possibility of driving.

It also explained why the path had looked as unused as it did. It was.

DeVille walked through a gate and entered the compound.

Silently, four men appeared and stepped towards DeVille. They came from behind the garage, wearing fatigues with winter camouflage. DeVille saw their approach too late. They each pointed a MP5 submachine gun at him.

DeVille recognized the guns, probably among the most used weapons in the world, after the AK-47. The SWAT team trying to arrest Khan in Utrecht, had been armed with these high-tech submachine guns.

At first he thought they were keeping watch over the helicopters. He quickly understood how wrong he was. Four armed men for such a task was overkill, especially in an area where there were no others except a shaman or two. The only other person he had seen was the man with the vodka and the dried beef.

Before he could think about doing a turn and run, they surrounded him. Not that it would have been smart to run. Outrunning four machine guns in an open landscape would put you at the top of the endangered species list.

One of the men lowered his gun, went over to him, and cuffed both his hands and legs. DeVille did not resist. The man nodded towards the main building.

*These guys are more than just helicopter guards.*

They pushed him towards the building. The leg cuffs did not have enough reach to make a full step, so DeVille could not follow the pace they wanted him to. He fell over twice. They approached what looked like an entrance. The exterior of the building was just white-painted concrete, but the door was ornamentally carved. He recognized the centerpiece of the door. It was the same as he had seen on Wang's cuff links in Shanghai. An image of a kneeling *Umai*—the ancient Tengriist goddess.

He was led through the door and into a small, sparsely decorated hallway. On the walls were paintings of mountain peaks. He recognized the peak in the largest painting—Khan Tengri.

He heard voices from behind another wooden door to their left. It was larger than the entrance door, with many small carvings of life during Genghis Khan's time.

DeVille knew the odds of a nice warm meal and a blanketed bed were diminishing by the second.

\* \* \*

Wang turned when the large entrance door to the grand hall opened. One of the Baghaturs walked in and waited for permission to speak. Wu was the one who nodded first.

"The prisoner has arrived and is in our custody," the Baghatur announced.

"Bring him in here," Wu said.

"Good luck, gentlemen," the CIA agent said as she logged off from the video conference just as DeVille was pushed into the room.

The man looked much more ragged than the man Wang had met in Shanghai. Wang recognized the coat as a Chinese army model and wondered where DeVille had gotten hold of it. He was filthy and looked exhausted.

*Why come up here?*

*If he knew we were here, what did he hope to achieve by coming alone?*

DeVille's blue eyes drilled into Wang, before fading away—sort of accepting defeat. The man sized up each of the other Khagans around the table.

When his stare came back to Wang again, DeVille looked at him quickly, tilted his head towards the big LCD-screen, and asked, "Was that Stella Hanson?"

\* \* \*

DeVille had only seen her for a split second, but the image together with the voice was enough to recognize her.

*It doesn't make sense.*

His brain struggled to compute what it meant. Nothing made sense right now.

He stared at Wang and waited for an answer he knew he would never get. He looked back at the three other men. It did not take a genius to figure out that they were the other men Sergei had told him about—Wang and another man were wearing suits, while the two others were wearing military uniforms. The man in blue was without doubt the Russian admiral.

The man in the green uniform, DeVille figured, was the unknown Chinese intelligence officer. His eyes did not seem to blink, boring into anything they looked at, and DeVille quickly moved his gaze away from him.

"Yes, it was," the man in the green uniform said and turned his attention from DeVille towards the admiral.

There was an awkward silence which confused DeVille further.

"Glad you could make it up here," the man in the green uniform continued, shifting his eyes, filled with cold death, back towards DeVille. "And you got rid of your guide? That probably saved his life."

It had been too easy, the escape. They had known about his movements ever since he had got away from the car. He was not surprised.

The man in the green uniform turned to the guards and said something in a language DeVille did not understand. One of the guards nodded, grabbed DeVille's shoulder, and pushed him back out the door through which they had entered.

They walked across the courtyard to the building he had assumed to be a workshop. Next to the building and the helicopters, DeVille saw two ATVs.

*Probably used to pull the helicopters to and from the tarpaulin-covered parking to the center of the courtyard.*

The only place in the compound where the helicopters could land and take off.

DeVille prepared himself for the worst.

*An execution in the open square? They have already tried to kill me once, or possibly several times, so why not?*

He expected panic to hit him any moment. It did not. He was as calm as he possibly could be.

*Why?*

He had no idea.

One of the guards opened a door to the building. Inside, it looked like some sort of woodworking shop—sawdust everywhere. They led him to the side and towards a large metal door. If it was not for the fist-sized window he would have guessed it was a vault.

It was a relief when they pushed him in. With three MP5s pointed at him, one of the guards removed his cuffs and closed the door behind him. He heard a heavy lock slide into place.

There were no windows except the tiny one in the door and there was no furniture. It was as barren as the mountain crevice he had spent the night in two days ago. The exception was a thin mattress on the floor which looked even less comfortable than the branches the shaman had made him sleep on. DeVille collapsed on the mattress and looked around at the four concrete walls. There was no way out.

*Why have they not killed me yet?*

*Why wait?*

The pungent smell in the cell caught his attention—it was coming from the hole in the concrete floor, located in the corner next to the door. The stench from it was so foul he vomited.

It was easy to work out what the hole was for.

# CHAPTER 38

*April 19ᵗʰ – 09:15*

DeVille woke up from the sound of keys entering the lock of the cell door. Sunshine flowed through the little window, so he knew he had slept for several hours. After they dropped him off in the cell, he first spent some time to see if he could find a way out. It was hopeless—it would be impossible to get out of this vault any other way except through an open door.

*Am I about to die at the hands of religious extremists?*

His mind drifted to the inevitable—why is Stella Hanson involved with these lunatics? Are there other things I'm missing in this case?

But he knew there could only be one reason why they had not killed him yet. He was onto something, or knew something, that could jeopardize their plan. Exactly what, he was not sure.

Two guards entered the cell and pointed their machine guns at him, while a third motioned for him to get up. A fourth guard appeared with a chair and a toolbox which he placed in the middle of the room, before recuffing DeVille.

A nudge from one of the machine gun barrels was enough motivation for DeVille to walk through the cell door.

They went out to the courtyard and DeVille noticed that the helicopters were still parked under the tarpaulin. Several men, dressed like a cross between monks and knights, walked across the courtyard carrying boxes, but he saw neither Wang nor his partners. He took a deep breath and smelled the mountains that surrounded the compound.

After about fifteen minutes of walking in a circle around the courtyard, one of the guards pointed to the building with the cell, and indicated it was time to go back.

*This is all the time outside the cell today?*

Hunger roared in his stomach and DeVille hoped it would be answered. In addition to appeasing his hunger, food would suggest they planned to keep him alive.

A thought struck him. There was one good reason for keeping him alive—they were using him as a bargaining chip with the chief of staff or someone. He was a hostage and they were demanding some sort of ransom. That could also explain why Stella Hanson was working with Wang and company—they would kill him if she did not cooperate.

The fresh air did wonders, making him contemplate in a more logical manner. If he got some food as well, perhaps he could figure out a way to escape.

His optimism quickly shattered as they returned him to his cell. The chair they had brought in was now surrounded by all four Khagans. DeVille's heart started to beat faster and sweat appeared on his forehead. This was not a courtesy call.

Before he had a chance to say anything, the guards pinned him down in the chair so hard that it almost toppled. The guards took off his cuffs and shackled his hands to the armrests and his feet to two rings in the floor. He was not going anywhere.

"Good morning, Mr. DeVille," the Russian admiral said casually. "Have you slept well? Are you rested? You'll need to be alert today."

DeVille stared straight past them and through the open cell door.

"Mr. DeVille, have you heard about *Ling chi*?" the man who had been wearing green fatigues yesterday asked. He was now wearing black overalls.

DeVille looked at him and shook his head.

"Slow slicing?"

Again, DeVille shook his head. This time slowly.

"Let me enlighten you then. It is a traditional Chinese way of torture and execution. I say execution because in the old days, they were not able to do it careful enough so that the condemned person did not die from the wounds. It was officially abolished as a government practice in 1905, but we…I…have perfected the methods. I can inflict you with maximum pain—while still keeping you alive."

DeVille felt fear take over his thoughts. He looked at Wang with pleading eyes.

"You might know the method by the name *death by a thousand cuts*," Wang answered his eyes casually.

DeVille had heard about that before. It meant to carefully remove portions of a person's body, one slice after another over a long period of time. Eventually death from blood loss, trauma, or the removal of an important organ occurred. It was a Chinese torture method that had been used for thousands of years. It had started with the Confucian principle that a body needed to be whole in the spiritual life after death. Not only did this method cause severe pain while living, it would also cause severe pain in the afterlife.

"Why?" DeVille whispered in desperation. "If there is anything you want to know I'll tell you. Just ask!"

"No. First you need to know the extent of the pain you'll be feeling if you lie to us. So we'll need to demonstrate that to you first."

An awkward silence filled the cell.

Then he spoke, "First *Ling chi*, then we'll talk."

* * *

Wang saw Wu pick up a scalpel from the table. He did not enjoy watching torture. It was beyond him. He always let his thugs take care of interrogations and executions without him present, but Wu had insisted they all be there so they could throw questions at DeVille.

Two of the guards removed DeVille's coat and shirt—his terrified expression sent shivers through Wang. Wu nodded to the guards and they took hold of DeVille in a tight grasp.

The scalpel removed a stamp-sized part of DeVille's skin on his left shoulder and revealed red flesh underneath. The muscles in the man's upper body twitched as if they were in spasm. It was as if the body wanted to shut down from the pain. Only a few drops of blood trickled out. DeVille did not scream, but it was easy to see that he was struggling not to.

Wu then moved to in front of DeVille and in a swift move cut through his right nipple and pulled it off with his fingers.

This bled more.

DeVille still did not scream.

He did scream when Wu took a pinch of salt and rubbed it into the two wounds at the same time. If they had not been inside a concrete vault, Wang was sure the scream would have carried for miles.

DeVille twisted his face and looked at him beggingly, so Wang asked Wu if it was time to start the interrogation.

"Just one more thing," Wu said.

He then swapped the scalpel with a small meat cleaver and placed DeVille's right hand facing palm down on the armrest. Wang knew what was coming, but did not have time to turn away. Wu chopped off DeVille's little finger just above the top knuckle. The finger pushed out a few squirts of blood. DeVille's eyes turned ash gray as they realized he was missing part of his finger.

Another scream followed.

"Now we talk, but if you don't tell us the truth we'll continue to chop off pieces of your body until you want to die." Wu stepped back, and indicated to Wang and the two other Khagans to start questioning DeVille.

"What's your relation with Sergei Ivankov?"

"Who do you really work for?"

"How did you find this temple?"

"What do you know of the missile's whereabouts?"

The questions flew in from all the Khagans. Even Bakunin who tended to stay in the background and let others talk, flung questions at DeVille. Some of the questions were genuine to see how much he knew, while others were intended to see if he was telling the truth or not. Wu had instructed them to make sure there were no quiet moments. DeVille was not allowed to have time to think. If he did not answer right away, they were to press him or move to another question, then ask the question again later.

Even in obvious pain, DeVille managed to answer most of their questions. Wang reddened when his cuff links were given as the answer to how DeVille had found the temple. Wu's black eyes did not leave Wang's for several moments.

DeVille could not answer how much the mafia knew, only that they were informed by someone in the FSB. He claimed the EU was not doing anything but keeping the trawler under surveillance. Wang felt certain it was the truth. Even with the best training to withstand torture, you would break after such a session.

Wang could tell Wu did not agree.

* * *

DeVille truthfully told them everything he knew. He sighed with relief—there was a pause in the blizzard of pain which kept striking him.

*The crazy Chinese guy cut of my fingertip and my nipple!*

He was about to pass out when a bucket of water was poured over him.

The cuts were painful, but when the bastard rubbed salt into the wounds, he thought he would die. He could taste blood. He was not sure if he had bitten his tongue or crushed some teeth while trying to bear the pain.

He was not sure if he was relieved it was over, or if he just wanted to die. What they had done to him was so horrendous that they would certainly not release him afterwards.

"Let's have another round."

*What did the man in the black overalls just say?*

There was no energy left in him to fight, and he just stared at the man as he walked towards him with the scalpel.

The burning pain came a split second after the knife entered his cheek. Two more swift cuts, and he thought he was about to black out. He opened his eyes quickly and saw what the man had put on the table in front of him. It was a piece of flesh with skin on it, about the size of a coin.

DeVille moved his tongue towards where the pain in his face was coming from. He withdrew it when it touched the inside of his cheek. The pain felt like being shot in the mouth with a stun gun. But the piece of flesh was what he feared it was—coming from a now gaping hole in the left side of his face.

"What's the EU doing with the information you've given them?"

"Who's in charge of handling the ship with the missile?"

"Will the mafia interfere?"

They started to shout questions at him again. They stood so close that DeVille could feel their breath through the gash on his face.

"I don't know." DeVille hissed out the words. The pain awakened a new emotion in him. "Give me a phone and I'll ask them," he said, exhaling.

"Trying to be a smart-ass, huh? I guess it is time to peel off some more skin." The man in the black overalls picked up the scalpel and the box of salt.

DeVille tried to head-butt him when he came close enough.

"I think we're done here for now," the admiral said. He kicked DeVille's chair hard, making it fall over.

Still attached to the floor by his leg cuffs, another shot of pain blitzed him as his perforated face slammed into the concrete floor.

All the men left the room and he heard the lock slide into place. He could not move. He was still shackled to the chair, but it did not stop him from screaming out loud.

Justice and vengeance—two new emotions awakened in him. He was not concerned anymore about whether he would live or die, but about doing the right thing. He would do all he could to try to make Carina proud. She had always been an angel of good, so if she was watching him now, she would surely be rooting for him to do something.

Exactly what, he was unsure.

* * *

Wang stopped for a moment and took a few large breaths of fresh air. He struggled to repress the urge to vomit. He had seen people killed before, but only with guns. Open wounds, like those today, were for underlings to deal with. He was above that.

Wu had always struck him as someone who could do such things, so no surprise there. A bigger surprise was that both Russians seemed unfazed by what they had just seen and done.

"I am pretty certain DeVille does not know anything more of value to us," Wu said, still wiping blood off his hands with a towel as they crossed the courtyard.

"I agree. We will have to leave shortly, that is why I cut short your fun. I will have to see what can be done to keep the mafia under control and try to identify their FSB friends." Alexandrovich looked at Wu with the unspoken question of what he was going to do with DeVille after they left.

"We will have to leave pretty soon too," Wu said.

Wang nodded his agreement.

Wu continued, "After lunch we will go over to the cell again and make him believe there will be another round of *Ling chi*. I just want to make sure he has not thought of something he wants to reveal to us that he forgot during the last round."

Wang could not stand the thought of lunch and vomited in the middle of the courtyard.

Wu smiled at him and said, "Then we will kill him."

# CHAPTER 39

*Norwegian Sea*

Through the binoculars, even in the early morning dawn, Umeira could see the outline of the gas platform they were heading towards. A large, multi-level accommodation building at one end rose upwards like a glacier, in contrast to the large and fiery orange gas flare at the other. They were separated by a spaghetti-like network of cranes and pipes of the production facilities in the middle. A helicopter with two rotors stood on the deck which stuck out from the side of the accommodation building. The helicopter, looking like a plastic model, explained the size of the platform. All of this stood thirty meters above water on four gargantuan concrete legs.

Umeira's new plan was to head due north for a day or two, then due south again, before detonating the ship next to the gas platform. This was just to give Abdul Aziz enough time to prepare a video statement which he would surely send to the largest news broadcasters in the world. His martyrdom would soon be discussed in classrooms and have specials on the Discovery Channel.

He got more and more excited about his initiative and the plan to not just detonate the bomb, but to also take down a platform full of infidels. Aziz would use this focus on their struggles in Chechnya in the best way.

There was one more thing he needed to take care of and he would do that now. He had wanted to do this for weeks, and finally the time was right to settle the score. He would take great pleasure in what he was about to do.

He walked down from the bridge and entered the deck below. It smelled like chlorine and looked synthetically clean. This was the accommodation deck for the crew. The cabin Umeira and his men occupied was a deck farther down. He walked to the end of the passageway and stopped beside the last cabin. He took two deep breaths, looked up at nothing, and smiled.

The door was unlocked, so Umeira opened it silently and entered. The sun would not be seen on the horizon for another thirty minutes, but the twilight flowed through the porthole and made it easy for him to spot the man asleep in the bunk.

He walked over and looked at the man for a second. He smiled and stuck his gun into the captain's mouth.

* * *

Zhang woke up choking. There was a hard metallic object in his mouth that he tried to spit out. He opened his eyes and stared right at the Muslim. "What the hell are you doing? Are you crazy? What are you doing in here?" Zhang said with difficulty as the metal object obstructed his tongue's movement. He froze when his sleep-encrusted eyes recognized what it was.

"Kill you," the Muslim whispered.

"What? Why?"

The Muslim just smiled.

Zhang was wide awake now—confused, but wide awake. "Who will sail the ship?" He then remembered that the Muslim did not speak much English. He also saw in his eyes that there was nothing he could say to change the man's mind. He looked around for something to defend himself with. His eyes landed on the half-empty bottle of *baijiu* liquor on his desk.

Two shots echoed in the cabin and pain shot through him faster than the speed of sound, like someone had lit his legs on fire. He looked down with eyes blurred from tears of fear.

He saw two holes.

One in each kneecap.

Zhang screamed and, while he looked at the laughing Muslim, threw his fist out in the hope of hitting him. He missed.

*Someone must have heard the shots and screams!*

*Why isn't anyone rushing to my rescue?*

He saw the Muslim take a bradawl out of his pocket. He became frantic with fear and tried to stand up. His blown kneecaps could not hold his weight and he fell to the floor. The Muslim immediately stabbed him just above the shoulder.

He felt the bradawl perforate his skin and continue into his body. The Muslim then tugged it back and forth before he pulled it out of him. Following the sharp, pointy tool was a large spray of blood. When the second squirt came in the same rhythm as his heartbeat, Zhang knew it was an arterial wound.

Zhang opened his eyes for a second and saw that it was raining red.

*A captain should go down with his ship—not the other way around.*

There were only four more heartbeats which pumped out blood before he was dead.

\*\*\*

Umeira looked down at the body on the deck of the cabin. It was covered in a pool of blood. There was graffiti on the cabin walls, spray-painted with thousands of droplets of blood. Through the blood-smeared face of the captain, he saw that the skin already had started to pale. The eyes of the Chinaman stared lifelessly up at him.

He laughed. The captain had pleaded for his life, asking who would sail the ship.

*Stupid infidel.*

There was a new captain onboard now.

He resisted the urge to take the captain's hat which was sitting on the nightstand.

His men were currently keeping the entire crew hostage in the mess room, except for the first officer who was on the bridge—with a gun barrel pointed at him. They would easily be able to maneuver the ship for the next few days. Even though the crew had to be killed, he believed he had learned enough to get the ship back towards the gas platform.

The young Chechen, who acted as his translator, had come up with the idea of destroying the radio system. That way, even if a crew member did manage to escape, something Umeira doubted, they would not be able to send out a distress signal.

He did not believe anyone would attempt anything foolish. If any of them even slightly acted up, he would take them down to this cabin and show them the dead captain and the dark red canvas of blood that was his last resting place. In a few minutes, he would bring the first officer down here—so he could spread the word of the grizzly scene.

Umeira opened the door of the cabin to leave, but stopped and turned around.

*The blood splatter only makes it better.*

He walked over and picked up the captain's hat.

# CHAPTER 40

*Khan Tengri Temple, Altai Mountains, China*

His stomach claimed he had been down on the floor for half a day, but DeVille knew it could not have been more than a couple of hours. He saw daylight streaming through the cracks around his cell door. Still in the same position as when the admiral kicked his chair, he was unable to move and unwilling to try, hands still cuffed to the chair and his feet to the rings in the floor.

The dusty concrete floor stung his wounds and he saw a mosaic on the floor, made up of many small droplets. The wounds had not bled much—salt, in the olden days, was used to stop bleeding in wounds soldiers got during battle. The torturer knew what he was doing. He kept him from bleeding to death.

*But why?*

Once, he blacked out from the intense pain, but his consciousness returned and the stinging pain was now just white noise. Every time he tried to move the white noise became louder.

So he stayed still.

The feeling that overpowered the pain was new to DeVille. At least in such an intensive form. But he knew what it was. It was pure hatred.

Not revenge, though it felt like it. He was going to die sooner or later. Probably sooner rather than later if he did not get away from here. But he had to prove to Carina that he had done something good with his life when he met her again. This was his only chance.

The only noise since the Khagans left the cell was that of a helicopter taking off. He had hoped to hear both helicopters leave, which would have meant that all four torturers most likely had left.

But he had heard only one helicopter. That meant that one of them, at least, was still at the temple. He suspected he knew which one.

All of a sudden two guards entered his cell.

*How much blood have I lost?*

*Why didn't I hear them open the lock?*

*Why didn't I hear them enter?*

They both looked at DeVille and then each other, all without a trace of expression on their faces and without a word. One of them pointed the MP5 at him and flicked the safety switch. The other walked over to DeVille, released the cuffs from the chair and the floor, and fastened them in front of him.

DeVille stumbled as he got up and he saw a slight smile on the face of the guard pointing his gun at him. He got a blanket thrown over his bare upper body. A blizzard of pain stormed through his body when the rough textile came in contact with his gashes.

They motioned for him to walk out the door. The second guard also flicked off the safety switch.

*The same thing all over again. Out for a quick walk, and then back for a torture session.*

"Move it!" one of the guards said in English.

"Fuck you," DeVille muttered. He felt like a different person now. This was all about doing the right thing.

For Carina.

His mind went into overdrive, figuring out a way to get out of another round of *Ling chi*.

When they got outside, the guards pointed him in the same direction as last time. He had not noticed it then, but the courtyard was covered in gray, fine dust. It resembled cement powder. If it was not for the patches of snow, it would have looked like what he expected the surface of the moon to look like.

DeVille made a decision. He was not going back to the crazy Chinaman. Not alive, for sure. When they reached a spot that was clear of snow he pretended to stumble in his shackles and trip over. The blanket fell off his shoulders and he felt the dust attach itself to his body.

One of the guards poked him with his gun and motioned for him to get up. With a look, DeVille let the guard know that he could not get up with the shackles on. The guard leaned over, arm stretched out to pull DeVille up.

When at an arm's length away, DeVille took a fistful of the dust and threw it in the guard's face. The guard's eyes and mouth were open. His hands instinctively reached for his face.

He was too slow.

With the same movement as he had thrown the dust, DeVille pulled the guard down to the ground. There was no resistance from the blinded guard. DeVille reached for the gun with his cuffed hands.

The other guard raised his gun, but did not fire, as his colleague was on top of DeVille and was blocking a clean shot. He hurried towards them.

DeVille fired three shots.

Two of them hit, one in the shoulder which made the guard twirl around, while the other hit from the back side just below the neck. He fell to the ground with a grunt.

The other guard got back on his feet, but DeVille rolled sideways and tackled him. He fell hard on top of DeVille, pinning him down. With both legs straight, DeVille quickly pulled them upwards, hoping to free himself from the guard. His legs hit the guard in the groin. He winced and moved just enough to the side so DeVille could roll him off. As soon as his arms were free, DeVille used the power of both to smash the MP5's magazine into the guard's face.

Both guards were down on the ground. Lifeless.

More guards would storm out of the buildings in a matter of seconds.

*They must have heard the shots.*

He got up and ran as fast as he could with his cuffed feet, the thirty meters towards the helicopter. The plan was simple—the chance of hitting the helicopter should deter them from sending shots in his direction.

He got under cover behind the helicopter and placed the gun barrel straight on top of the chain that kept his feet cuffed. One shot and the chain was broken.

Sounding like horses on a track, men approached fast. There was no time to try to shoot the handcuffs off. He looked at the ATV.

With the MP5's switch set to 'continuous fire' he let rip a quick spray of fire towards the guards coming from the other side of the helicopter.

He straddled the ATV, saw the key in the ignition, and pressed the start button. It roared to life.

The path he had entered on was blocked by the approaching guards. With one hand on the handlebar steering, he tried to hold the MP5 away with the other. He almost lost the gun as he had no room for movement thanks to the thirty-centimeter chain between the cuffs.

At the diagonally opposite side from where he had entered the compound, he spotted another path. The ATV wobbled as he steered and accelerated towards it.

A couple of shots whizzed past him. A quick glance over his shoulder revealed at least four men about to lower their guns and fire at him. He was already two hundred meters away.

*They will have to be good shots if they are to find their target.*

A bullet grazed his shoulder, making him jerk to the side, and he almost fell off. He let go of the accelerator and the ATV slowed markedly. He regained his balance and hit the accelerator again—the off-road tires spun and quickly hurled the vehicle forward.

The adrenalin in DeVille's veins numbed the pain from the wound made by the grazing bullet. He was still bare-chested, after he lost the blanket in his pretend fall to the ground, but the icy wind felt nice as it anesthetized the pain.

An engine roaring, and the sound of gravel being spun away, told him that more guards were in pursuit on the second ATV. Not shooting out a tire or the engine of it when he had the chance, could very well be the mistake that got him killed. That could have given him the head start he needed.

*The helicopter!*

He should have done something to that as well.

This path was much better than the path up to the temple had been. It was clearly carved into the steep mountainside. There was little gravel or snow on the path, and the ATV gripped well in the corners.

After about five kilometers, the path narrowed as if it soon would disappear and the turns got more frequent. Some of them being one-hundred-eighty-degree hairpins. He slowed down as he could not see around some of the corners. Only having one hand on the handlebars did not make it any easier.

The other ATV was now only a hundred meters behind him. He had to get the handcuffs off—he could not shoot and steer at the same time.

*There's no time to stop.*

He took another quick glance behind at the two men on the other ATV. They were closing fast and he saw the passenger aiming his gun, ready to fire. In front of DeVille, the path was about to hit a heavily-angled, blind corner.

*This is my only chance.*

He reached the corner, turned the handlebars, and rolled off the ATV. The MP5 slammed into his ribs. The path was peppered with apple-sized rocks. He thought for a split second he had broken some ribs, but the adrenalin quickly took his mind away from the pain.

The ATV continued at a forty-five-degree angle, and flew off the cliffside. Within a second, DeVille heard the sound of plastic and metal being crushed in the impact with the mountain.

*At least two hundred meters down to the next ledge.*

He crawled back towards the mountainside and clenched the gun with his cuffed hands. The cold, sharp surface of the mountainside cut into his back.

The other ATV slowed to a halt, out of DeVille's sight, about where his ATV had gone over the cliff. He heard the two guards get off their vehicle and saw them walk slowly towards the edge.

They were both looking down into the valley below when DeVille got them in the crosshair of his MP5. Neither of them noticed him.

Unsure how many rounds were still in his magazine, DeVille silently switched the gun to 'manual.' He fired a single shot into the back of the closest guard, enough to make the man stumble and tip over the edge. He heard the scream as the man fell, but not the landing.

Surprised, it took the second guard an extra half-second to turn around and aim. DeVille fired two shots at the guard. The third press on the trigger only delivered a click.

*I'm out of ammunition.*

It did not matter.

The two shots had hit the guard in his thigh and his shoulder. The guard's MP5 rattled as it fell on the large rocks and the man took two steps sideways before he knelt in evident pain.

DeVille did not waste a second. He used all the energy he had left and rushed out from the cliffside and kicked the guard's head with all his force, like it was a football. The head seemed to stop for a moment, before it dragged the rest of the man's body over the edge with it.

DeVille bent over in time to see the body slam against the mountain a few hundred meters farther down.

DeVille cursed loudly. The men probably had keys to his handcuffs and he now regretted kicking the man. There was nothing he could do about it now, so he turned and walked over to the ATV the guards had arrived on.

DeVille noticed a saddlebag on it. He opened it and saw on top something he could use. In between snow gear, such as a shovel and metal snow chains for the tires, there was a handgun. In a plastic container there was ammunition for both the handgun and the MP5.

He picked up the gun and switched the safety off. He had seen this done in movies a few times, and hoped it would work as well as shooting off the chain between his feet had.

*Aim at the chain, shoot, and my hands should be free.*

It did not take many seconds before he realized it would not work. The chain's length made it impossible for him to hold the trigger and angle the gun at any part of the handcuff chain. He would end up shooting himself if he tried.

A thought struck him. He sat down and took his right boot and sock off. He angled his left leg so that the sole of the boot was vertical and then leaned the gun against it. With his hands he held the barrel of the gun as far in as he could so that the chain was tight in front of the muzzle. He bent his big toe and clasped the gun with his foot and stuck the toe into the trigger guard. With a quick squeeze of his toe, the gun fired.

The shot knocked him backwards and pain exploded in his bare foot, his wrists, and his face. The recoil of the gun had flung it towards him, slamming it into his face. His foot looked bad—covered in lots of stinging small wounds from shrapnel, either from the bullet or the chain. His wrists felt like someone had whipped them with steel wire.

He put his boot and sock back on and felt relieved.

*I've managed to escape.*

"Now what?" he asked out loud, looking across to the mountains behind which he had been told Mongolia was hiding. He expected more people to come after him on foot. They might even have another ATV stashed away somewhere.

The chance of a successful escape to Mongolia was slim to none. His chance of just getting off this mountain was slim. He had no food or water. He had no clothes except for boots and pants.

He went back to the ATV, hoping there would be a first-aid kit as well in the saddlebag. It did have one, but DeVille was happier at what he saw at the bottom of the saddlebag—a snowsuit.

He did his best attending to his wounds and put on the snowsuit. Several signs of frostbite were already beginning to show on his upper body.

He started the ATV and drove off—still in the opposite direction to the mountains blocking him from Mongolia.

*Better to get as far away from the temple compound as possible.*

DeVille's options were limited to either continuing on the path farther up, or trying to climb down the mountainside. He chose option number one.

He was only another kilometer or two away when he heard it.

The helicopter…

# CHAPTER 41

DeVille twisted the accelerator and made the ATV work the path at a speed that would seem reckless on a highway. One slip, or misjudgment of speed around a bend, would lead to certain death.

It was another minute or so before the helicopter came into view. There was nowhere for the helicopter to land, so that did not worry DeVille. What worried him was that they probably had men ready to fire at him from the helicopter.

About five hundred meters ahead, DeVille saw the cliffside flatten out. It was still steep, but now it looked like it was possible to climb up or down.

But he also saw something else. Because of the less steep cliffside, a rockfall had stopped its downward descent in the middle of the path.

There was no way to drive around it and the helicopter was approaching fast. DeVille knew he was trapped and a sense of helplessness dawned on him. He had been so close to getting away, but now that seemed impossible.

He slowed down and got off the ATV. He could turn and go back, but he knew that the helicopter could easily make a U-turn and catch up with him again. It would be a cat and mouse game he would lose.

With the MP5 around his neck and the handgun in the pocket of the snowsuit, together with spare ammunition, he climbed over the rockfall. The moment he got over, several rocks exploded in dust, screaming bullets ricocheting around him.

More shots came in DeVille's direction, but he was now well-covered behind some of the big rocks. He switched the MP5 to 'continuous fire,' took aim, and fired all of the bullets from one of the new magazines towards the helicopter.

Some of the rounds must have hit the helicopter, making it waver to the right and forcing it to make a large three-hundred-sixty-degree turn. That gave him time to eject the empty magazine and insert a new one.

When the helicopter faced DeVille's direction again, it slowed to a stop and hovered like a wasp over the path. A wire was lowered out of the side, and three men began rappeling down.

DeVille switched the MP5 to 'single shot' and took aim. The rappel line was in the middle of his two in-line sights. A figure came into the crosshair and DeVille pressed the trigger four times.

The man lost his grip, plunged past the other two, and hit the rocky ground with a thud.

Before DeVille could aim again, the two men were down and, without bothering to check on their fallen Tengriist, approaching the rockfall fast.

They were about fifty meters away when DeVille saw he had an unobstructed view of the ATV. Another flick of the switch back to continuous fire, and he took aim at where he assumed the fuel tank of the ATV was. A jerry can with extra fuel was attached to the side of the ATV.

He fired a full round towards the vehicle.

Nothing happened.

DeVille swore.

Movies had tricked him into believing he could blow up a vehicle by shooting at its fuel tank.

The salvo from the machine gun made the approaching guards take cover on the other side of the twenty-meter-wide rockfall.

DeVille took the handgun out of the pocket of the snowsuit and fired a single shot at the ground under the ATV. It hit a rock, creating a spark which lit a fire in the fuel that was dripping from the bullet-ridden fuel tank. Within a second the ATV was completely covered in flames. The pungent, yet addictive, smell of gasoline disappeared as the flames grew, and the smell was replaced by that of burning plastic.

He inserted a new magazine into the MP5 and waited, with a gun in each hand, for the guards to climb over the rockfall.

*No chance of me going back to the Chinaman alive.*

An explosion penetrated the roar of the hovering helicopter. Parts of the ATV flew over DeVille. The shock wave seemed to slow down time as the flying debris glided down and landed without a sound. He knew what had happened. During his machine gun salvo, he must have missed the jerry can. The heat of the burning ATV had created pressure on the vacuum in the can. When it reached the right temperature and pressure, it exploded—making the whole ATV a flying fireball.

Thick black smoke came from the other side of the rockfall. The helicopter backed off and disappeared behind the screen of darkness. DeVille made up his mind. It meant they could not see him either. He slowly crawled over the rockfall, his fingers on the triggers of each gun, and had a quick look.

The two men were facedown, unconscious, and hugging the rocks. Shrapnel had ripped open their faces.

DeVille saw two spare magazines on each of the men. It made him realize that he had crossed the rockfall low on ammunition. Knowing he had been so close to death spurred him on in a way that frightened him. He ejected his magazine and took one from the closest man and inserted it. The three others he stuffed in his pockets.

He looked through the downed men's pockets in hopes of finding something useful, but with no luck. One of the men had a water bottle, which DeVille took. He opened it, took a big sip, and clipped it to the side of his snowsuit. Another find was a half pack of cigarettes and a lighter—he stuffed both in his pocket.

The noise from the helicopter waned.

*Perhaps shrapnel hit it too?*

The ATV was still burning and DeVille knew he needed to use the opportunity. With the MP5 slung over his shoulder, and his pockets full and bulky, he started to climb down from the path. It looked like it was about two hundred meters to the bottom of the valley.

It would take several hours to get to the bottom and he would be a very easy target if the helicopter returned. Up was no option. There was no choice.

*I have to get to the bottom before they come back.*

With an icy stare, he looked towards the mountains that blocked his view of Mongolia.

# CHAPTER 42

*Altai Tavan Bogd National Park, Mongolia*
*April 21ˢᵗ – 13:05*

There was a circular roof made of hide with a hole in the center, kind of like a tipi, and it was the first thing DeVille saw when he opened his eyes. He was in a hut—it was oval with walls made of hide or felt—supported vertically by crisscrossing sticks. In the center stood a small stove, rusty after years of use in the wilderness. Between four supporting posts, which looked almost like Roman columns, a chimney stuck out of the hole. The walls were filled with floral motifs of traditional Mongolian banners.

*Am I in Mongolia? Have I made it?*

He was on a bed made of straw and on top of him was a fur blanket. Underneath, he was still wearing the snowsuit. The boots had been removed. His body ached and he touched his chin.

*The Tengriists.*

Not being tied down in any way, he was not someone's prisoner. His memory struggled with who might have rescued him. The last he remembered was coming down the mountain on what he thought was the Mongolian side and onto a flat pasture with a river running through the middle.

He had been extremely fatigued. The last time he had eaten was just before he and the shaman split up. He collapsed on the grass. The sun burned him and the only thing his body wanted was to sleep.

He caved in and closed his eyes, even as it struck him that he might never wake up again. How long he had been out, he did not know. Someone had found him and taken him to the hut. Whoever that someone was, had saved his life.

Because of the hut, he guessed it was a herder. Not because of the colorful, but spartan, decoration, but because of the sound of goats bleating outside.

Luckily, there had been lots of streams with fresh, cold water while he crossed the mountains, otherwise he would never have managed to get this far.

When he had started to descend the mountainside, after the battle with the Tengriists, he expected the helicopter to return at any moment. But it did not. It took him several hours to get to the bottom.

Afterwards, it was a fairly simple hike through the valley. The ground was soft in places, soaking his feet. He took many breaks so he could dry off his feet. The last thing he needed was a case of trench foot. Late in the afternoon, he reached the end of the valley and was faced with the dilemma of starting to climb the mountain, or trying to get some sleep.

As there was still a chance that the Tengriists would come after him, he decided to climb until he found a hidden spot to camp.

It took him longer than expected, so it was already dark when he found a good spot. There was some brush around and he thought about using the lighter he had taken to make a fire. He decided against it, fearful of revealing his position.

He slept only for a few hours, but surprisingly well—despite his wounds sending jolts of pain through him at intervals of just a few minutes, and a rock hard ground. When he woke up, there was still moonlight so he climbed through the rest of the night.

It was an easy climb and he reached the top as the sun rose. He abandoned the MP5, but kept the handgun. Each time he stopped for a rest, he used the time to try to pick the lock of the hand and foot cuffs; the bracelets were still on him. He used the spring from one of the MP5's magazines. Eventually he managed.

The climb down was a lot harder. He was forced to make serious detours to get around some steep cliffsides. His legs threatened to give way on him several times.

He reached the bottom and a flat pasture, feeling like a zombie. Apathy took over and the sun drained away the energy he had left. That was when he collapsed.

The goats bleated louder and louder and he heard footsteps outside. He reached into his pocket and gripped the handgun, surprised it was still there.

A man entered the hut. The large leather and fur coat seemed to hang heavily from the hood and dragged his head down. He wore high boots, almost like riding boots.

*Definitely a herder.*

Without speaking, he acknowledged DeVille being awake with a nervous smile, and placed two bowls on the ground next to where DeVille was lying. One contained the same kind of jerky DeVille had gotten from the shaman. The other was what DeVille assumed to be warm goat's milk, thick as cream—steam rose fast towards the hole in the hut.

"Excuse me, do you speak English? *Français?*" DeVille asked hopefully. No reply. DeVille tried again in Arabic, Norwegian, and Dutch—all the languages he knew. There was still no sign of a reply. He sighed.

DeVille wolfed down the food and the warm goat's milk. His survival instinct was on high alert. It tasted like the smell of old diapers, but his body gladly accepted it. He had gotten rest, but his body also needed to replenish all the energy spent over the last couple of days. The herder sat with him while he ate.

The food and the warm milk recharged his brain. And with that the thought of the torturer returned. And a new sentiment—a need for revenge.

*What to do next?*

He had escaped the Tengriists, but he was somewhere in no-man's-land in Mongolia. He thought about how to get back to Brussels, but the thought lasted only a second. He needed to regroup, rearm himself, and return to China.

Wang and the other Chinaman needed to be stopped and, more importantly to DeVille, pay for what they had done to him.

He did not worry too much about the Russians. They were in on it, but he did not feel the same need for revenge as he did with Wang and the other Chinaman. He never thought he would risk everything for revenge, but then again he had never been tortured before.

And of course there was the matter of the missing nuclear missile which was about to be detonated somewhere. *And* stopping these Tengriists taking over most of Asia.

How to do that was beyond him. He was in the middle of nowhere with a man whom he could not communicate with and without any means of going anywhere.

When he finished all the food and drink, the herder took the bowls and left the hut with no expression on his face. DeVille was as revitalized as he could hope for.

A thought slammed into him like an uppercut. He had two allies, of which only one could help him. The chief of staff would help him get home, but the one who would help him with revenge was the one he had met just a week and a half ago.

Sergei. And his Russian mafia.

Sergei would gladly see damage done to the Tengriist Four who threatened his livelihood. Even though DeVille deplored the activities of the mafia, he was willing to accept any assistance he could get.

He needed to get to Russia. DeVille knew the border could not be too far away as the Chinese, Mongolian, Kazakh, and Russian borders all met each other in the Altai Mountains.

DeVille spotted his boots, got up, and put them on. He pulled aside the hide that covered the entrance and for a second got blinded by the noon sun. He looked around at the landscape and it was nothing like he remembered it from when he got down from the mountain.

It was a narrow valley with a little stream cutting it in two. The air was sweet and smelled like a barn full of hay. All the herder's goats were on the other side of the stream from the hut. DeVille looked around for the herder. He saw him seated on a rock, his upper body moving from side to side as he milked one of the goats.

DeVille crossed the stream and walked towards the herder and his goat. He sat down on a rock not far away, in direct line of sight of the herder. If they could not communicate by words he needed to find another way. Eyes could say a lot. It would be a good start.

The herder looked him straight in the eyes while his hands continued to milk the goat in a rhythmic motion. The squirts of the milk dinged the bottom of the metal bucket each time the herder pulled one of the goat's two teats.

They looked at each other for what felt like several minutes. There was no movement in the face of the herder. His skin was wrinkled and weatherworn after a hard life working outdoors in all kinds of weather. He looked like he could be seventy years old, but DeVille guessed he probably was closer to forty. Most people in Mongolia never lived to reach Western retirement age.

DeVille sighed and was at a complete loss to how he was going to explain to the herder that he wanted to go to Russia. There was a flicker of sympathy in the herder's eyes.

"*Rossiya*?" DeVille all of a sudden asked. If they were close to Russia, perhaps the Russian name of the country would sound familiar to the herder.

The herder let go of the goat's teats and stood up. He smiled and pointed in a direction across the pasture towards where the valley ended. The goat used the moment of freedom from the herder's hands to walk away and blend in with the herd.

It was not unlikely that the herder understood a bit of Russian, when DeVille thought about it. Herders in this area crisscrossed back and forth over the borders with their goats.

The only problem was that DeVille did not speak any Russian. In fact, it was the only word he knew, besides greeting phrases. He wanted to ask how far it was and if it was at all possible to get there.

The herder moved towards him. He walked three steps, lay down on the ground, and pretended to sleep. This was repeated once.

DeVille figured it meant that it would take two days to hike there. DeVille pointed at the herder, then at himself. The herder shook his head and pointed to the goats.

DeVille stood up and bowed to the man. He knew the man could not leave his goats. He was determined to get to Russia, and if he had managed to escape China and get this far, he should be able to do another two days of hiking. There were no mountain peaks to speak of in the direction the herder had pointed.

He stared towards the end of the valley, and unfamiliar feelings started to brew in his mind. It felt like the feeling a former smoker would get when having a cigarette after several months. The rush made him feel a little light-headed, but good.

*Excitement before the fight?*

He remembered the pack of cigarettes he had taken from the Tengriist guard and fished it out of his pocket. He lit one and quickly sat down from the wooziness after inhaling just twice.

The thought of Wang and the torturing Chinaman made him shiver. He would do everything to stop their plan, and at the same time, hopefully, inflict pain on them.

*But what about Stella Hanson?*

A sound that resembled a post horn interrupted DeVille's thoughts. He turned around to see the herder standing in the opening of the hut with a straight horn which looked like it was made of bronze.

The herder blew the horn twice more before he went back into the hut.

# CHAPTER 43

*Shanghai, China*
*April 22$^{nd}$ – 21:50*

The Hublot showed it was almost ten in the evening. Wang was sitting in his office and had eaten half his dinner. He sighed. No matter how much he seasoned it, the taste remained bland. It was normally his favorite dish—slow-boiled ducklings in a ginger and star anise- flavored broth. The fragrant liquorice together with the moist and savory meat always made his mouth water. Not this time. Most of it would end up in the trash.

He glanced back at his dinner before his eyes looked out of the window to the millions of lights that lit up the Shanghai skyline. Throughout the day, doubt about what the Tengriists were doing had emerged.

*Have we been too ambitious?*
*Will I lose all I have?*

Wang knew it was a test from Tengri, but he still was not sure how to respond. The events of the last few days had definitely played a part. But no one had foiled their plan, at least not yet, and it looked like they would succeed.

He had not slept much since he returned from the temple. That could not continue. He needed to stay sharp and focused. The plan was about to enter the most critical phase.

The food felt like it had grown in size, yet he swallowed a mouthful, and thought about DeVille's escape from the temple.

*Is he still alive?*

The helicopter had been forced to return to the temple after the explosion, as the pilot feared that shrapnel had been sucked into the air vents. DeVille was a lucky man.

Upon their return, a furious Wu dispatched two foot patrols of Baghaturs. They had returned empty-handed.

Wu later informed his friends in the armed forces to be on the lookout for a man in the area—a man suspected of terrorism, something that tended to mobilize a large search party. They also came up with nothing.

It was a possibility that DeVille had managed to cross the border into Mongolia, but Wu doubted that. The area was inhospitable and DeVille had not been equipped to make such a journey. The likeliest possibility was DeVille lying dead somewhere in the mountains, either from fatigue or from an accident.

The uncertainty fueled the doubt that crept onto Wang like a spider slowly moving across its web.

He pushed the plate away. Whatever had happened to DeVille would not stop their scheme. Nothing would. It was impossible to stop now.

There were two things that nagged at Wang. DeVille was one. The other was the Euphausia. Wang had seen the GPS tracking of the krill ship, which showed that she was on course towards the Norwegian coast. She would never reach the location in the Arctic Ocean and spread radiation across the area in time for the auction of the mining rights.

He was also unable to contact the ship. When he informed the other Khagans of this, Alexandrovich acted immediately. Abdul Aziz's camp had been raided the night before by a group of Spetsnaz Special Forces and Aziz was killed in the shootout. In fact, all the militants in the camp were killed, including Alexandrovich's informant.

Alexandrovich retrieved the satellite phone they had provided Aziz with earlier and found out that the rebel leader had ordered the ship to get close to shore. Wang assumed that the captain of the Euphausia and the rest of the crew had either been killed or taken hostage.

This jeopardized the whole mining plan. The auction for the prospecting rights was in less than two weeks. It would not work if the bomb exploded just a few days before the auction. Russian authorities would need about a week to determine the radiation levels. It was only after that that the rights would be worthless—for everyone except Wang and Bakunin.

Now they could only hope that the price they needed to pay would be something they could jointly afford. If they did not get this income source, it would delay the plan. Because it was his ship, it was his responsibility. The other Khagans would blame him. The other Khagans were ruthless when it came to failure.

He had to make sure the bomb got blown up somewhere. The terrorist attack still had to happen. Wu and Alexandrovich needed it as a motive to wipe out the Uighurs and the Chechens.

To be on the safe side, the Khagans decided to find an alternative revenue stream as a plan B. They had given Wang the task—one of the reasons why he was having dinner in his office tonight.

So far he had only come up with a few ideas, but he deemed them all to be too risky. One of them was to take over privately-owned industry, through some faked-up charges, something both Wu and Alexandrovich could easily do. But it could draw unwanted attention. Another idea was to steal some of the activities of the Russian mafia or the

Chinese triads, but that could end in a full-blown war. Besides, they were already in a conflict with the Russian mafia.

Wang slammed his fist down on the table. The cutlery jumped on his plate. Not only was he struggling to come up with a good idea to get money into their organization, but he was also annoyed about all the money he had spent on radiation-proofing his mining ship.

*A waste of money.*

Wang's phone rang. He picked it up and clicked the green button without saying a word.

"Good evening, Khagan," the voice on the other end said, unmistakably Wu's.

"Good evening to you as well, Khagan." Wang was not up for a chat with Wu right now. If anyone could pick up on his doubt, it would be Wu.

"I guess you've heard what Alexandrovich has achieved?"

"Yes, he's done well. But we still can't contact the ship."

"Relax. We're still good, Khagan. When the ship and the bomb blow, we'll still be able to blame the terrorists, giving us the reason we need to hit them back hard. And if the ship heads at full speed towards the Arctic now, we could still get it to the location in time. Impersonating Aziz, giving orders to the terrorists aboard."

Wang needed to hear that glimmer of hope. But before he got to say how pleased he was with the news, Wu continued, "But, we cannot risk that."

"Why?" Wang realized the question made him sound desperate, so he hurriedly added, "I mean, wouldn't it be best to follow the plan? It has worked great for us so far."

"There are two reasons, Wang."

*Wu didn't use my title.*

"Firstly, we know that both European and American authorities are keeping an eye on the ship," Wu went on. "But they will not dare do anything as long as the ship is at its current location, near a gas platform. If it goes back into open seas, they will probably use the opportunity to raid it. Secondly, there's a fair chance the crew is killed, so the ship is just going in circles, sailed by some terrorist mountain goat that's never been to sea before. They would never get to the Arctic Ocean."

Wang saw the logic in Wu's assessment, although he did not like it.

"Alexandrovich is trying to contact Aziz's man onboard right now."

*He didn't call Alexandrovich Khagan either.*

"To tell them to blow up my ship as soon as possible?" Wang asked.

"No. We need them to wait for a few days, maybe even a week."

"Why?"

"Come on, Wang, do I have to explain everything to you? We need to create an evidence trail so it seems realistic for us to later blame both the Uighurs and the Chechens. We also need to remove any trace from Aziz's camp that could link us with them. Thirdly, any intel suggesting that we or the Russians could have known about the attack cannot exist. You see the difficulty in doing that?"

Wang was not interested in being berated anymore, so he changed the subject. "Has *Khagan* Alexandrovich been successful in dealing with the mafia?"

"No." There was a moment of silence before Wu added, "I'll give him a week or so before I'll send my guys in Dubai to have a little talk with this Sergei person."

Wang was not a fan of Wu's methods, but in this situation he would happily support the use of his techniques.

"Have you found us new revenue streams?"

"Yes, but I need a little more time to finalize the plans," Wang lied, cursing Wu silently for having brought the topic back up.

"All right, we trust you."

Wang sensed the suspicion in Wu's voice. "Thanks. I won't let Tengri down. Have a good evening, Khagan."

"The same to you, Khagan."

Wang put the phone down and immediately thought of DeVille. Three times he had met the man and something told him there would be more encounters. The doubt he felt earlier was now turning into fear and anger. Tengri would punish them all if this man ruined their plan.

The maid knocked on the frosted glass door and Wang motioned for her to come in. She cleared the plate and cutlery from his desk and put a tulip glass of cognac in front of Wang.

*Louis XIII de Rémy Martin.* Two thousand American dollars per bottle.

It was part of his dinner routine. There were a dozen empty bottles in the kitchen. The beautiful bottles were probably worth five hundred dollars each. He had instructed the maid not to throw away the beautiful crystal, shaped into an oval, with a rim just like a crocodile's scute.

Wang took a sip of the powerful liquid. It tasted floral, as if he were drinking a concentrated rose garden. He watched the maid pick up the tray and when she turned to leave, he knew how to become calm—how to boost his confidence.

For Tengri's sake.

"Put down the tray, Zhen," he said, and got up from behind his desk.

# CHAPTER 44

*Gorno-Altaysk, Russia*
*April 24<sup>th</sup> – 17:35*

The old warehouse had been turned into an auto workshop and storage facility. The four old trucks stowed away on the left side looked like they had been there since communism fell. They were greenish gray, although the light blue patches from where someone had brushed themselves against the trucks revealed their true color. They matched the shelves, full of oily engine parts and tools on the other side of the warehouse.

Knowing who occupied the warehouse, DeVille guessed it was not a legitimate business. Either it was a chop shop for stolen cars or a cover for some of the mafia's other activities.

Around him stood three men. One of them held an AK-47 while the two others had handguns stuffed down the front of their black jeans. They all wore identical short, black leather coats. Even though it was overcast outside, and the warehouse was windowless, they all sported sunglasses.

*These guys are straight out of* The Matrix.

These wannabes must have seen the movie a few times too many. The fact that they were all short, chubby, and bald did not seem to hinder their aspiration for getting a role in a sequel. Sergei's men had different 'uniforms' in Russia compared to Dubai.

DeVille's body ached, he needed sleep, and he was hungry. He had been waiting in the warehouse for a couple of hours. The three cast members from *The Matrix* had not given him any information. Or any refreshments.

Two hours after the Mongolian herder blew his horn, a man on a horse had appeared. The herder and the horseman talked for a few minutes before DeVille was motioned to get onto the horse.

* * *

DeVille was not a big fan of horses, but he was not a big fan of the situation he was in either, so he reluctantly took the horseman's hand and was pulled up onto the horse. The herder smiled at him when they rode off and DeVille was unsure if it was because he was happy to get rid of the foreigner, or because he had provided what DeVille had wanted.

They rode for what DeVille believed to be five or six hours, without any stops, until they got to a road. They dismounted, took a break, and drank some water. The horse looked like it had been leading the Dubai World Cup, the richest horserace in the world, and lost it on the final stretch.

A car pulled up, a tiny saloon of some make DeVille had never heard of, and two men stepped out of it. They shook hands with the horseman and talked for about twenty minutes.

One of the men then popped the trunk and motioned for DeVille to climb in. He looked at the tiny space and then at the horseman. The horseman nodded.

Unenthusiastically, DeVille climbed in.

They drove for several hours. The road was bumpy and DeVille got flung around in the trunk every few seconds. The tiny space did not allow him to move much, giving him cramps in his legs more than once. A few times it felt as if the car's four wheels all left the ground at the same time then suddenly hit Earth Mother again. How he did not get a concussion was beyond him.

The car finally stopped and when they opened the trunk it was pitch-dark outside. He stumbled out, falling over, his legs not ready to hold his weight right away. They gave him some water and after a few seconds he was able to stand.

"*Rossiya*," one of the men said and pointed towards a building with light streaming out of it, maybe a kilometer away.

The man started to march in front of him, pretending to shoot and then shook his head.

*Border post—manned by armed soldiers.*

The man then pointed in another direction and nodded towards a trailhead. DeVille hoped it led to a safe route across the border. If he had interpreted the man correctly, it did.

A small leather satchel, containing a bottle of water and a large piece of bread, were handed to him. Before he could thank the men, they got in the car and drove away as if they had just stolen it.

*Where's the vodka?*

He wondered what, and who, they thought he was. If he got out of this alive, he made a mental note to come back here to thank these guys one way or another. Or he could ask Sergei to do something for them.

He was not sure he would get the chance.

After he ate a few pieces of the bread, he walked for two hours until he saw the lights from the border post were well behind him. There was a little path to follow, so navigating across the border was easy. He sat down under a tree and slept until he felt the sun warming his face.

A while later he got to a road where he decided to hitchhike. It must have been thirty minutes before the first vehicle appeared: an old pickup truck with a few wooden crates in the bed.

Without rolling down the window, the young driver motioned for him to get up in the back. DeVille scrambled up. He had no idea where the pickup was going, but since the driver did not ask, the road could only lead to one place. Hopefully, a city or a town.

DeVille snapped out of thinking about the last few days when a fourth man entered the warehouse with a laptop in his hands, holding it like it was a tray of coffee. He was dressed just like the others, as if he were from *The Matrix*. The man nodded towards a small table covered with tools and the guy with the AK-47 walked over and pulled it in front of DeVille.

On the table were a drill and a blowtorch—easily within his reach. He was not a prisoner, but after what happened in the cell in the Altai Mountains, he found comfort in knowing that a weapon was close by.

The fourth man placed the laptop on the table and flipped it open.

*Skype.*

DeVille recognized the face on the screen.

"How did you find me?" Sergei asked with a smile.

"I see the weather is nice in Dubai," DeVille said, looking at the golf course and the skyline behind Sergei's villa.

"It always is. What are you doing in the middle of Russian nowhere?"

"A long story, but I need your help."

"Humor me with the story first. Then I'll see what I can do for you, my friend."

It was the first time a leading Russian mobster had called DeVille a *friend,* and he was not sure he appreciated it. Right now, though, it was more than he could hope for. He told the second-in-command of the Russian mafia all that had happened since he left the villa in Dubai. He told him about the attack on the way to the airport, the attempt to arrest him at the airport in Altay City, the escape, what had happened at the temple, and the escape to Mongolia.

"You've been quite busy over the last week. And very resourceful. We could use someone like you in our organization." Sergei sounded genuinely impressed.

"Thanks, but I think I prefer to work in a less violent environment." Deep down, he was flattered by Sergei's job offer.

"If you ever change your mind, let me know. Obviously you know how to find me. Not many can do that. So, how did you do that?"

DeVille told him how he had gotten help from the herder and his friends.

"When we approached the city I figured it was big enough for you to have some *business* here. After I got dropped off, I waited until the evening and approached a group of working girls. I then asked to see their boss, saying I had an important message for Mr. Mogilevich. They did not seem to know who that was, but reluctantly agreed. After a few hours, I was introduced to their pimp."

"You took a large risk there. Those hookers could have worked for a competitor."

"I thought you and your organization were in overall charge of all the local mafia?"

"As long as there is profit to be made, there will always be someone trying to encroach on our business model," Sergei said, again sounding like a corporate CEO.

"Well, what's done is done. It worked. I met the pimp. Not a very pleasant man, but I told him as much as I could about you and eventually he seemed satisfied. He then made me wait until early this morning when the gentlemen here came and took me to this warehouse. They've had me wait until now."

"I'm sorry about the poor hospitality, but they had to make sure you were who you claimed to be. It's part of their job."

"Fair enough."

"It was a smart approach, but too easy. I will have to see what I can do to improve my personal security. Thanks for highlighting the holes in our system, though." Sergei paused, seemingly thinking of how to make it more difficult to find him. "I guess you want help to get safely out of Russia and back to Europe? For a friend, I can do that."

"Actually, that wasn't what I had in mind." DeVille let the answer hang in the air. He knew that if Sergei agreed to his request, there would be no way back. He would either have blood on his hands or he would be dead.

But he had to do it.

After a couple of seconds he saw that Sergei understood and he saw the face of the Russian turn into a smile.

"Again, if you ever need a job, we always need people like you."

"Let's keep our cooperation focused on this issue first."

"Sure. In return for my help, just promise me you'll consider it."

"Agreed. Will you help?"

"I assume you want to go back to China? The challenge has turned personal?" Sergei seemed to know the answer, so he did not leave time for DeVille to answer. "I can get you back into China, I can send with you a couple of good men, I can arm you, and I should be able give you intelligence about Wang's whereabouts."

"I also need to take out the other Chinaman," DeVille said.

"Okay, that can be done."

"And a CIA agent."

# CHAPTER 45

*Norwegian Sea*
*April 26ᵗʰ – 09:55*

The half-digested breakfast landed on top of a wave and was immediately swallowed by the sea. Umeira retched twice more. He wiped his mouth, leaned back from the railing, and took a couple of deep breaths. The air was fresher than the freshest air he had ever experienced in the mountains of Vedeno in Chechnya. It was the only good thing about the sea. He still felt sick, but there was nothing left in his stomach, so he went back onto the bridge.

White, foamy waves were all he could see. He was soaked after his five-minute bout outside. The positive thought about the fresh air disappeared—he hated the sea.

The storm had lasted almost three days, and had drifted the ship farther north than Umeira thought possible. They turned back this morning. He had given the first officer a thorough beating in the cabin where the decaying body of the captain was. Pretty quickly he told Umeira they were around three days away from the gas platform.

Just before the storm, he received a message from Abdul Aziz to stay close to the coast and possible targets, but to wait for his orders before detonating the bomb. Normally this would not cause Umeira to believe anything was amiss. But his leader was known for never waiting if there was a possibility to make a successful strike. Aziz believed waiting only reduced the chance of success—one of many reasons why there was friction with other rebel groups in the Caucasus.

Another reason for Umeira's skepticism was that the message was written in grammatically correct Arabic. He knew Aziz was a scholar, but he used to include a lot of words typical of the Medina area in Saudi Arabia's western region, where Aziz had grown up.

Then they saw a news broadcast on CNN, and Umeira's suspicions were confirmed. A taped message from a leader of a rival separatist group was shown. It said that all jihadists would unite to revenge the killing of Abdul Aziz by Russian forces. Although they disagreed on a number of issues, anyone who was killed fighting the Russians on behalf of the Almighty would be revenged. The CNN anchorman continued by saying the Russian military declined to comment.

Umeira did not feel any sadness—only rage.

It meant that Aziz was not the sender of the message.

The Russians were trying to deceive him and have him wait before detonating the bomb.

*Probably so they can attack first.*

He was now determined to blow up the ship and the gas platform as soon as possible.

*But why do they want us to stay close to the target?*

Umeira could not figure out the reason, but it did not matter. He had to make a decision and so he did. He was going to make Aziz proud and earn both of them the right to enter the heavenly kingdom.

The first officer, who was very accommodating now after the earlier beating, said they were not able to do more than eight knots in the storm. The Euphausia was about five hundred fifty nautical miles away from the gas platform. The weather forecast claimed the storm would continue at its current strength for the next few days.

Umeira figured it out himself. It was three days back to the platform. He had managed to pick up quite a bit of navigational skills while aboard this ship. There was no need to beat the answer out of the first officer, but it seemed like a good idea. A way to release some of the anger he felt for Aziz's death.

The important part was that in less than seventy hours, there would be an explosion which would terrify the world. There would be an explosion which would help the Chechens, and their Uighur brethren, in their fight for freedom.

There would be an explosion which would revenge Abdul Aziz's death.

# CHAPTER 46

*Shanghai, China*
*April 26th – 20:20*

Every thirty minutes, the window of the black Toyota saloon rolled down a few centimeters and the large Russian, who called himself Konstantin, lit up a cigarette. The smoke filled the car and it seemed like none of it even attempted to escape through the open window. It bothered DeVille, although he was not sure if it was because of the stink in the car or because it made him want a cigarette himself.

*Probably the latter.*

The radio was broadcasting, on low volume, a song, probably, that sounded like stomping feet, interrupted every few seconds by a human scream. The radio station was preset, and on, when they took over the car. Strangely enough, neither of the two Russians sitting in the front had even attempted to change the channel or just simply turn it off.

They had been sitting in the car, outside Wang's building, for nearly three hours, and DeVille felt like a smoked mackerel—but smelled worse.

*So much has happened since I stood outside the same building three weeks ago.*

The two Russians sitting in the car with him were both Sergei's men. Obviously thugs and hardened criminals, but a class above the Matrix-men from Sergei's garage. Sergei had kept his word and sent him two good soldiers.

Konstantin towered a head above DeVille, and when he was not smoking he sat and rubbed a reddish goatee that framed his always open mouth. It amazed DeVille that the beard had not worn off with this constant rubbing.

The other Russian called himself Alex and was the same height as DeVille, but with his wide shoulders he looked twice the size. Sitting in the driver's seat, he would turn back every few minutes and look at DeVille, with the face of a kid who suspected him of hiding candy. Except the candy was to kill a man. His eyes, on the other hand, said nothing.

Neither Konstantin, nor Alex, wore black leather jackets or black jeans.

It had been very easy to travel back to China. Within three hours of disconnecting from Sergei on Skype, a Russian passport with a Chinese tourist visa was handed to him by one of the 'Matrix-men.' DeVille thought the name printed in the passport, *Igor Igorovich*, had a nice ring to it.

Around two in the morning, Konstantin and Alex arrived and shook hands with him. Within minutes, the three of them were driving to the local airport. From there, they took a flight to Novosibirsk, connected with a flight to Hong Kong and then to Shanghai. The passport did its job without a glitch.

One of Sergei's men at the airport in Novosibirsk had delayed the flight to Hong Kong by two hours so they could make the connection, Alex told DeVille. How was not mentioned, and DeVille decided it was better not to satisfy his curiosity.

They arrived in Shanghai early in the afternoon and a man waiting for them at the airport, introduced himself as

Sergei's *ambassador* to China. Apparently well briefed by Sergei, he got down to business right away. His expensive silk suit with its modern cut, made him look more like an interior designer than a gangster. A large Mercedes took them to Wang's building.

China was not only the world's factory, but also the world's biggest producer of pirate copies. Everything from movies to books to artillery weapon was copied here. The Russian mafia shipped billions' worth of fakes into Russia every year. DeVille remembered the number from the fact file he had read before meeting with Sergei in Dubai. That was the reason why they had *branch offices*, as Alex called them, in most large Chinese cities.

They knew Wang was inside his building. One of the ambassador's men had kept track of Wang since yesterday and confirmed that Wang was in the building. It was three hours since they had relieved the man and taken over his car. Konstantin had been busy polluting it with cigarette smoke ever since. By now, without having seen the pack, DeVille was positive Konstantin smoked Marlboro Lights.

Sergei had been a busy man after they disconnected from Skype. He arranged to send both Alex and Konstantin with him, had the fake passport made, and ensured his men in Shanghai were ready to assist them.

*Am I somehow in debt to Sergei and the mafia?*

Not really, he decided. He was actually doing the mafia a favor if the Tengriist conspirators were put out of action.

Also, DeVille was about to risk his life again.

*Sergei is sitting safe in Dubai.*

It rained, just like that day three weeks ago when he had waited for Wang for the first time. At least this time he was sheltered in the backseat of the car. Droplets of water trickled into the car through the opening in Konstantin's window.

The plan was simple—probably too simple, DeVille thought. But he could not think of any better way. The two

Russians had not suggested differently when he told them the plan.

Ideally, Wang would lead them to the other Chinaman. That would be lucky. But it was unlikely the two of them would meet up in plain sight, and even if they did, there would be security around.

*Just like at the temple.*

More realistically, they would have to capture Wang and coerce him into revealing the other man's identity and whereabouts.

DeVille doubted Wang would be very cooperative, but he was hoping Alex and Konstantin were well versed in methods of getting people to talk.

Konstantin flicked the cigarette butt out of the gap between glass and car and pressed the button to roll up the window. He moved around in his seat and said a few words in Russian to Alex.

*A sign that they're getting impatient.*

He had explained plan B to them and neither of them had flinched, even if it was beyond difficult and dangerous.

Konstantin pulled out his gun, checked the magazine, and then put it back in his pocket. He turned to DeVille, looked at him with pleading eyes, and asked, "Can we go in and take him down now?"

# CHAPTER 47

Wang paced the living room of his large apartment. He had done it—he had found another income source. The income from the Arctic mining was almost certain to be less than anticipated now.

*If any at all.*

The joy he felt got even better looking at the minimalistic harmony of the interior in front of him. His apartment was sparsely furnished—only two large, sharp-edged white couches, and a square, chrome coffee table.

The couches were facing away from the wall-to-ceiling windows overlooking the skyline of Shanghai. Instead, anyone sitting was given a view to some of the art that decorated the three white walls.

*My priceless possessions.*

The art had no connection to his Tengriist beliefs. It was all contemporary art by young talented Chinese artists. The common denominator with all the art was hidden messages of social critique. Only someone who knew what they were looking for could see this.

One of the paintings showed a woman with a scar on her stomach, possibly after a cesarean, with the stitches painted in a dark bronze color. The stitches looked like they had been hastily sewn by an amateur. If you turned the painting upside down, the stitches resembled the Chinese characters for *democracy*.

Making art that criticized the government was dangerous in China. That pushed prices of such art up, but Wang believed them to be worth every yuan he had paid. The hidden critique of the government, he disagreed with, but an artist willing to sacrifice himself and his family for a statement of criticism fascinated him.

Wang let the dark wooden floor warm his bare feet as he walked over to one of the couches and sat his naked body down. The leather felt cold, but at the same time good. He was both joyous and relieved. With the alternate revenue source, they could, as soon as the Euphausia exploded, move ahead at full speed.

He had celebrated by having sex with the maid. It was the sixth time in four days. He wondered if he was addicted. There was something arousing about having full control of a young, innocent woman. Whether or not she enjoyed it, she never attempted to avoid him when he wanted her, and she performed her domestic duties just like before. Obviously she enjoyed it, he convinced himself.

The maid interrupted him, coming out of the bedroom. Her uniform was a bit untidy and Wang could tell she had not brushed her hair. The classy, but ragged, look made him warm inside. She gave him a half-second, awkward smile as she passed him. He concentrated on staring straight through her and onto his art.

Wang peeked into the bedroom—the bed was made and his clothes nicely folded. It did not look like anything had happened in the room just a few minutes ago. He could not hide a smile.

*This girl knows her place in a man's house. Genghis Khan would have been proud of me.*

He walked into an adjacent room, converted into an altar to Tengri. There were no windows, and the walls were covered in dark mahogany. He closed the door and, still naked, knelt down on the bare concrete floor and draped a white scarf over his shoulders.

A bare spotlight in the ceiling illuminated the little room. He pulled out today's sacrifice from the built-in refrigerator. He looked straight into the eyes of the little feline. It curled around his hand as he pulled it out of the little cage, only big enough for a guinea pig. It was barely alive, having been chilled down for several hours. It reacted as if it were drugged.

Tengri demanded a live sacrifice and at the temple they used goats, but in the city that was not practical. Shanghai suffered from a large population of stray cats, meaning a steady supply of kittens was available.

The cat livened up, warmed by his hands and uttered a sickly meow. With a butcher's precision, he slit the throat of the cat and quickly parted the animal in one large and four smaller pieces while repeating a prayer to Tengri.

*Guide me in the right direction.*

The large piece represented Tengri's power, while the four smaller ones represented himself and the three other Khagans.

A red river of blood trickled towards the drain in the corner, following the same route as so many other rivers of blood. Even though the room was washed after each sacrifice, a clear red vein in the concrete led towards the drain.

When finished, he walked satisfied into his bedroom and showered off the cat's blood, the scent of sex, then dressed. He went to his study and picked up the phone. It was a phone call he was excited to be making.

*Finally I have something good to tell Wu.*

Wu picked up after two rings.

"Good evening, Khagan," Wang said a little too fast, realizing his excitement was probably easily noticed by Wu.

"Good evening to you as well, Khagan Wang. It sounds like you have good news. I have been waiting for you to call. I have good news as well, but please share yours first."

"I have solved our cash flow issue." Wang enjoyed a few seconds of silence.

"How?"

"There is something which we will have access to after you and Khagan Alexandrovich start your offensive against the terrorists. And it will be plenty of it too. Do you know what that is?"

"I do not know. Spit it out, Khagan."

"Terrorists and political prisoners. Or in my scenario— laborers. I am sure we cannot kill them all, so why not use these prisoners for our own good? It is better they work than sit in a jail and rot. They can do that after we have exhausted them."

"What do you want them to do?" Wu sounded skeptical.

"I still own that huge piece of farmland in Tibet. It would be perfect for a labor camp or a prison. The government leases the land for a labor camp at above market rate, we use the prisoners to work the fields and sell whatever we'll have them grow."

"And that will generate enough cash?"

"It should be more than enough to cover any interest on money we would have to borrow to get the Arctic Ocean mining rights."

"Okay, then. It is not a bad suggestion."

*The bastard! Why will he never give me the full credit I deserve?*

"And I know just how we can arrange that," Wu continued. "I have volunteered to take charge of a newly established anti-terrorism section. I can sign the lease for your land."

"Excellent. That makes it easy." Wang's mood improved again.

"And it gets better—the position raises me to an advisor to the president on national security issues, and I will be the public face in the battle against terrorism. *I could not have planned it better.*"

Wu told Wang he would start in the new position in a week's time and he was allowed to take with him all the men he trusted from his current department. "A week works out well as I would not want that ship of yours to blow up while I am on duty. It is better that I come in and clean up afterwards," Wu told him before they hung up.

Wang stood up and felt optimistic for the first time in several weeks. He looked out of the window and at the sky, mumbling an apology to Tengri.

He had passed the test.

A celebration was fitting, so he decided to go to his favorite French bistro, Rogier's, for dinner and drinks. Their food could be better, but their wine cellar had the best selection of any restaurant or hotel in Shanghai. Although a French bistro, they stocked the American Joseph Phelps Insignia range—Wang's favorite red wine.

He put on his coat, grabbed an umbrella, and looked into the kitchen. The maid had not started cooking dinner yet.

*She looks exhausted. But I can still see the girlish, rosy glow on her cheeks.*

"Don't bother with dinner. I'm going out for a couple of hours. Relax a little bit and save your energy for when I return."

# CHAPTER 48

"No." DeVille saw the disappointment on Konstantin's face, but it would be suicidal to try to break in during daytime. Wang would still be in his office and there would be many of his underlings there. Like in other Asian countries, DeVille knew it was unacceptable to leave the office before the boss.

After midnight it would be easier, as Wang should be in his apartment. Still very dangerous, so he hoped plan A worked.

Konstantin said something in Russian to Alex who responded with a giggle.

*Probably not a compliment.*

*Bloodthirsty gangsters giggling like schoolgirls.*

*Are they as good as Sergei promised?*

He decided to compromise with the Russians. After all, he needed them if this endeavor was to have any chance of success.

"All right, guys. Here's what we'll do. We won't try to follow Wang. It could be days before he meets up with the other Chinese guy anyway. So we'll grab Wang as soon as we have the opportunity. Okay?" DeVille looked at the faces of the two Russians for confirmation that they understood him.

Konstantin rubbed his goatee twice before he nodded. Alex just shrugged.

Twice more Konstantin polluted the inside of the car with his cigarettes before DeVille jumped up in the backseat.

"Him! The man in the beige coat and the Burberry umbrella that just came out," DeVille said. "The checkered umbrella," he added, unsure if the two Russians knew what Burberry was.

*Idiot. Of course they do.*

These guys had probably copied thousands of Burberry items and were experts on designer fashion brands.

"Got him," Alex said, flicking his gun's safety switch.

DeVille waited until Wang crossed the street to the side where they were and they saw him walk in the opposite direction.

"Go! Go! Go!" Adrenalin rushed through DeVille's body.

The two Russians exited the car without a sound and headed towards Wang at a fast, but natural, pace. Within ten seconds, they caught up with Wang and sandwiched him.

The three of them stopped and the Russians made Wang turn around. They said something to Wang, whose face changed into a concerned expression. They walked back towards the car and, only because DeVille knew, he saw the outline of gun barrels in the Russians' pockets—poking into Wang's side. To anyone else it just looked like three men who knew each other well. The desperate look on Wang's face was of no concern to DeVille. Most people on the street would do their best to avoid eye contact. No one would register that something was amiss.

Alex opened the rear door and Konstantin pushed Wang's head down, forcing him in. Wang was now squeezed between DeVille and Konstantin.

"Surprised that I'm alive?" DeVille could not help himself and smiled. The expression on Wang's face, like a kid who had just woken up from a nightmare, made DeVille know that he was justified in doing this.

Wang tried to get out past Konstantin, but then he seemed to remember the guns and gave up the attempt.

"We're going to have a little talk. You, me, and my two Russian friends here." DeVille saw that Wang stiffened as he heard the nationality of Alex and Konstantin.

Alex slammed the automatic gearbox into 'drive' and the car sped off from the curb. Even though it was only two hours to midnight, the traffic was heavy. It took them thirty minutes to drive the kilometer or so to the nearest highway. Sergei's branch office was located in a warehouse close to the port area, just across from Gaodong Park.

An hour later, they pulled up to a windowless building that looked more like a bunker. It had a sign on the roof with both Chinese and Cyrillic writing.

*The legitimate face of the Russian mafia.*

DeVille was sure the inside was far from legitimate.

Alex pressed a button on a small square remote Velcroed to the dashboard. A garage door slowly opened. Alex steered the saloon over a speed bump with care and entered the garage.

Strong fluorescent tubes in the ceiling switched on and killed their night vision.

*Motion sensor?*

The garage was neatly organized, a Great Wall pickup truck parked to their left and a work desk in front of them. No tools visible, but there were drawers in a cabinet next to the work desk. To the right of him was an unpainted concrete wall with a door in it. DeVille guessed the garage took up about a third of the warehouse.

"We won't be bothered here," Alex said and killed the engine. Konstantin pulled out his gun and stepped out of the car. He motioned for Wang to follow. When the

Chinaman hesitated, the Russian grabbed him by his collar and pulled him out.

"Sit down," Alex ordered Wang and unfolded a camping chair taken out of the trunk of the Toyota. Again hesitation and again Konstantin used the grip he had on Wang's collar to force him down in the chair.

"You idiot. You think you're going to change anything by killing me?" Wang shouted at DeVille.

Alex returned to the trunk and grabbed a roll of duct tape. Konstantin aimed the gun at Wang while Alex taped the Tengriist's arms and legs to the chair. DeVille stood expressionless and watched panic grow in the eyes of the Chinaman. He wriggled around, obviously to see how well he was attached to the chair.

"You fuck," DeVille said in a low voice. He planted his fist in Wang's face and felt it crush the bones in his nose. A good feeling. Blood ran down Wang's face, hissing noises coming out of his nostrils.

"Who was the other Chinese guy? The bastard who tortured me?"

Wang spat a mix of blood and saliva towards DeVille, but most of it did not get farther than DeVille's shoes.

"Listen, you creep. If you're going to have any chance of getting out of here alive, you'll tell me what I want to know." The smile on DeVille's face disappeared and the adrenalin in his body mixed with rage. It scared him that, for a second, he would rather see Wang dead than get the answers he needed.

He kicked Wang so hard in the chest that the chair toppled over backwards. His head slammed into the concrete floor and DeVille worried he had overdone it.

Then Wang groaned. Alex and Konstantin lifted the chair up again. DeVille asked again, but Wang still refused to talk so he nodded towards the Russians and they joined in with a few hits to his face and Wang's already broken ribs. It was obvious that it was not the first time the two Russians had physically interrogated someone. They only hit hard enough to inflict pain, while at the same time they kept the Chinaman alive and conscious.

*Can I do it? I have to.*

"Last chance." DeVille made sure he stared straight into Wang's eyes.

"No," he hissed. "Go ahead and kill me. I'm not talking."

"You're not going to be that lucky. We'll do something else instead. I'm not as good as your friend was, but I'm sure I can cause some pain. We have all night, don't we? Alex, please hand me the tool."

Wang's blood-soaked and swollen face watched Alex fetch a scalpel from the trunk of the car and hand it to DeVille.

"Your friend introduced me to a new hobby. Let's do some Ling Chi."

# CHAPTER 49

*Norwegian Sea*

It was minus twenty-five degrees Celsius in the storage hold and it felt exactly how Umeira imagined it would do. Despite the thick boots, prised off the crew member who was about to die, he could not feel his feet. They were as numb as they would have felt if they were asleep. His fingers felt like they were welded to the meat cleaver, and the frost stung his face as if he were in a sandstorm. His nose was stuffed up with what felt like frozen droplets.

Umeira feared for his stomach contents, but luckily there was no fish smell in the large hold. The ship seemed to rock a little less down here compared to on the bridge.

*Is it a shame to blow up a brand new vessel that could help feed the hungry?*

*Sure.*

He hated the sea. The ship itself was different. He had grown fond of it. It was, after all, the vessel which would transport him to heaven. In a way he was at one with the ship.

His focus changed back to the meat cleaver which seemed like an extension of his arm. He needed to be quick in this temperature. The six crew members who stood around him shivered. He could not risk losing his audience.

A cry pierced the perfect silence. Umeira looked at the source of the cry; the crew member lying in front of him. Two tight ropes were attached to opposite bulkheads of the storage hold and to the man's wrists, holding him down on his stomach.

The man was guilty of a crime in Umeira's eyes. The man had disobeyed him and tried to escape. Two hours ago, this man and two other members of the crew managed to sneak out of one of the portholes in the galley where they were supposed to be preparing dinner. They got up on deck unnoticed, and tried to lower an inflatable raft into the sea. One of Umeira's men saw them from the bridge and fired at them.

They approached the sailors and Umeira knocked the closest man unconscious with the butt of his rifle. That was the man who was now underneath his boot. The two others cut the lines to the raft and as it fell down they threw themselves after it.

*Are there sharks in the North Sea?*

If there were, then these two men were definitely becoming someone's lunch. Several rounds of machine gun fire were sent towards the raft—sinking it and most likely killing anyone in or around it.

He was now about to let the six remaining crew know the consequences of disobeying him. They were all going to die soon anyway, but the crew did not know that. He needed them to cooperate until that final moment. The scene he was about to display in front of them should do the trick.

With two fingers, Umeira touched the bloody captain's hat in a salute to the men around him.

Umeira's stiffened arms raised the meat cleaver and he held it over his head for a couple of seconds before he threw his arms forward. He struggled to keep his balance as the ship danced to the rhythm of the waves. The cleaver entered the man's neck just above his shoulder blades. The cleaver was sharp enough to go straight through and decapitate the man.

The cook was a professional and kept a good tool.

The first gush of blood moved the head twenty centimeters to the side, giving the audience a clear look at the headless body. As the heart stopped and the burst of blood changed into a trickle, it looked like a raw, bloody rib-eye steak had replaced the head on top of the man's shoulders. One of the crew retched twice before giving in and vomiting on his own boots. The others whimpered and turned away. Umeira's pupils had learned their lesson.

The crew members were taken back to the mess room. It was made sure the galley was locked.

*No more escaping through the portholes.*

Umeira stepped onto the bridge where a cup of hot coffee from a thermos helped return the feeling to his feet and fingers. The radar screen told him there were five hundred twenty miles left.

*It is taking forever to get back to the platform.*

Soon, hundreds of infidels would die, and he would become a great martyr.

# CHAPTER 50

*Shanghai, China*

DeVille chuckled without knowing why. The terror in Wang's eyes, when he mentioned Ling Chi, was not something which would normally amuse him. On the other hand, nothing that had happened over the last few weeks could be characterized as normal.

*It's just a way for my mind to blow off steam.*

Both Alex and Konstantin smiled.

*Do they know what Ling Chi is?*

If they did, it should build respect with these hard-core mobsters.

"Are you up for some Ling Chi, Wang?" DeVille approached him with a firm grip on the scalpel, moving it back and forth in front of Wang to make sure his eyes were focused on the shiny blade.

DeVille cursed silently at himself as he let out another chuckle. He noticed that Wang's dark brown pants were now a shade darker around the crotch.

*I'm being childish. But at least I didn't wet myself when they performed Ling Chi on me up in the mountains.*

He positioned the scalpel neatly behind Wang's ear and grabbed hold of the lobe with his other hand. Wang did not move. A red droplet slowly emerged as DeVille carefully perforated the skin with the tip of the scalpel.

He hoped it was enough to get Wang to talk.

It was not. Wang just sat there, staring into space.

Alex grabbed the scalpel out of DeVille's hand and cut off half of Wang's ear in one swift movement. The Chinaman screamed and tried to move his tied hands up to his ear, but had to give up. It bled a lot. DeVille was taken by surprise and stood back. Konstantin laughed. Alex moved towards the other ear. Wang screamed even louder.

DeVille hurried forward and put a hand on Alex's arm. "Don't take the other ear. He needs to hear our questions. How about a finger or something instead?"

Alex stopped and looked at him before seeming to agree and positioning himself in front of Wang's hand.

Wang's scream turned into a hissing noise and he seemed to struggle to look DeVille straight in the eyes. "Okay! Okay. Stop. I'll tell you whatever you want to know."

"The other Chinese guy?" DeVille was happy Wang was willing to cooperate. He took the scalpel from Alex and hoped they would not need it anymore.

*Has the good in me returned?*

He held the scalpel in front of the Chinaman so the blood on it could drip onto Wang's shirt.

"His name is Wu. He's a lieutenant general of state security in Beijing."

"Is he in Beijing now?"

"I think so. I don't know. I don't know his routine. I don't even know where he lives."

"Come on, you got to give me a little more than that." DeVille moved the scalpel closer to Wang.

"Okay, okay. Please. He works in the headquarters in Xiyuan, next to the Summer Palace."

DeVille had never been to the Summer Palace, but he knew it well. It was on his bucket list of places to visit. Something told him he would not get to delete it from the list anytime soon.

"What's Stella Hanson's involvement?" This was the question that was burned into his mind like the intensity of a desert sun.

"The CIA agent? I don't really know. I heard about her for the first time up in Altay a few..." Wang stopped mid-sentence, like he did not to want to remind DeVille about what had happened in the mountains.

*As if I could forget…*

"Come on. Don't bullshit me. You'd never let anyone into your circle of Genghis Khan wannabes unless you knew all about them."

Wang glanced at the scalpel and said, "She told us that she is Alexandrovich's niece and that the two of them have been sharing intelligence for a number of years. It was the first time we all heard about it."

"More?"

"There's nothing. I think she tried to kill you in Dubai in order to prove to us that she was trustworthy—but she failed." Wang spat out the last word.

*The CIA was behind the assassination attempt in Dubai? Is Stella a double agent?*

It did not make sense for the CIA not to know about her having a prominent uncle in the Russian navy. That was a liability. Their vetting would have discovered that, he assumed.

Anyway, all that mattered was that he had a name and a location for where to start looking for this Wu. A picture was not needed—the image of the man was burned into DeVille's cornea for eternity.

***

Wang knew he had said too much, but they had cut off his ear.

*What was I supposed to do?*

He needed to calm down and analyze the situation. He was not concerned about these men finding Wu. He was sure he could handle them, but he had to keep something back, to use to bargain his way out of this situation.

He was still surprised that DeVille was alive. Nobody should be able to survive such wilderness without any equipment or food. They had underestimated him, but still…

*Wu will not be happy when he finds out.*

"Where's the ship with the bomb going?"

"I do not know. The terrorists seem to have taken control of it. But I use the cook to spy on the captain for me. If you take me back to my office, I can contact him by satellite phone and find out." Wang hoped this little lie could be the key to his escape, but he had no idea how much DeVille knew about the Euphausia.

"Don't bullshit me, I'm sure you know everything about your expensive ship and where it's heading."

"No, I do not. I could not care less. It is part of the plan for the terrorists to blow up the nuclear missile somewhere. Where they do it does not really matter."

"I don't really care either. We're going to keep you in this warehouse with a gun and a scalpel close to your head. If we don't find Wu in Beijing, I'll make sure the scalpel is used first."

"Fine," Wang said, but he knew DeVille would never let him go, after finding Wu.

*I have to get out of this now.*

The two Russians came up to him and bent down to remove the tape which held his legs to the chair. He was heading for the trunk, but he had no idea if he would be alive or dead inside it. The Russians looked at him with disappointment, like two children who had just been told that they could not play any longer.

When they had cut loose both feet, Wang managed to wriggle his arms loose from the tape holding his wrists. While sitting, he launched both feet towards them—hitting them in the chest so they stumbled backwards.

By throwing his right arm around, he grabbed the chair and swung it back—slamming the Russian with the goatee on the side of his face. He tumbled over with a dark, wet, red cut on the side of his face. Wang felt the adrenalin pumping through him.

*I know I can get out of this. I am sure.*

* * *

"No!" DeVille shouted, knowing it was too late. Two rapid shots filled the garage with noise, smoke coming out of the barrel of Alex's gun.

Wang clutched his chest as he knelt down. Blood seeped through his fingers, before he collapsed facedown onto the concrete.

Konstantin staggered to his feet, holding the gash in his face with both hands. He looked at Wang before he kicked the lifeless head with all the power he had. DeVille pictured it separating from the Chinaman's body, but it only bobbed back to where it had been before the kick.

"Great. Now it just got twice as difficult to get the second guy," DeVille said with annoyance in his voice.

Alex stared at him with eyes far from apologetic. Konstantin found a first-aid kit in the trunk of the car and quickly bandaged his wound, making him look like a mummified zombie.

"We must leave now. Fast. Someone might have heard the shots," Alex almost whispered.

DeVille sensed the seriousness in the Russian.

He looked down at Wang's body, and the blood crawling out from underneath it. It reached Wang's outstretched left arm, where the dark blood contrasted with the deep gold of a huge Hublot decorating a now pale wrist. The sheer size of the dial on the skinny arm made Wang look like a child who had borrowed his father's watch.

"Why the hell not?" DeVille said out loud, smiled, and slowly shook his head.

# CHAPTER 51

*Beijing, China*
*April 28<sup>th</sup> – 10:15*

"Not many know that there are two summer palaces in Beijing, one called the Summer Palace and the other called the New Summer Palace. Both built in the early eighteenth century, but the *newer* of the two has history as an imperial site as far back as when Beijing was made the capital of the Jin dynasty in the twelfth century." DeVille was bored, but the look he got from Konstantin made him stop the history lesson.

Instead, DeVille forced himself to keep his focus on the other side of the road. The entrance to the headquarters of the Chinese state security. Their best chance of finding Wu would be to keep an eye on the building where he worked.

The setup was the same as in Shanghai—Alex and Konstantin in the front of the car and DeVille in the back. Except this time they were cramped in a tiny hatchback. Alex had suggested that a small car would blend in better.

The tight confinement meant that Konstantin's cigarette smoke, filling up the car every thirty minutes, was unbearable. DeVille told him so. Konstantin just looked at him and rolled the window all the way down, but the wind outside made the smell of the Marlboros drift back into the car again.

*Why hasn't Wu shown up yet? Is he even here?*

They had traveled the thirteen-hundred-kilometer distance between Shanghai and Beijing in just over five hours. At an average speed of two hundred fifty kilometers per hour. It was even more impressive if you counted the fact that they stopped at six or seven stations on the way. The Chinese high-speed trains could reach a top speed of almost four hundred kilometers per hour.

He wondered if it would have been better to confront Stella Hanson first, but he had decided against it. It was only a matter of days before Wu would know Wang was gone. It was quite possible he already knew. A man of Wu's caliber, who could smell danger around a corner, was not something DeVille needed.

Wu was dangerous enough as it was. He was a psychopath. There was a fair chance they would not make it out alive—another reason to go for Wu first. If Stella was in on this, she could kill him in a heartbeat. He could not risk that, before getting to Wu. Of the two of them, it was Wu he wanted the most.

At least by going after him first there was a better chance of accomplishing his goal—the promise he had made to Carina: stopping these evil men's plan. But right now, to avenge the humiliation from the mountains was just as important.

*Wu has to pay.*

*Just like Wang has done.*

DeVille knew it sounded wrong and he knew it was wrong, but most people had never been in such a situation—if they had, they would feel the same way.

*Feeling it and acting on it are two different things, though.*

That was what separated humans from beasts.

Today he did not care.

273

The need for revenge and the hatred was temporarily subdued after Wang was killed. But with the hunt on for Wu, the feeling reappeared. Deville was calm inside, genuinely hoping he would get out of this alive. A couple of days ago, he could not have cared less. But the change of heart added another emotion—behind calmness lurked fear.

The fear burst through without DeVille knowing why. Then he understood. He was staring straight at Wu. He was about seventy-five meters away, but DeVille would recognize that face from across a packed football stadium.

The high and clearly visible cheekbones stretched his face towards his ears. It looked diamond shaped. His narrow eyes, angled upwards, and his thin lips, were highlighted by the stretched face.

He would never forget that face.

"That's the guy. In the green coat. But we can't grab him here."

"Why?"

"There's bound to be CCTV all over the place. It's so close to a state building. It'll be way too dangerous. Okay?"

Both Alex and Konstantin looked at him expressionlessly. Finally, Alex nodded.

"Good. We need to hurry. I want Alex to follow him on foot. Stay as far away as you can, and if he enters a building make sure you wait outside. Okay?" Before DeVille could get an answer, the Russian was already out of the car. Letting Wu out of their sight would be dangerous, and DeVille was certain the three of them needed to work together to take down Wu.

"I drive," Konstantin said without expecting an answer and climbed over to the driver's side. He got in and started the car. He squeezed the hatchback out of the parking bay they had occupied for almost three hours. DeVille could still see Wu's back. Beijing traffic was the worst. DeVille once read about someone who was stuck in traffic for three days. The traffic today was perfect, moving at the same speed as if they were walking. They would neither lose Wu nor overtake him.

After about five minutes, they were still a hundred fifty meters behind Wu—Alex somewhere in between. The sidewalk Wu was on had few pedestrians.

With the speed of a diving eagle, suspicion struck DeVille.

*Something doesn't make sense.*

A spymaster like Wu, guaranteed to have enemies, had never looked back to see if anyone was following him. Neither did it make sense that a high-ranking Chinese official would walk somewhere. He was of the chauffeured elite.

It made DeVille wonder what had happened to Wang's body. Either Sergei's *embassy* had taken care of it in a professional way or someone had found it. If it was the latter, Wu knew that his fellow conspirator was dead, and that he was most likely the next target.

*Does Wu know he's being followed?*
*Does he know that it's me that's following him?*
*Are we walking into a trap?*

# CHAPTER 52

DeVille could only hope that Alex still had Wu within eyesight. The traffic came to a standstill and Wu rounded a corner. When the traffic moved again and they got the car around the corner, they saw neither of them.

There was the possibility that Wu had turned right. Not just once, but twice. He could not have kept going straight. There were no people that far up front. Best chance was that Wu had crossed the street. With slow-moving traffic, it was not like he would have had to wait for the pedestrian lights to turn green.

"We must take the second left," Konstantin said as he drove and read a text message at the same time. "Alex says that the Chinaman walked into a building."

"Did he say what kind of building?"

"No."

There was not much they could do if Wu entered a store or another crowded place, besides wait for another opportunity. At least they had located Wu. Since he was on foot, they could easily follow him when he exited the building. He would probably head for his apartment, a good place to intercept him.

*Can we grab Wu on this street or are we still too close to the state security building?*

"We probably should wait until he gets to his apartment," DeVille said monotonously.

"There's Alex," said Konstantin with his index finger in one direction while his eyes scanned farther down the road for a parking spot. Half a block down, a car pulled out from the curb. Thirty seconds after they had parked, DeVille was standing next to Alex.

"He's in there," Alex said calmly as he pointed to a building covered in scaffolding.

DeVille took a long look at the structure, trying to determine what type of building it was, but the scaffolding did a good job of keeping it a mystery. There were no workers on the scaffolding either.

Then it dawned on him that Wu was working overtime. They had struck lucky. It was Saturday. They could have been stuck outside the state security building until Monday before Wu would have shown up.

"I'll go in and have a look, you two wait here in case Wu comes out of another door." DeVille made a decision, "If he comes out, grab him. I'll be right back."

The double door was not locked and DeVille stepped inside. It was well lit inside, considering there were no lights on and the windows were covered in scaffolding. DeVille saw what kind of building it was.

A theater.

Red velvet, dark wood, and gold-colored metal was everywhere. An attempt to copy a western-styled theater. Three huge chandeliers hung from the ceiling.

*An unsuccessful attempt at replicating the* La Scala *in Milan.*

When he passed the ticket booth and the foyer, and entered the theater hall it reminded him more of the stage from *The Muppet Show* than *La Scala*. It was shaped like a half-circle with four rows of theater boxes that went from one side to the other, and he felt caged. The stage looked, in the dim lighting, like it could easily be fifty meters wide.

He knew there and then that he would never be the same person as before. He had changed in a way he believed was irreversible.

*Someone will die soon and that someone is possibly me.*

*Will this help me to come to terms with Carina's death?*

*Probably not.*

*Forgive me…*

The heavy, red carpets made it easy for him to walk quietly. Two silhouettes appeared down in the orchestra pit. One of the shapes was Wu, and DeVille was certain the second person was a woman. They were talking, but DeVille could not make out the words.

He took a long, careful look around to see if there were any others. The private boxes got an even more thorough scan from him, but he could not see anyone or anything suspicious. He crouched and moved forward.

The silhouettes walked up onto the stage. DeVille inched closer and saw it *was* Wu. He also saw that the other person was a woman—Stella Hanson.

He had found the two of them together.

*Is that good or bad?*

*Can I take them both out?*

*Or will the two of them have an easy time taking me out?*

The grip of the gun in his jacket pocket felt cold as he pulled out the Glock pistol, supplied by Sergei's ambassador in Shanghai. He hid behind the eighth row and listened. Now he could hear them.

"Alexandrovich speaks highly of you, but it's in my nature not to trust anyone. Not even Alexandrovich. Not even my fellow Khagans. I always demand proof." Wu spoke in a monotone voice, giving DeVille the chills. The same voice he had spoken in during the torture.

"What kind of proof do you want?" Stella sounded frustrated.

"How about you give me something that you think can convince me? Then I will decide myself if I am convinced."

"What if it doesn't convince you?"

"Then you have a serious problem, my dear."

"I can give you any information you want. What about the number of marines on duty at any time of the day at the embassy?"

"Not good enough. Why would I care about that?"

"Okay, I can do better. What about a copy of your dossier with the CIA?" Stella put on a smile, beaming confidence.

"Tempting, but we both know that you can alter it before I get it. Or just give me a fake one."

"True, but I can guarantee you that there will be a surprise or two in there. I'm sure you'll find it interesting."

There was a small beep and Wu reached for his pocket and fished out a phone. Wu's face stretched into a smile.

"I don't need any information, but I have the perfect test for you. If you succeed doing this, you'll have proven your loyalty."

"Sure thing. Bring it on."

Wu raised his arm, and DeVille sensed movement behind him. The hand holding his pistol was kicked before he could turn around. The Glock rattled along the floor and the echo went on forever in the hushed theater. DeVille tried to turn around, but froze. The ice-cold steel felt like it was about to choke him. A knife was held to his throat.

"Stand up," the person behind him whispered into his ear.

"Welcome, Mr. DeVille," Wu said. "I did not think I would see you so soon after our encounter in the mountains. But I am very glad that you showed up. You will be the perfect test for the enchanting lady over here. I believe the two of you have already met?"

DeVille was pushed forward. Wu said something in Chinese. There were two men behind DeVille, both with murder written all over them.

They must have been hiding somewhere on the floor in between the seat rows. That was why he had not noticed them. The second man picked up DeVille's pistol from the floor and threw it to Wu.

DeVille breathed heavily. His hands moistened and images of what Wu had done to him up in the mountains flashed in front of him. The man he hated so much was in front of him—in control.

DeVille was scared.

He was shoved into the orchestra pit and was now within meters of Wu and Stella.

*Damn!*

*Why did I tell Alex and Konstantin to wait outside?*

*How long do I need to wait before they will come and rescue me?*

*What can I do to buy enough time?*

"This is how you can prove your loyalty to our cause," Wu said with a smile to Stella.

"What do you mean?" she asked.

"The way to earn my trust is simple. You've told us that you've already tried to kill DeVille once."

"Yes?"

"Kill him now. With his own gun."

# CHAPTER 53

"How did you know DeVille would show up?" Stella asked, accepting the gun handed to her by Wu.

"I did not. As I told you, I do not trust *you*. So, I made sure I had a couple of men follow me here from a distance. They also staked out the theater in case you were to try anything."

"Still doesn't answer the question."

"They spotted three people following me, and I immediately thought it was your guys. Turns out that it was my *skinless* friend DeVille."

DeVille's hope of being rescued by Alex and Konstantin disappeared fast, Wu being aware that they were around. Alex and Konstantin were hardened gangsters who had seen their share of bloodshed, but something told DeVille that even they would have a tough time against Wu and associates.

Wu seemed to read the worry on his face. "If you are hoping to be saved by your Russian friends, you can forget about it. They're both dead." Wu's finger made a slitting gesture, slowly, across his throat.

The knife blade pressing against DeVille's throat seemed even colder than ice.

"You damn idiot," Stella told DeVille and walked towards him. The man behind him released the pressure of the knife and withdrew a few paces to the side. She slapped him so hard that he stumbled back and onto a first-row seat.

"You have a death wish, don't you?" She pointed the pistol at him. "Head or chest, Wu?" she asked to the great amusement of the two Chinamen standing next to DeVille.

"Head will do just fine," Wu replied coldly, apparently not sharing the amusement.

DeVille closed his eyes. He heard Stella breathe and he braced himself for what it would feel like to get shot. He opened his eyes again and saw Stella put pressure on the trigger. He gave her his most pleading look.

Instinctively, he crouched down just as the gun fired. Two quick shots exploded and a growl rang in his ears.

*Where did the bullets hit me?*

He sensed the trickle of warm blood at the same time as an iciness shot up his arm.

But he was able to open his eyes. The two Chinamen who had been standing next to him a second ago both clutched their chests, before they fell to their knees—finally toppling facedown into the red velvet. DeVille looked at his arm and saw a light tear in the sleeve of his jacket.

It was not a bullet wound.

It was from the Chinaman's knife.

"Don't move!" Stella pointed the pistol at Wu.

"I guess I was right doubting your loyalty."

"Damn right. Now, keep those hands up."

"You know you'll never get out of here alive?" Wu smiled.

"No? You think you're the only one who came prepared? Well, that was dumb of you. The three guys you had outside, who slaughtered the Russians, they've been detained by the men I brought. They were there a long time before your guys arrived."

Wu's smile disappeared. DeVille decided he needed to get out of the theater. Wu and Stella were still locked in a staring contest, so he started a slow crawl towards the exit.

"DeVille! Don't make this difficult. You're staying."

His little flight attempt had been noticed and he stopped crawling and stood up. He looked to the stage and saw a smile return to Wu's face as he grabbed for something in his pocket.

Stella did not interpret the alarm in his eyes. DeVille leaped towards her, turning her around, and squeezed his finger into the trigger guard. He pushed her finger onto the trigger twice, at the same moment as Wu fished out a gun.

Both shots entered Wu's chest.

Wu's gun dropped to the floor, as if in slow motion, and he fell over. His thin lips got soaked in blood, before he twitched and coughed. Then he was completely still.

DeVille got to his feet and started to run. He was about five meters away from the exit when he was tackled to the ground. Stella was on top of him trying to get his arms together. In an attempt to wrestle free, he rolled to the side, and as soon as he was on his back he got his arms ready to deliver a punch.

Stella was quicker and he knew it was over when he felt the burning muzzle of the pistol pressed to his temple.

He froze.

"You damn idiot," Stella Hanson hissed.

# CHAPTER 54

"How dumb are you? I just saved your ass and you're trying to escape from me? I should probably shoot you for being a dumbass!" Stella spat out the words. She seemed to be struggling to repress the urge to slam the pistol into his head.

"Who did you say saved who?" He accepted that there was no way he would get out of the theater alone, so he regained his composure and spoke calmly. "I'm confused, who do you actually work for?"

"I'll explain it in a bit, but now we need to get out of here as fast as possible. We don't know how many men Wu had backing him up."

"No. First tell me why you tried to have me killed in Dubai?"

"It's complicated, but I'll explain that too when we get safely back to the embassy."

"No. You'll tell me now." DeVille wanted to know why the CIA agent had tried to have him killed, before he went anywhere with her.

"Listen, dumbass. I'm obviously not on Wu's side, since he's lying dead over there. And I have a gun pointed at you, so you're not in a position to protest about anything. So do what I tell you to do."

DeVille saw her point and, having no cards to bargain with, he shrugged and motioned that he would follow her.

They sneaked out through the foyer where DeVille spotted Alex and Konstantin lying lifeless, facedown. There was no blood visible, but the red velvet carpet was markedly darker in a large circle around each of the Russians' throats. Their deaths saddened him.

"They're your guys?" Stella pointed at the bodies.

"Yeah. Sort of." He had no idea how he was going to explain his hookup with the two Russians. Something he was sure he would have to do.

"Russian mafia?"

"Yes."

"How did you find Wu?"

"Long story." DeVille started to feel exhaustion overtake him like a tsunami on a beach, so he did not feel like telling the story right now.

"Wang?" Stella looked at him with part curiosity and part respect.

"Yes?"

"He's dead, isn't he?"

"Yes."

Just before they reached the entrance door, Stella motioned for him to stop. She fished a cell phone out of her belt holster and pressed a button twice. She opened the double doors just enough for a thin ray of light to penetrate and peeked outside without revealing herself to whoever was outside. Within forty-five seconds they both heard a car.

"On three, run through the doors and get in the backseat of the gray car with the black license plate out there."

Before he had time to argue, Stella started the countdown with her fingers. As she raised the third finger, she pushed him through the doors. He immediately saw the silver Infiniti saloon. Stella followed him through the doors.

They both ran the fifteen meters to the car and vaulted into the front and rear passenger seats.

"Back to base. Fast, but discreet," Stella said to the driver who pulled the car back out from the curb into traffic. How he would go fast anywhere was a mystery to DeVille, as traffic was as bad as it had been earlier. He placed his head solidly on the headrest and felt his body enjoy the sumptuous leather seats. The smell of hide was intoxicating. Ten seconds later, his body succumbed to exhaustion and he was asleep.

* * *

DeVille woke up as the car went over a speed bump in a dimly-lit parking garage. He had no idea how long he had been out. He checked his wrist and smiled. Probably a good hour.

"The embassy?" he asked without getting an answer. The driver parked the car and Stella exited, signaling for DeVille to do so too. They walked to a guarded elevator where two marines let her pass after inspecting her ID card. A fingerprint scanner opened the elevator doors and they both stepped in. DeVille noticed she pressed the button for the seventh floor.

His sleep-clouded mind saw there was a fourth floor and he remembered it was common in China to omit floor number four. An unlucky number, often associated with death. Number seven on the other hand was a number which meant luck in regards to love and relationships.

*Wouldn't the CIA be better placed on the fourth floor?*

They arrived at the seventh floor and he was guided into a meeting room only ten meters away from the elevator. The only other door around had another one of the fingerprint scanners.

Stella Hanson pointed to a chair, "Have a seat. I'll be back in a few minutes."

After ten minutes a man came in with a tray full of sandwiches and soda cans. DeVille's stomach rumbled at the sight, and the man smiled.

"Dig in," he said.

It took four sandwiches and about two hours before Stella returned.

"Let's get down to it. You thought I worked for these guys? Like a double agent?" She spoke the moment she walked in the door and sat down in the chair next to DeVille. It took him by surprise. Having expected her to sit opposite him, he had hoped to have the table between them as a buffer. She crossed her legs a little slower than what seemed natural.

It took him a second to regroup his thoughts. "I saw you on the screen up in the Altai Mountains."

"Oh yes, of course. I was very impressed. Both with the fact that you found their temple *and* the fact that you managed to escape alive."

"If you knew I was up there, why didn't you do something?"

"First of all, I'd already told you twice to stay out of this. Secondly, taking down this group of conspirators was deemed more important than saving your life. Sorry."

"Back to your part in this, please," DeVille said with a cold voice, having completely forgotten the intimidation he felt when she first sat down next to him.

"I'm the Russian admiral's niece."

"I know. Wang told me. But your uncle seemed pretty resolute that you were on their side."

"How I ended up in the US and him in the Russian navy is a long story, but that's unimportant. I didn't even know I had an uncle until he contacted me when I first joined the CIA twelve years ago. After a while of getting to know each other, he suggested discreetly that both our careers might benefit from some information sharing. I brought this to the attention of my supervisors. My uncle was already someone they were watching since he was quickly climbing through the naval ranks. They agreed to the information sharing to see what he was up to. We've only given him semi-classified material. Nothing harmful."

"I'm still not sure I understand."

"After some years, I think my uncle genuinely thought I was on his side and eventually he started to share more and more about the Tengriists and their plans. When the CIA understood the scope of their plans, an alarm went off, and I was tasked with finding a way to stop them." She paused, seemingly considering if she should tell DeVille more. "When the nuclear missile got stolen and it seemed like the Tengriists were behind it, we assumed they had some type of grand plan. It was that event that triggered action from our side."

"Well, Wu and Wang are dead. What about your uncle and the other Russian?"

"We're dealing with them. None of your business. Anyway, this is a debriefing, so I need you to tell me your story. How did you get to Altay? How did you kill Wang and how did you find Wu? All the details, please. Got it?" She waited for DeVille to nod, then turned on a voice recorder sitting on the table.

"What about the bomb?" It all of a sudden struck DeVille that even if they had taken out Wu and Wang, the terrorists whom the Tengriists tricked into stealing the bomb were still on the loose on the krill ship.

Stella switched the recorder off. "We're working on that, but it's not as dangerous as you think. It was a training missile they stole. It's still dangerous and is capable of serious damage, but it doesn't have a nuclear warhead."

"Was that part of the plan? Did you know that they were to steal a *fake* missile?" DeVille was confused.

"No, not at all. In addition to a very expensive fighter jet, the Dutch also lost one of their best pilots. We also believe that a couple of the crew on the krill ship are dead. Even if they worked for Wang, it doesn't make them guilty."

DeVille pictured Alex, Konstantin, the cabdriver in Dubai, and the man in The Hague. It seemed like Sergei had lost the most.

"You might think we don't have any scruples," Stella Hanson continued, "but you'd be wrong. Luckily for us, although not the dead fishermen, they took the missile to sea. There we can control the damage. If they had decided to blow it up in a city it would have been devastating."

The little smile that followed did not convince DeVille.

Stella continued, "The training missile was to be delivered to a base in the UK. When the missile went missing from the crash site, and we found an Uighur in custody who appeared to be part of this, I immediately suspected the involvement of the Tengriists. Not just because planning this whole operation was way out of the league of the Uighurs, but I also sensed from my uncle that they were close to doing something big. A few days later he told me how they had duped the Chechens and the Uighurs into stealing it, and he also told me how it would help their plan. Or our plan, as he told me. Remember, he thought I was part of it."

"So, it was just a stroke of luck that they stole a training missile and not a real one?"

"Sort of, and when you showed up, it gave us the perfect way in to try to foil their plan. At the end of the day, the Tengriists were more dangerous than the missile. If they'd gotten to power, more people than the missile could have killed would have died."

"*I* gave you the *way in*?" DeVille did not like the insinuation that they had puppeteered him this whole time. Sergei had also said it was lucky DeVille showed up in The Hague when he did.

"After you left the interview of the terrorist in The Hague, I followed you—part of standard procedure. Just to make sure you were who you claimed to be. To be honest, we don't really trust the EU's security vetting. But it was only when you were approached by this mafia guy we already had under surveillance that I got the idea. The original plan was to use the mafia to take down Alexandrovich and Bakunin. But the mafia is too cautious to work directly with the CIA, so cooperating with them through you without them knowing of our involvement seemed like a good plan."

"So why did you shoot the guy then?"

"First of all we didn't know if he was going to hurt you or not. I also had to make it look real."

"Right. Like with the cabdriver."

"Yes, *right.*"

"If so, why wasn't I allowed to leave the hospital?" DeVille thought it seemed like ages since his escape from the hospital in The Hague.

"We wanted the mafia to try to contact you again, so we could start the cooperation. The hospital seemed like somewhere you could be easily reached, while we had the perfect excuse to keep an eye on you to see who contacted you and when."

DeVille wondered if Stella knew about the flowers and the card he had received in the hospital, but he chose not to ask. "What will happen to Alexandrovich and Bakunin?" he asked instead.

"They're a lot less dangerous now without Wang and especially Wu," she said and added with a smile, "Also, I don't think the mafia is finished with them yet."

"Why did you try to kill me in Dubai?" He could not hold it in any longer.

"How did you know?" Stella's face showed a sign of surprise for the first time.

"I know, let's leave it at that." It was the first time DeVille felt he had the upper hand in this talk.

"The mafia?" She turned the tables on him before he had any time to enjoy the moment.

He just looked at her and decided not to tell her anything about the mafia.

"Doesn't matter. It was indeed the CIA who tried to *capture* you, but it was not on my orders. My supervisors made the decision without consulting me. I wanted to use you longer."

"What? Why?" DeVille wondered if being in the offices of the organization that had tried to kill him, or capture him as Stella claimed, was the smartest place to be.

"They knew you met with a high-ranking mobster." She looked at him with eyes that told him not to be cocky, eyes that told him that the CIA knew. "They also knew that you were on your way to China. They were nervous that you would screw up the plan. If the Khagans got suspicious that the CIA knew about their plan, they could have made contingency plans. They just wanted to question you and see what you knew and what you were up to. I also think they wanted to see if they could feed you some info that you could pass on to the mafia."

"Like what?"

"Doesn't matter anymore."

"They tried to kill me!"

"No, they didn't. They needed to make it look as credible as possible if you were captured. As I said, the mafia would never agree to cooperate with the CIA, so they needed to know for sure that you were not a friend of ours."

"Your guys certainly didn't behave friendly, so I guess they accomplished their assignment."

"And, you had been told to stay away from the case," she said, completely ignoring his attempt at wittiness. "Repeatedly. And they only shot at you in self-defense."

"And they killed the cabbie just to get to me?" DeVille saw images of the hole in the back of the cabdriver's head flash before his eyes.

"He wasn't as innocent as you think. He was working for the mafia. I guess the Russians didn't completely trust you either, so they made sure an accomplice drove you around to keep an eye on you. That worked out great for us, as then Sergei got reliable information that someone was indeed after you."

DeVille was shocked by the brutality of the CIA, but the feeling receded as he remembered his little session with Wang.

*I'm not any better.*

The cell phone on the table vibrated noisily twice and Stella Hanson looked at the screen for thirty seconds, seemingly scrolling down a long message. She smiled and looked at him. "Well, within a couple of hours that bomb, the ship, and the terrorists onboard will not be a problem anymore."

# CHAPTER 55

Umeira had barely fallen asleep for a well-deserved rest when one of his guys ran into his cabin and woke him up. The young English-speaking Chechen ranted about a helicopter, but Umeira did not see any logic or sense in what the soon-to-be-martyr was saying. Confusion clouded him like the grayness that hung over the ocean he had been staring at for weeks now.

The Chechen finally got Umeira to his feet and rushed him to the bridge. He went straight out onto the wing and saw it himself. A combat helicopter hovered in front of the ship. Umeira's knees weakened. Hanging from the helicopter's sides were batteries of menacing missiles.

"Stop the ship immediately and surrender," a loudspeaker said. "You have two minutes to stop the ship and have all men facedown on the aft deck."

\* \* \*

DeVille looked on with curiosity as Stella turned a computer screen towards him. It was three hours since they had finished the interrogation, or debriefing as Stella called it. An image of a ship filled the screen.

"This is the FV Euphausia," Stella said. "The picture is courtesy of a Predator drone."

The quality of the image baffled DeVille. He could clearly make out two men on the bridge wing, several on deck, and the helicopter hovering in front of the ship.

Light flashed from where the men aboard stood. Machine gun fire. The men were shooting bursts of automatic fire towards the gunship. It slowly increased its altitude before it tipped its nose and flew away.

\* \* \*

The threat only angered Umeira.

*Who do they think they are, trying to scare a man with a nuclear bomb?*

*I will be dead within hours anyway.*

Umeira knew a gunship would not be harmed by machine gun fire, so he expected it to come back. They were only an hour or so away from the platform, so all he needed was to buy some time.

"Here's what we're going to do. Ramzan will start getting the bomb ready to detonate. Mokhmad, you will get all the ship's crew up on the cargo deck. If the helicopter comes back we'll start shooting them one by one. That should hold them up long enough for us to get close enough to the gas platform. Understood?"

Umeira's men nodded.

"Yalla!"

Umeira stood on the bridge for the ten minutes it took for the crew to be assembled on deck, all bound and blindfolded. Mokhmad, being their best shooter, pointed his rifle at the first in the row. Umeira knew he could take them all out in a second or two.

Ramzan stepped out of the container, giving him the thumbs up. The bomb was ready and so was he. He saw his fellow Chechen lock the container and arm the booby trap.

Umeira smiled, knowing he was only a few moments away from carrying out one of the most spectacular attacks against the infidels in modern history—rivaling the twin tower attacks in New York. The cause of all the believers in the Caucasus would be front-page news all around the world.

*Russia will be humiliated.*

He would be a martyr reaping his rewards in heaven.

\* \* \*

"Look there," Stella said and pointed to the stern of the ship.

DeVille barely made out the small round head and the harpoon-looking thing that seemed to shoot four or five cans onto different spots on the boat. Then the head disappeared underwater again.

"US navy SEAL," Stella explained. "The canisters contain a completely odorless chemical agent which will seep through the ship and incapacitate everyone within thirty seconds. It's a much improved version of the one used during the Moscow theater hostage crisis."

"But a lot of people died from it in Moscow, didn't they?"

"I said improved, didn't I? And I also said incapacitate. It's still dangerous, but now it is fine as long as whoever is exposed gets respiratory assistance within half an hour. If not, they risk brain damage…and possibly death."

Next, five SEAL operatives inflated a life raft and placed the unconscious crew, now with oxygen masks, in it, before they entered themselves—and drifted away from the advanced fishing vessel.

"They're only taking the crew with them? Not the terrorists?"

Stella ignored his questions. "The SEALs have handheld minisubs which they'll use to propel the life raft as far away from the ship as possible. To avoid the shock wave."

* * *

One of Umeira's rewards was that he did not have to witness what happened seven minutes later. Fifty miles away, a submarine launched a Tomahawk cruise missile. It hit the FV Euphausia, blowing it up, together with Umeira, his men, and its cargo.

# EPILOGUE

DeVille loved the leather texture of his favorite chair. It was the one piece of furniture he never wanted to part from. The Eames lounge chair was something most people recognized, and many owned fake ones as well. His was not only an original, but it was from the late seventies, with Brazilian rosewood. The hues of dark orange with dark, almost black, stripes made the polished wooden back of the chair resemble tiger skin. That particular type of wood was rare and sought after as it had not been available for the last two decades, thanks to an embargo.

He had bought his at an auction three years ago at the stiff price of almost four thousand euros. He reckoned that it would be worth twice that amount in no time.

The view from his apartment was not great. Only the building across the street was visible through the large baroque windows in his living room. It was a brick building, its windows encased in blue drapes, and it smiled at DeVille with its sunburned face. It was not exactly overlooking the

Grand Place, but he would take the quietness of this neighborhood any day.

He had done a lot with the interior and he still had some ideas to improve it. It was not a large apartment, but he had knocked down all the walls that were not load-bearing. The living room looked huge with its white walls, whitewashed hardwood floors, and the old-fashioned ceilings. It used to be three rooms, but now the living room, kitchen, and study were all one.

DeVille was reading an online news article about two separate car bombings in Moscow. Both explosions happened at the same time, which led the media to speculate wildly about conspiracies and the potential connection between the two assassinated men.

One of the bombs killed the chief of the general staff of the Russian armed forces, while the other killed a prominent businessman. No one had claimed responsibility yet.

It was four days since DeVille had returned from Beijing, and he had been busy giving a report of all that had happened—with some minor omissions—to the chief of staff. After he finished, he got some verbal abuse from the chief of staff for not having updated him enough and for the fact that several people had been killed.

At the end of the day, though, it seemed they were satisfied with his work, as the chief of staff had signed off on his whopping sixty thousand euro invoice. DeVille would not want to do it again, but the pay was good.

*Not bad for a month's work.*

He flipped to another tab on his browser. It was about time to decide where to go as a reward. There were three places on his shortlist for a two-week vacation: the Maldives, the Azores, and Hawaii. He had never been to any of them. Each had a warm climate, rich history, great restaurants, and was known to provide five-star luxury and service. DeVille was torn.

He wondered if she would come with him. He could not ask.

He finished the article about the Moscow bombings and stared out into the gray Belgian morning. He remembered the soccer bet he had made the last time he was in the city. The last time he was home before all of this had happened.

Turkey against Austria. It took him a little while to find the results from over a month back. Eventually he found it on UEFA's homepage. Turkey had beaten Austria two goals to nil.

"Yes!" he shouted, behaving like a little boy who had just found his favorite toy car under the bed. After all, he had only won forty-five euros. Less than point-zero-one percent of what he had earned over the last month.

At that moment, his phone rang. He recognized the number. It was her.

"You sound happy this morning," a voice full of giggles said on the other end.

DeVille closed his eyes and pictured a Stella Hanson without clothes.

"It's nothing. Just some soccer results I came across. I'm a little bit behind on scores." He turned back to the iPad and shut it down.

The two of them had left Beijing together on the same flight. She had been due in Brussels to brief NATO on the latest development in the case.

During the flight they talked about everything and nothing, and Stella revealed a side of herself that DeVille did not expect her to have. She seemed compassionate and lovable, and could obviously leave work in a separate drawer when she wanted to.

DeVille had felt very comfortable in the seat next to her. They did not sleep for a second, constantly talking. Their teenage-like behavior must have been a nuisance for the other passengers, but they did not care.

He had wondered several times after their return if she had flirted with him or not.

"Do you want to grab dinner tonight after I'm done at NATO?" she asked.

"That sounds great," he said excitedly. "What time do you think you'll be done?"

"How about you pick me up outside the Radisson at eight? I should be done by then."

DeVille looked down at the large Hublot with the red-gold casing and black dial that sat on his wrist and smiled. He had not taken it off for over a week. The even deeper red-gold hands told him he would see her in less than twelve hours. "Sounds like a plan. I'll show you a good time."

"I'm sure you will…"

After the call, he stood up and walked towards the bedroom. He stopped by the large unopened package which stood on the dining table. His excitement vanished.

He knew what the card said, yet he looked at it again—unsure if he were going to open the package or not.

The card read:

*Your first paycheck.*

*Sergei*

# ACKNOWLEDGEMENTS

A special thanks to Simon van Wijlen, Ida Johanne Sivertsen, Sharon Buchanan and Kat Mellon for the help they've given me polishing this novel. Without them it would look nothing like it does now.

A special mention to my good friends at Critique Circle who has helped me along the way.

Most important, I'd like to thank Eryn and Victoria for giving me the opportunity and the support to fulfil my dream.

*Vetle*

# ABOUT THE AUTHOR

Vetle Sivertsen is a thriller writer who believes that all good stories not only must contain suspense and an escape for the reader, but should also include context to a real-life issue.

He pursued a career in international business before he changed paths and started doing what he really loves; to write. The interest in thrillers and mysteries started at a young age when he devoured books about *Biggles* and *The Hardy Boys*. He got older and fell in love with the works of writers such as Agatha Christie and Alistair MacLean. From early on he knew that he sooner or later would take up their profession.

He has a Norwegian passport, but considers himself a citizen of the world. He has lived in Sweden, India, The Netherlands and he currently resides in Dubai together with his wife and daughter.